Praise for *The Monster in the Box*

"One of the best-written detective series in the genre's history . . . *Monster* brings both Rendell and Wexford back in strong form. . . . Ultimately, everything weaves together in Rendell's imaginary town, but more so than ever in *The Monster in the Box*."

—Michael Sims, *The Washington Post*

"Ruth Rendell slyly sends up two iconic figures of English society—the animal lover and the guardian of political correctness—in her new Inspector Wexford mystery. . . . It's a pleasure to have flashbacks to a boyish Wexford in hot pursuit of girls of a certain alluring type. It's also a revelation to see how meticulously Rendell reconstructs that long-ago period and place."

—Marilyn Stasio, *The New York Times Book Review*

"[Targo] is as good a villain as Wexford ever tried to pin down . . . hauntingly nasty."

The Spectator (UK)

"In spare but arresting prose, [Rendell] elucidates Wexford's past while telling a compelling story of the present. A master of psychological suspense, Rendell brings her profound talents to bear."

—Jay Strafford, *Richmond Times-Dispatch*

"If the British did not actually invent the mystery novel, they certainly were the ones who converted it into an art form and, over the years, have been among the genre's most accomplished performers. Of these, none ranks higher than Ruth Rendell. . . . Durability alone would be sufficient to earn her respect, but to it Rendell adds storytelling skills that make her unique on today's literary landscape. As proof, consider her latest offering. . . . A most pleasing tale, adroitly plotted and deftly rendered, peopled with characters both original and convincing. Rendell has been hailed as the best mystery writer of our time. While such ratings are always subject to argument, she belongs on any short list."

—Robert Wade, *The San Diego Union-Tribune*

"Those coming to this masterful series for the first time doubtless will be delighted to make Wexford's acquaintance."

—Tim Rutten, *Los Angeles Times*

"Ms. Rendell always excels in the difficulties of the mind. . . . [She] puts a fresh cast on the topic of what lies in the mind of a serial killer."

—Muriel Dobbin, *The Washington Times*

"*The Monster in the Box* rewards loyal readers with a generous trip back to the origins of the Kingsmarkham copper."

—P. G. Koch, *Houston Chronicle*

"Fans will enjoy Wexford's long look back at his early obsession with the woman who looked like his perfect mate, with hilariously disastrous results."

—Hallie Ephron, *The Boston Globe*

"Wexford fans won't want to miss this one."

"Rendell easily outdistances most mystery writers with her complex characters."

"Rendell is in fine form (when hasn't she been?)."

"Targo haunted this world, as he haunts the reader: the monster is out of the box and it's impossible to put him back once this book has been closed."

BARBARA VINE NOVELS

THE
MONSTER
IN THE
BOX

An Inspector Wexford Novel

Ruth Rendell

Scribner

New York London Toronto Sydney

SCRIBNER

A Division of Simon & Schuster, Inc.
1230 Avenue of the Americas
New York, NY 10020

First Scribner trade paperback edition July 2010

SCRIBNER and design are registered trademarks of The Gale Group, Inc., used under license by Simon & Schuster, Inc., the publisher of this work.

For information about special discounts for bulk purchases, please contact Simon & Schuster Special Sales at 1-866-506-1949 or business@simonandschuster.com.

The Simon & Schuster Speakers Bureau can bring authors to your live event. For more information or to book an event contact the Simon & Schuster Speakers Bureau at 1-866-248-3049 or visit our website at www.simonspeakers.com.

Text set in Janson Text
Book design by Ellen R. Sasahara

Manufactured in the United States of America

5 7 9 10 8 6 4

Library of Congress Control Number: 2009018818

ISBN 978-1-4391-5033-7
ISBN 978-1-4391-5037-5 (pbk)
ISBN 978-1-4391-5437-3 (ebook)

To Simon, my son, who told me about the box

THE MONSTER IN THE BOX

1

H<small>E HAD NEVER</small> told anyone. The strange relationship, if it could be called that, had gone on for years, decades, and he had never breathed a word about it. He had kept silent because he knew no one would believe him. None of it could be proved, not the stalking, not the stares, the conspiratorial smiles, not the killings, not any of the signs Targo had made because he knew that Wexford knew and could do nothing about it.

It had gone on for years and then it had stopped. Or seemed to have stopped. Targo was gone. Back to Birmingham yet again or perhaps to Coventry. A long time had passed since he had been seen in Kingsmarkham, and Wexford had thought it was all over. Thought with regret, not relief, because if Targo disappeared—more to the point, if Targo never did it again—what hope had he of bringing the man to justice? Still, he had almost made up his mind he would never see him anymore. He would never again set eyes on that short, muscular figure with the broad shoulders and the thick, sturdy legs, the coarse, fairish hair, blunt features, and bright blue eyes—and the mark that must always be kept covered up. Wexford had only once seen him without the scarf he wore wrapped round his neck, a wool scarf in winter, a cotton or silk one in summer, a scarf that belonged to one of his wives perhaps, no matter so long as it covered that purple-brown birthmark which disfigured his neck, crept up to his cheek, and dribbled down to his chest. He had seen him only once without a scarf, never without a dog.

Eric Targo. Older than Wexford by seven or eight years, a much-married man, van driver, property developer, kennels proprietor, animal lover, murderer. It was coincidence or chance—Wexford favoured the latter—that he was thinking about Targo for the first time in weeks, wondering what had happened to him, pondering and dismissing the rumour that he was back living in the area, regretting that he had never proved anything against him, when the man appeared in front of him, a hundred yards ahead. There was no doubt in his mind, even at that distance, even though Targo's shock of hair was quite white now. He still strutted, straight-backed, the way a short man carries himself, and he still wore a scarf. In his left hand, on the side nearest to Wexford, he carried a laptop computer. Or, to be accurate, a case made to hold a laptop.

Wexford was in his car. He pulled to the side of Glebe Road and switched off the engine. Targo had got out of a white van and gone into a house on the same side as Wexford was parked. No dog? Wexford had to decide whether he wanted Targo to see him. Perhaps it hardly mattered. How long was it? Ten years? More? He got out of the car and began to walk in the direction of the house Targo had gone into. It was one of a terrace between a jerry-built block of flats and a row of small shops, an estate agent, a nail bar, a newsagent, and a shop called Webb and Cobb (a name which always made Wexford smile) once selling pottery and kitchen utensils but now closed down and boarded up. Mike Burden had lived here once, when he was first married to his first wife; number 36, Wexford remembered. Number 34 was the house Targo had gone into. The front door of Burden's old house was painted purple now, and the new residents had paved over their narrow strip of front garden to make a motorbike park, something Burden said he resented, as if he had any right to comment on what the present owners did to their property. It made Wexford smile to himself to think of it.

There was no sign of Targo. Wexford walked up to the offside of the van and looked through the driver's window. It was open about three inches, for the benefit of a smallish dog, white and a tawny colour, of a feathery-eared, long-coated breed he didn't recognise, sitting on the passenger seat. It turned its head to look at Wexford and let out a single, sharp yap, not loud, not at all angry. Wexford returned to his car and moved it up the road to a position on the opposite side to the white van between a Honda and a Vauxhall. From there he could command a good view of number 34. How long would Targo stay in there? And what had he been doing with the laptop or the laptop case? It seemed an unlikely place for any friend of Targo's to live. When he had last seen the owner of the whitish tawny dog and the white van, Targo had been doing well for himself, was a rich man, while Glebe Road was a humble street where several families of immigrants had settled and which Burden had moved out of as soon as he could afford to.

Wexford noted the number of the white van. He waited. It was, he thought, a very English sort of day, the air still, the sky a uniform white. On such a day, at much the same time of year, late summer, he had visited Targo's boarding kennels and seen the snake. The scarf round Targo's neck had been

of black, green, and yellow silk, almost but not quite covering the birthmark, and the snake which he draped round it
had been the same sort of colours, the pattern on its skin
more intricate. Accident or design? Nothing Targo might do
would surprise him. The first time he had seen him, years
and years ago when both were young but Wexford was very
young, Targo wore a brown wool scarf. It was winter and
cold. The dog with him was a spaniel. What was it called?
Wexford couldn't remember. He remembered the second
encounter because that was the only time Targo had for a
few minutes been without a scarf. He had opened the front
door to Wexford, left him standing there while he picked a
scarf, his wife's, off a hook and wound it round his neck. In
those few seconds Wexford had seen the purple-brown naevus, shaped like a map of some unknown continent with pen-
insulas running out to his chest and headlands skimming his
chin and cheek, uneven with valleys and mountain ranges,
and then Targo had covered it. . . .

Now the front door of number 34 opened and the man
emerged. He stood on the doorstep talking to a young
Asian, the occupant or one of the occupants of the house.
The young man, who wore jeans and a dazzlingly white shirt,
was at least six inches taller than Targo, handsome, his skin a
pale amber colour, his hair jet-black. Targo, Wexford noticed,
might have grown old but he still had a young man's figure.
The T-shirt he wore showed off his heavily muscled torso,
and the black jeans emphasised his flat stomach. He had left
the laptop behind. While he was in the house, he had taken
off his blue-and-white scarf. Because it was warm, no doubt,
and, incredibly, because it was no longer needed for concealment. The birthmark had gone.

For a moment Wexford asked himself if he could possibly have made the wrong identification. The yellow hair had gone white, he couldn't see the bright blue eyes. The purple naevus had been the distinguishing mark which primarily identified him. But, no, this was Targo all right, squat, stocky, muscular Targo with his cocky walk and his confident stance. The Asian man walked a few steps down the short path with him. He held out his hand, and after a short hesitation Targo took it. Asians shook hands a lot, Wexford had noted, friends meeting by chance in the street; always men, though, never women. Someone had told him the Asians at number 34 owned the defunct Webb and Cobb next door—for what that was worth. No doubt they received rents from the tenants of the flats above.

Targo came across to the van, opened the driver's door, and climbed in. Wexford could just about see him stroke the dog's head, then briefly put his arm round it and give it a squeeze. If any doubt was left, the dog identified him. A memory came to Wexford from the quite distant past: the first Mrs. Targo, by then divorced, saying of her ex-husband, "He likes animals better than people. Well, he doesn't like people at all."

The white van moved off. It might be unwise to follow it, Wexford thought. He hadn't much faith in his powers of following a vehicle without its driver spotting him. It would be easy enough to find out where Targo now lived, harder to say what use discovering his address would be. He sat there for a few moments longer, reflecting on how seeing Targo again had instantly made him aware of his own physical shortcomings. Yet when he had first seen him, all those years ago, he had been a tall, young policeman, very young and very fit, while Targo was squat and overmuscled and with that horrible facial mark.

Sometime in the years since they had last encountered each other, Targo must have had the naevus removed. It could be done with a laser, Wexford had read in a magazine article about new remedies for disfigurement and deformity. The man had been making a lot of money, and no doubt he had spent some of it on this improvement to his appearance as others had their noses reshaped and their breasts augmented. The stranger thing, he thought, was that Targo still sometimes wore a scarf even on a summer's day—until he remembered and stripped it off. Did he feel cold without that neck covering he had been wearing for most of his life?

A girl was walking past Wexford's car, starting to cross the street between it and the Honda. She looked about sixteen, wore the dark blue skirt and white blouse with a blazer which constituted the uniform of Kingsmarkham Comprehensive and, covering her head, the hijab. In her case it was a plain headscarf, the same colour as her skirt, but unflattering as it was, it failed to spoil her looks. Her dark brown eyes, surmounted by fine shapely eyebrows, glanced briefly in his direction. She went towards the house Targo had come out of, took a key from the satchel she carried, and let herself in. Too old to be the daughter of the handsome young man. His sister? Perhaps.

Five minutes later Wexford was parking the car on his own garage drive. Instead of letting himself in by the front door, he walked round the back and surveyed his garden. It was a large garden, which Dora had been doing her best to keep tidy and under control since their gardener had left three months before. It had been a losing battle. Those three months were the time of year when a garden needed constant attention: lawn mowing, weeding, deadheading, cutting back. Little of that had been done. I suppose I could spend the weekend making a real effort, he thought, then added, no, I couldn't. We must get a gardener and soon. He took a last look at the ragged lawn, the dead roses dropping petals, the nettles springing up vigorously among the dahlias, and went into the house by the back door. Dora was in the living room, reading the local evening paper.

"We have to get a gardener," said Wexford.

She looked up, smiled, said in a fair imitation of his voice, "Hallo, darling, how lovely to be home. How are you?"

He kissed her. "OK, I know that's what I should have said. But we do need a gardener. I'll get you a drink."

In the kitchen he poured her a glass of sauvignon from the fridge and himself one of merlot from the cupboard. No good putting nuts or crisps into a bowl because she'd snatch it away from him and hide it somewhere as soon as she saw it. He thought again of Targo's muscly body, then he carried the wine into the living room.

"What do you think about Moslem girls wearing the hijab?"

"Is that the headscarf? I think they should if they want to, really want to for themselves, I mean, but shouldn't be coerced into it, certainly not by fathers and brothers."

"It must be the most unbecoming headgear for a woman to wear. But I suppose that's the point."

"Or if you're Moslem, you don't find it unattractive. Which brings me to Jenny. She's been here talking about some girl, a Moslem girl, she's sixteen, in her class at school. She seems to think you ought to know about it."

"Know what?" Wexford had liked Burden's wife since he'd first met her twenty years earlier when he and Burden started working together. He knew she was intelligent and a good teacher, but if only she wouldn't try to get him involved in investigations which wasted his time and usually came to nothing. "What's wrong now?"

"This girl—she's called Tamima something, Tamima Rahman, and she lives with her family in Glebe Road, next to where Mike and Jean used to live. . . ."

"I've seen her. I saw her today."

"How can you know, Reg?"

"Well, unless there are two sixteen-year-old Moslem girls living next to where Mike used to live in Glebe Road and attending Kingsmarkham Comp, I can be pretty sure I've seen her. What's Jenny's businesss with her?"

"She says Tamima got seven or eight GCSEs, A's and A stars, and if all goes well, she'll be going on to sixth-form college. That's all right, but the girl seems unhappy, uneasy even, worried about something. She's got a boyfriend, a Moslem like herself so that ought to be all right, but Jenny doesn't think it is. She thinks you ought to see the family, find out what's going on. Mike, apparently, isn't interested."

"Good for Mike," said Wexford. "He's better than I am at being firm with people who want to waste his time. Now, how about this gardener? Shall I put an ad in the *Courier*?"

2

H<small>E COULDN'T GET</small> Targo out of his head. Incapable of doing much on a computer himself, he hesitated over asking DC Coleman or DS Goldsmith to find where the man was now living, his marital status, his means of livelihood. He had no real reason to know these things, only hunches, suspicions, speculations, built up over the years. Instead he asked one of his grandsons, and he, like all bright children, went to his computer and came up with the answers in a few minutes. Eric William Targo was now married to Mavis Jean Targo, née Sebright, and they lived at Wymondham Lodge, formerly the old vicarage of Stringfield.

Wexford knew the house, as he knew most of the big houses in the environs of Kingsmarkham. No vicar had lived in the place for many years. The Reverend James Neame, incumbent of the parish of Stringfield, now had four churches in his care, each attended by no more than ten people at Sunday-morning service, that service itself taken by a lay reader when Mr. Neame was preaching elsewhere. His home was a small redbrick house between the (now closed) village shop and the parish hall. Several families had occupied the vicarage since the previous vicar left it for good, but it was only dignified with its present name when a rich man from London bought it in the early nineties and gave it a rigorous makeover. When Targo bought it perhaps less than a year ago, it was Wymondham Lodge with extensive grounds, sculpted gardens, two garages, three bathrooms, and a guest suite.

The next day was Sunday and Wexford decided to drive over to Stringfield and—what? Spy out the land? The chances of seeing Targo just because Wexford had his house in his sights were slim, but he felt he couldn't rest until he at least went there and tried. Incongruously, he wondered how many animals and of what kind the man was keeping within the old stone walls of the vicarage garden. The day was fine, hazy and mild. Leaves were still a long way from falling, but they had grown dark and tired-looking. Everywhere had that late-summer appearance of untidiness, grass long and brownish, flowers gone to seed, windfall plums rotting at the foot of trees. He took the bridge across the river Brede and was in Stringfield within ten minutes. There was little traffic. The heart of the village had its usual neglected, even abandoned, look, the church tower in urgent need of repair, gravestones leaning over at angles, several of the once sought-after cottages with For Sale notices in their front gardens. He turned down the lane which led to Wymondham Lodge, a narrow byway in which it was impossible for two cars to pass each other. It widened a little when the edge of the stone-walled grounds was reached.

The land rose a little beyond the wall, giving Wexford a view of a pair of llamas grazing. He did a double take when he saw a Bambi-like creature, a miniature deer, nearby. He pulled the car onto the grass verge, thinking that he wouldn't be surprised to see a leopard or even an elephant. But there was nothing like that, though he caught a glimpse of tall wire fences, like the kind enclosing a tennis court, in the distance. The roar he heard he decided he must have imagined. Driving on towards the house itself, there was less to be seen. Not Targo or his wife, that was too much to expect. But the white van he had seen in Glebe Road was parked on the gravel drive with a silver Mercedes beside it. The old vicarage looked as a dwelling only can when its owners are wealthy and able to spend money on it constantly. The brickwork had been repointed, the white trim recently repainted, the slate roof was glossy and sleek, free of moss. There was no sound—but what sound could there be in this remote spot unless it might be a cry from some animal?

He moved the car along the road out of sight of Wymondham Lodge's windows. It was a former home of Targo's that he was thinking of, not the medium-sized detached place in Myringham where the kennels were, not old Mrs. Targo's cottage in Glebe Road from which he had stalked Wexford, but the little place in Jewel Road, Stowerton, not much more than a cottage itself, where he had started out. Young but a married man with a child and another on the way and, of course, a dog, a spaniel.

Number 32 had been his, and the Carrolls lived at 16. Wexford remembered perfectly now. They were all the same, those houses, a row of them, two tiny living rooms and a kitchen, two bedrooms upstairs. Some of them had a bathroom but most didn't. The gardens were small rectangles with a gate at the end, opening into a lane where dustbins were put out and deliveries made. Everyone had coal and coke delivered in those days.

Elsie Carroll had been found dead in her bedroom one evening while her husband was out at his whist club. Did anyone play whist anymore? The police had come, Wexford

with them, a young policeman then, excited and a bit over-
awed. He hadn't seen the woman's body, only seen it carried
out, covered in a sheet, after the pathologist had examined it.
Leaving the house later, sent home by Ventura when George
Carroll, the husband, had been found, he had encountered
Targo exercising his golden spaniel in the street. At midnight
on a damp, cold night. That had been his first sight, his very
first, of the man who now lived in some grandeur behind
those stone walls.

Of course he was wearing a scarf. A thick waterproof
jacket, Wellington boots, and a scarf wound round his neck.
The scarf had been brown wool with a lighter check pattern.
The man looked at him, met his eyes, stared. While he stood
still and stared, the dog was lifting its leg against a tree in the
pavement. The stare was absurd, sinister, it went on so long.
Wexford found himself making an impatient gesture, turned
away towards the car which would take him home. Once, he
looked back and saw the man still there, still gazing at him.
And he remembered saying to himself, that man, he did it.
Whoever he is, he killed Elsie Carroll, then Wexford said to
himself, don't be ridiculous, don't talk—don't even think—
such nonsense.

Driving home half a lifetime later, he thought, I've never
told anyone but I'm going to. I'm going to tell Mike. I'll have
my Sunday lunch with Dora and Sylvia and the kids, I'll con-
template my awful garden, and I'll draft an ad to put in the
Courier for a gardener. Then, after all that, I'll phone Mike
and ask him to come out for a drink. Now Targo is back and
I've seen him, the time has come to tell someone, and who
but Mike?

■ ■ ■

"If it's about that Rahman girl, I'd rather not," Burden said.

Wexford had almost forgotten her, so full his mind had been of Targo. "Who?"

"That schoolgirl Jenny seems to think is being victimized in some way. The one from the Asian family that live next door to my old house."

"It's not about that, Mike. It's got nothing to do with that. This is something quite different. I've never told anyone about it but it's not new, it's been going on for more years than I care to remember, and now I think it's going to start again. Doesn't that whet your appetite?"

"D'you mean you're going to tell me?"

"If you'll listen," Wexford said.

They chose the Olive and Dove, the little room called the snug which over the years they had made almost their own private sanctum. Of course others used it, as the yellow-stained ceiling and the lingering smell of a million cigarettes bore witness. In a few years' time a smoking ban would come in, the walls and ceiling be redecorated, new curtains hung at the clouded windows and ashtrays banished, but in the late nineties there was no hint of that. Outside the window it was mostly young people sitting at tables under coloured umbrellas on the Olive's veranda, for the evening was as mild as the day had been, while their elders crowded into the saloon bar. All those people or those who succeeded them would ten years in the future be obliged to huddle on that veranda, rain or shine, snow or fog, if they wanted to smoke.

Wexford asked for his usual red wine, Burden for a half of lager. He was no big drinker, though he had a large appetite, and Wexford would have been surprised if he had before coming out eaten less than a two-course dinner with bread that he himself had given up and potatoes that he was forbidden. For all that, the inspector kept his slim, elegant figure. To Wexford it was almost indecent that a man of Burden's age had no discernible belly and could still wear jeans without looking ridiculous.

Having said earlier that he wasn't coming if the conversation was about Tamima Rahman, Burden nevertheless plunged straight into the subject.

"I hope I'm not being disloyal, but I sometimes think that people who are as intensely antiracist as Jenny is, actually discover examples of Asian or black people being ill-treated where no ill-treatment exists. Moreover, I'm afraid I think, and I told her what I think, that if this Tamima was a white girl who seemed a bit depressed and—well, unable to concentrate, Jenny wouldn't take a blind bit of notice. There you are, I suppose that is a bit disloyal."

"It's politically incorrect, Mike. I don't know about disloyal. As for this girl, I only know what Dora passed on to me from what Jenny said."

"There isn't any more to know, as far as I can see." Burden tasted his drink and gave a small approving nod. "So what was it you wanted to tell me?"

"It will take quite a long time," Wexford said reflectively. "It can't all be told tonight." He paused, then went on, "You have to understand that I've never told anyone, I've kept it entirely to myself, and I thought I never would tell anyone. That was in part because the man in question had gone away. That wasn't the first time, he'd gone away before, but he'd never stayed away so long. I was beginning to think—no, I'd decided—that it was all over. Now he's come back. I've seen him."

"What did you mean by 'in part'?"

"Because I could think of no one to tell who would believe me," Wexford said simply.

"And I will?"

"Probably not. No, I doubt if you'll believe me. But I know you'll listen and you'll keep it to yourself."

"If that's what you want, I will."

The story Wexford was going to tell started when he was young, living at home with his mother and father because he couldn't really afford to live anywhere else. He got on with his parents, there were no difficulties there, but he moved away for two reasons: it wasn't "grown-up" to live at home, and besides that, he was engaged. At twenty-one he was engaged. But he wouldn't tell any of that. He wouldn't talk about the sexual revolution which was coming but hadn't yet arrived, and how it was out of the question for his parents to let Alison stay the night. Even when he had found himself a room with a baby Belling stove and use of the bathroom down the passage, he couldn't have had Alison to stay the night. Her parents would have expected her home by eleven at the latest. His landlady would have turned her out and him too probably. There would have been gossip. Girls still had a reputation to keep, girls still knew what the word meant and, if they tried to forget it, were still told by their fathers—never *dads* in those days—what would become of them if they lost it.

But he and Alison had their evenings. Mrs. Brunton, his landlady, was one of those who believed that sexual intercourse only ever took place after ten at night. He was young and probably thought the way magazines were beginning to say men thought, that is, about sex every six minutes. He had known Alison since they were sixteen and he liked the sex but not as much as he had thought he would. There must be more to it or what were all these people on about?

He tried not to think about it. He was *engaged*, and he had old-fashioned ideas about engagements. Not that he was quite back in the days when defaulting men got sued for breach of promise, but still he would have thought it dishonourable for the man to break an engagement when the woman obviously wanted to keep it. Or did she? She said she loved him. He tried not to think about it but to think about his work instead.

And it was about that work that he would talk to Burden. The inspector waited, watching him and helping himself to the nuts Wexford was not allowed to eat.

"It was mostly taking statements," he began, "from people who had been receiving stolen goods or knew someone who had or had broken into a house and stolen five pounds from a wallet. And making house-to-house-calls and once, rather more excitingly, taking my turn in sitting beside a hospital bed in which lay a man who had been stabbed in the street. A very rare event in Kingsmarkham in those days. And then Elsie Carroll was murdered."

It was the first murder in their area of mid-Sussex for two years, and the previous one hadn't really been murder at all but manslaughter. This one was murder all right. She was found by a next-door neighbour. The neighbour, Mrs. Dawn Morrow, had been expecting Elsie Carroll to come in and have a cup of coffee with her and a chat.

"Those were the days when a couple of women would never have met for a drink, that is wine or beer or spirits. No one drank wine, anyway, except French people or the sort that went to posh restaurants. Dawn had two children, three and one, her husband went to see his widowed mother on a Tuesday evening, and she couldn't leave the house except perhaps to 'pop next door.' Elsie was invited for seven thirty one February evening, and when she hadn't come by eight, Dawn went to find her, leaving her children alone for a couple of minutes, as she put it. Both couples were on the phone, but both believed it was wrong, absurdly extravagant, almost immoral, to make a phone call to the house next door."

At this point, Burden broke in. "Where exactly was this?"

"Didn't I say? It was Jewel Road, Stowerton."

"I know it. Smart cottages with different-coloured front doors, very popular with commuters to London."

"It wasn't like that then. It was—it is—a terrace. Some people had outside lights either in the porch or on an exterior wall. The Carrolls at number sixteen didn't. The back gardens were small, and all of them had a gate in the rear wall leading into the lane where dustmen collected the rubbish and deliveries were made. No one locked these gates and everyone left their back doors unlocked. Nothing ever happened, it was neurotic to be afraid of some intruder coming in.

"Dawn rang the Carrolls' front-door bell and, when she got no answer, went back into her own house, out by the back way, and into the Carrolls' garden by way of the lane and the gate in the rear wall. The back door had a glass panel in it and light was coming from the kitchen. That door was not, of course, locked. Dawn went on, calling out, 'Hallo,' and 'Where are you, Elsie?' No one said 'hi' then. When she got no answer, she called out again and went through the kitchen into the hallway that everyone who lived in that terrace called 'the passage.' A light was on here too.

"I'd never previously been in any of those houses, all identical in layout, but by the evening of the next day I knew this one well. There were two small living rooms on the ground floor that subsequent owners have converted into one through room. Upstairs were two bedrooms, a bathroom, and a tiny boxroom, big enough for a small child to sleep in. The Carrolls had no children so Dawn had no reason to keep her voice down as she went upstairs calling Elsie. It was just after eight."

Wexford paused to drink some of his wine. "Next day, DC Miller, Cliff Miller, took a statement from Dawn Morrow and I sat in on it, learning the ropes. The next statement that was needed I'd have to do myself. Dawn said that a ceiling light was on in Mrs. Carroll's bedroom and she went in there. At first she didn't see her. The bed was in a bit of a mess. It looked as if it hadn't been made. Pillows had been thrown about and the eiderdown had fallen half onto the floor. That was very unlike Elsie, leaving her bed unmade. Dawn walked round the bed and then she saw her lying on the floor between the bed and the window. 'I thought she must have fainted,' she said. 'I went up to her and looked more closely but I didn't touch her. They told me afterwards that she was dead, but I didn't know that. She was lying facedownwards with her face turned into the rug so I couldn't see it.'

"That's more or less what she said, Mike. Maybe I'm not remembering precisely. And I'm stating it coldly, leaving out what she must have felt, shock, amazement, fear. She went next door to number eighteen where some people called Johnson lived, and the Johnsons both came back with her. They went upstairs together. Mrs. Johnson had been a nurse before she married; she looked at Elsie Carroll and said she thought she was dead but to go out of the room while she tried to see if she had a pulse. A bit later she came out and she told her husband Elsie was dead and to phone the police and he did."

Elsie Carroll had been strangled with the belt of her dressing gown, which had been lying across the bed. That was the opinion of Dr. Crocker, whom Wexford had never before met but who later became his friend. Crocker, who was there within not much more than half an hour, gave an approximate time of death as not more than an hour before and possibly as little as half an hour before. By this time Detective Sergeant Jim Ventura had arrived with DC Miller, DC Pendle, and Wexford himself. Within a few minutes Detective Inspector Fulford had also joined them. This murder was something very out of the ordinary, a sensation, in that place and at that time.

"We had no scene-of-crimes officer at that time. DC Pendle—Dennis was his name—and I went around the house, paying particular attention to the bedroom, taking fingerprints. DNA had been discovered, but Watson, Crick, and Wilkins had yet to win the Nobel Prize for their work. It would be a long time before it could be put to forensic use, and it's not foolproof yet, is it? But fingerprint detection had been around for a long time. While we examined that bedroom, a pretty little room which Elsie Carroll had papered in pink patterned with silver leaves, Ventura and DI Fulford waited downstairs for Elsie's husband, George, to come home.

"Almost the first thing Ventura had done was speak to Harold Johnson and Margaret, his wife, the former nurse. It was twenty minutes to nine. Johnson told him that George Carroll regularly attended the Stowerton whist club, which met in St. Mary's church hall, and he would be there now. The church hall was no more than a mile away, if that, and George Carroll had gone there, as usual, on his bicycle. Margaret Johnson said he was usually home by nine thirty, though sometimes it was after ten. Ventura sent DC Miller to St. Mary's Hall to find George Carroll, tell him what had happened, and bring him home."

"Things would be a bit different today, wouldn't they?" Burden said. "Everyone would have a mobile phone. The church hall would have had a landline, which it certainly hadn't then, and all those whist players mobiles."

"Elsie Carroll wouldn't have left her back door unlocked or the gate in the wall unbolted. There would have been more streetlights."

"In other words," said Burden, "you could say, contrary to what one is always hearing, that life was actually *safer* then."

"In some ways."

"So are you going to tell me George Carroll couldn't be found?"

"Don't be so impatient. Let's say he couldn't be found immediately. D'you want another drink?"

"I'll get them."

When Burden came back, he found Wexford scrutinising the photocopy he had made in preparation for this meeting of the chapter on the Carroll murder in W. J. Chambers's *Unsolved Crimes and Some Solutions*. Looking up, he said, "You didn't think I could remember all that after so long, did you?"

Burden laughed. "Your memory is pretty good."

"I'm giving you all this preamble because it's necessary, but what I really want to talk about is the man I suspect committed the crime. No, not suspect. I know he did it as I know he did at least one other. His name is Eric Targo and we'll come to him in a minute." Wexford said almost humbly, "You're happy for me to carry on?"

"Sure I am, Reg. Of course I am."

3

MILLER CAME BACK to Jewel Road, having been unable to find Carroll, and we waited there for him, that is, Fulford, Ventura, and I. Elsie's body had been taken away. By our present-day standards, they were a bit cavalier about taking measurements and photographs, but I daresay what they did was adequate. The bedroom was sealed off as a crime scene. It was then that Harold Johnson dropped what Ventura called his bombshell. He asked if he could speak to Ventura, found him less intimidating than Fulford, I suppose. Fulford was more like an old-time army officer, a sort of Colonel Blimp, than a policeman.

"Johnson and his wife had been at home all the evening, watching television. Of all the residents of Jewel Road, they were one of the few families who had television, and it sounded as if they were enthralled by it, glued to it every night. There were all sorts of rules and restrictions about television-watching at that time. For one thing, you were supposed to sit as many feet away from the set as there were inches in its diagonal, never sit without lights on, and various other stuff that turned out to be nonsense. Still, the Johnsons wanted to do it properly, and they believed they should draw the curtains and switch on what Margaret Johnson called 'soft lighting.' But I suspect and thought so then, I remember, that although they would have denied this vehemently, they wanted to leave their curtains open as long as possible so that anyone passing could see the glow of the cathode tube and recognise it for what it was. Something I forgot to mention—the Johnsons were also among the few residents who had converted their two living rooms into one so that they had windows back and front with curtains to be drawn.

"It was about seven, he told Ventura, when he got up off the sofa to draw the curtains. He couldn't be sure of the time but he knew it was a bit after seven because the programme they wanted to watch had started. First he drew the curtains at the front bay window, then he moved to the back. These were French windows and the curtains floor-length and rather heavy. He pulled the curtains, but the right-hand one got caught up on something, the back of a chair, and when he went back to free it, he looked out into the darkness and saw the figure of a man coming away from the back door of number sixteeen and making for the gate in the rear wall. At the time he thought it was George Carroll, who went out that way if he was going on his bicycle, which he kept in the shed by the gate. But now he was less sure.

"He thought the man he had seen was short, no more than five feet four, while George Carroll was five feet seven. But it was dark and Harold Johnson said he wouldn't be able to take his oath—that was his expression, 'take his oath'—on its being Carroll. The time he could be sure of: just after seven. Elsie, of course, couldn't say what time her husband had left the house, but Dawn Morrow told Ventura next day that he usually left before seven, maybe as much as ten minutes before."

"So when did Carroll come home?"

"A good deal later than was expected. About ten forty-five. It looked to me as if it was a terrible shock for him, but as Pendle said to me afterwards, whether he'd killed her or not, finding the place a blaze of light and his home full of cops would have been a shock anyway. Fulford told him he could see his wife's body if he wanted to, but Carroll refused and began to cry. Fulford wasn't sympathetic. He said brusquely that he'd like to ask him some questions and he wanted to do it now, that was unavoidable. He and Ventura questioned the man, and Pendle and I were sent home.

"If you're interested, you can read what Carroll said in Chambers's book. You can have this photocopy I made for you. But the real thing of importance is that Carroll told Fulford he had spent the evening with a woman called Tina Malcolm. The term *girlfriend* wasn't used so much then and Carroll told Fulford he was the woman's 'lover.' That put Fulford against him from the start. He was exceptionally straitlaced and puritanical—worse than you."

"Thanks a bunch."

Wexford laughed. "This woman, Carroll said, would confirm that he had been with her from seven thirty until ten, and he was glad it had 'all come out,' it was better this way with his wife knowing. Then he remembered his wife was dead and began crying again."

"My God," said Burden. "That's a bit grim."

"Well, it was. I was glad to get out in the fresh air. The car we'd come in was parked outside. Pendle got into the driving seat—he lived fairly near me in Kingsmarkham High Street—and I went round to the passenger door. No remote opening of car doors then, of course. . . ."

"I had been born, you know, I even remember the moon landings."

"Sorry," said Wexford. "Though why I should apologise to a man for treating him as if he were younger than he is I don't know. Pendle had to reach across and lift up the thing—don't know what it was called—that locked the door, and while he was doing that, I noticed a man standing outside number sixteen. He had a dog with him on a lead, and he was waiting while the dog took a pee up against a tree. His name was Targo, Eric Targo, though I didn't know it then. Mostly someone you encounter like that will immediately look away when he knows you've seen him. Especially when you've been watching his dog foul the pavement, though that wasn't thought of as an offence in those days. Targo didn't look away. He stared at me. You'll think I'm exaggerating but I'm not. You know how you sometimes read that someone's eyes pierced into your very soul?" Burden plainly hadn't read that and didn't know it. "Well, never mind, but that's what Targo's did. He stared at me—it was under a streetlamp—and then he nodded slightly. Oh, it was a very faint nod, not much more than a tremor, and as he turned away, I saw the birthmark. He had a scarf round his neck—he always wears a scarf or he did—but it slipped a little because he turned his head. At first I thought it was some sort of shadow, a trick of the light, but when he moved, I saw it for what it was. Cancer the crab crawling across his neck, shaped like a crab with pincers or an island with promontories." Wexford shrugged. "Take your pick."

They had been alone for the hour and a half it had taken to narrate all this, but now three people came into the snug, a woman and two men. Although the room was small, it contained three tables, any one of which the newcomers might have chosen, but they picked the one nearest to the policemen. Burden said quietly to Wexford, "Shall we go back to my place and you can go on with the story there?"

Burden's house was nearer to the Olive than Wexford's. The difficulty was that Jenny would be there, unable to leave her young son on his own, but as it happened, she said nothing to Wexford beyond "Can I come and see you about something, Reg? To the police station?"

He named a day and a time more to keep her quiet for the present than because he wanted to hear what she had to say. He knew it already. Burden and he went into a little room the Burdens called the study, though as is so often the case, nothing was studied there. It was a place where one of them could watch a different television programme from that showing in the living room. Burden left him there while he went to fetch drinks and the snack he could eat but Wexford must not.

Alone for a while, Wexford reflected on that midnight so long ago. He had never forgotten that look, the light from the streetlamp falling on the man's thick fair hair and his rather rugged coarse face with the scarf not quite hiding the dark stain mantling his neck. Then, the faint nod as if to say, "We know each other now. We are bound together now." Of course that was nonsense, a nod couldn't mean all that.

Next day had been Wexford's day off. He would have preferred to go in, he didn't want to miss the next steps in the proceedings, but nor did he want to say that to Ventura. It sounded a bit—not overkeen but maybe *presumptuous*. He was too new in the job and too low down the scale to attract that sort of attention to himself. He spent the day with Alison instead, going for a drive (in her father's car), and the evening alone in his room. That was the time when he'd been doing the next best thing to going to university: reading, reading,

reading. It was Chaucer that evening, "The Squire's Tale." But later on he lay awake a long while and his mind went back to the old worry, how he could marry a woman he didn't love and would soon, he was afraid, cease even to like anymore.

Burden reappeared with a bottle of sparkling water and for Wexford a glass of red wine, the last of his self-imposed ration for that day. Wexford poured himself a tumbler of water. From the array of bowls of nuts and cheese biscuits, he took a handful of salted almonds.

"You'd got to the bit where you and this Targo were staring at each other," Burden said, his tone sceptical if not exactly scathing.

Wexford ignored it. "The following morning, at what Fulford called his tasks-for-the-day roundup, Ventura said he wanted me to come with him to interview Tina Malcolm, girlfriend or 'lover' of George Carroll. Back at the mortuary the pathologist was carrying out a postmortem on his murdered wife. Ventura and I went to Powys Road. This woman Tina Malcolm lived in a two-room flat with kitchen. No bathroom, but that wasn't unusual in those days. There was a bath in the kitchen with a cover over it to make a table. It was neither shabby nor smart, just ordinary. It would have been interesting to a young person going in there today because, although the bedroom was quite a generous size, she slept in a single bed."

"Have some more nuts."

"You know I'd better not." Wexford sighed, but inaudibly. "Tina Malcolm was about thirty-five, dyed-blond hair, heavily made-up. Women wore much heavier makeup then than now. Lots of girls wouldn't let themselves be seen outdoors without it. More of it on the lips than on the eyes, though.

Her heels were so high that they made you wonder, then as now, how women could take more than a couple of steps in them without falling over. She knew we were coming and I think she'd dressed up for us, not because we were policemen but because we were men.

"She took us into her sitting room and offered us tea, which Ventura refused. You always think of Latins as being warm and effusive, but he was a taciturn devil, dour and brusque. Accepting tea might have put her at ease. She was very nervous. As well she might have been in the circumstances."

"In the circumstances? You mean she was involved with Elsie Carroll's death?"

"Well, no, rather the reverse. Or so it seemed. What happened next was extraordinary, Mike. It was the first time I'd ever come across anything like it, but more to the point, it was the first time Ventura had. He told me so in the car afterwards and mostly he hardly opened his mouth with lowlife like me."

Burden laughed. "So what was it? I can't bear the suspense."

"She hadn't heard anything about the murder. Or said she hadn't. You have to remember that there was nothing like the proliferation of news then that there is now. Radio, yes, and TV, of course, but only two channels and no breakfast television. Newspapers, but no use to you if you didn't have one delivered by nine in the morning. It was half past when we got there, and there was no paper to be seen. Ventura asked her if she had heard about the murder of Mrs. Elsie Carroll, and she just stared, her eyes went as big as saucers, and she whispered something about not knowing. Her hands had started to shake.

"Ventura gave me a look which indicated I was to say

27

something, so I asked her if Mr. George Carroll was a friend of hers. She nodded and whispered yes, and Ventura told her to speak up. No one used that term *relationship*, meaning 'affair,' in those days, and Ventura asked her what was the nature of her friendship with Mr. Carroll. This time she did speak up. 'He's a good friend,' she said. 'There's nothing wrong.' That was the way people spoke then when they meant there was nothing sexual. Neither of us had told her when Elsie Carroll's death had taken place. Ventura asked her when she last saw George Carroll, and she said she couldn't be sure, not very long ago. 'Did you see him two evenings ago?' Ventura said. She drew herself up and looked shocked. I suddenly began to see that she was no shy violet, she was a clever woman. Ventura ignored that stuff about not seeing Carroll in the evenings. 'Did you see him between seven thirty and nine thirty?'

"She shook her head quite calmly. 'Please answer the question, Miss Malcolm,' Ventura said. With a slight smile she said, 'I have already told you I never saw Mr. Carroll in the evenings. That wasn't the nature of our friendship. The answer's no.' She was just a touch indignant by then. Another glance from Ventura and I said, 'Are you absolutely sure of that, Miss Malcolm?' I got a nod and an impatient shrug.

"Ventura believed her. What astonished him was what he called the barefaced effrontery of Carroll trying to set up an alibi with an entirely innocent woman whose loyalty he thought he could count on. I thought it was a classic case of a woman who was happy to be having an affair with a married man when all went smoothly, but the sky changed when a bad storm came up. I didn't say so, however. I knew it would be useless. Still, he was too good a policeman to leave this without further confirmation, and I was left behind to call at all the flats in the block and ask if anyone had seen George Carroll two nights ago. In about three-quarters of the flats a woman was at home, a man in only one of them. I questioned them, but no one had seen George Carroll or any man go into Tina Malcolm's flat. Or maybe I should say no one said they had.

"People like publicity these days, they're hungry for it. But not then. That fifteen minutes of fame—or is it fifteen seconds?—no one wanted it then. They wanted to keep themselves to themselves, keep out of the public eye. Don't get involved was what mothers said to their children.

"It was next day that we did the house-to-house in Jewel Road and I encountered Kathleen Targo and her son. But not Eric Targo. Nearly all the men were at work as he was. Hardly any women were. Those of the men Ventura thought we ought to see we went back to talk to in the evening. No one was fingerprinted—there was no evidence pointing to anyone except perhaps George Carroll. These days we'd no doubt have taken DNA from everyone, men and women, on both sides of that street and streets beyond as well, but not then, not possible then."

"So you saw Eric Targo in the evening?"

It had been an ordinary, seemingly insignificant, meeting. While Pendle was talking to a man called Green at number 25 on the other side of Jewel Road, Wexford was knocking on the door of 32 and being admitted to the house by Targo. Somewhere downstairs, probably in the kitchen, a child was screaming and there was a sound of water running.

"Don't like his bath," said Targo.

Those were the first words Wexford ever heard him speak. As was often the case in marriages, his accent was uglier and coarser than hers, the local mixture of old Sussex and south-London cockney. The man was short, just coming up to Wexford's shoulder, and had perhaps compensated for his lack of height by developing his body with weight-bearing exercises. Big muscles stood out on his arms and the calves of his legs. He wore shorts—unheard of at that time of year in Kingsmarkham and its environs—which showed his thick thighs and bulging calves.

"He opened the door to me, and the minute he did, he remembered his neck was bare. As soon as he saw me, he snatched up a scarf which was hanging from a hook with a lot of coats and tied it round his neck. The shorts made it even more odd that he should also be wearing a cotton scarf tied round his neck. A woman's scarf it looked like, red and black and white. Then I had realized it was to hide the birthmark. Maybe I imagined it, but I thought the look he gave me was full of hatred because I'd seen the birthmark."

"You imagined it," said Burden.

"Maybe, but you weren't there."

Wexford had been led into a living room, which, like every living room in that street, in the whole town probably, was heated either by a coal fire or an electric two-element heater. In this case it was the latter and the room was cold. The spaniel was stretched out in front of the "fire." Targo was the sort Wexford would have expected to be cruel to animals or at least callous with them, but to his surprise the man bent down and stroked the dog tenderly on its silky head before sitting down and asking him bluntly what he wanted.

"I asked him how well he knew Mrs. Elsie Carroll. 'That the woman what was murdered? Never spoken to her,' he said. I didn't feel like calling him sir, but I'd been told I had to. My personal assessment of someone didn't come into it.

'May I ask you where you were on February eighteenth, sir, between seven and eight p.m.?' I said.

"Targo stared at me. It wasn't the same sort of look he had given me under the streetlamp, not a fleeting nod, but a brief stare of dislike and contempt. His eyes were a bright icy blue, still are, I daresay. 'What d'you want to know for?' he said.

"I'd learnt the formula by that time. 'Just routine, sir. To eliminate you from our enquiries.'"

Burden laughed. "What else?"

"Targo said he was at home with his son. I'll never forget his words. They were so expressive of the man's character. 'The wife had gone to her whatsit class—dressmaking. I don't mind that'—incredibly, he winked—'teach her to make her own clothes and the kid's, save my money.' The screaming and splashing from the kitchen had stopped. There were footsteps out in the passage and Kathleen Targo came in with her son.

"'Oh, pardon me.' She recognized me. 'Is anything wrong?'"

It amused him that people had begun to look on him, especially when on their home territory, as a harbinger of doom.

"I told her nothing was wrong and then I asked him if he'd mind telling me what he was doing while he was at home with his son. There was just an outside chance, Mike, that she'd deny that he had been—but, no. Not a flicker of wonder or doubt. 'I was doing press-ups and leg curls—if you know what they are—in the kitchenette.' They called kitchens kitchenettes then, even if they weren't particularly small.

"Mrs. Targo told the boy to say good-night to his dad, and Alan went up to his father. He didn't say anything but—well, to my surprise, kissed him on the cheek. Then he fondled the dog's neck, and that pleased Targo. He smiled and nodded. Alan went up to his mother and held up his arms, but she shook her head. 'Not the way I am now, Allie,' she said. 'You're too heavy.'

"She was very unhappy with Targo. I guessed that then, and what I thought was confirmed when I met her again by chance years and years later. She and Targo were divorced by that time and she'd married again. That evening in Jewel Road I could see she was exhausted but he didn't get up. 'You can make yourself useful for once, Kath,' he said, 'and show the officer out. I'm tired. Oh, wait, though,' he said to me. 'There's one thing you may want to know. I said I'd never spoken to that Elsie Carroll and I never did, but it's well-known down this street her two-timing husband was carrying on with a woman in Kingsmarkham. Dirty bitch. No better than a streetwalker.'

"'Eric! Not in front of the boy,' Kathleen said.

"'He don't understand. That Carroll'd have been happy as Larry to see the back of his wife, that I can tell you.'

"I thanked Targo and said he'd been very helpful, the way we were supposed to, though he hadn't. All he'd done was teach me something about his own character. It was after that that Kathleen took me out into the hall and sent the boy upstairs before she opened the front door and let the cold air in. I turned back on the doorstep and I asked her what she thought of the Tuesday-evening dressmaking class. I said my mother was thinking of signing up for it.

"'Oh, it's lovely,' she said, showing more enthusiasm than I'd seen from her before. 'Eric's so good staying here with Alan. I never miss.' I had the impression she only said that to make me think all was fine with them on the domestic front. It was all part of that pretend-everything-in-the-garden's-lovely attitude people adhered to then. 'Well, I'll have to miss it for my confinement.'

"They still said that then. Well, some of them did, the really old-fashioned ones, the sort who still put on a hat to go to the shops. There were women in the villages round here, in the cottages without running water or electricity, where they referred to their husbands as 'my master.'"

"OK," said Burden. "I can see that Targo could have left his son for ten minutes, say, and gone along the back lane to number sixteen—sixteen right?"

Wexford nodded.

"And gone through the gate into the back garden—maybe even concealed himself and watched George Carroll leave on his bike before going into the garden. He finds poor Mrs. Carroll upstairs and kills her, strangles her. Then he leaves the way he came where he is seen by Harold Johnson, who doesn't recognize him in the dark. It could be done. Easily. But why, Reg? *Why?*"

4

B URDEN WAS LOOKING at the photocopy of the chapter from Chambers's book Wexford had given him. It was ten pages long. "There's absolutely no motive," he said at last. "Of course finding a motive's not strictly necessary, but you have to admit it helps. Where's your circumstantial evidence? There's none against Targo unless you count Harold Johnson seeing a man cross the garden, but, according to Chambers, he was never prepared to swear in court that it was George Carroll or anyone else. Or is Chambers wrong there and he took his oath it wasn't Carroll?"

"No, he never did," Wexford said. "All he would say was that he thought it was a short man, but he was a very tall man himself and five feet seven or five feet four might have been equally short to him."

"Targo's got the same sort of alibi as any other man in that street. He was at home with his family, in his case at home looking after his son. How old was the boy, by the way?"

"I wasn't very good on children's ages in those days. Four? Maybe a bit less."

"So you're basing this theory on a look the man gave you, by night, in the light of a streetlamp? Leave for a moment why he would—well, glare at you. Why would he kill Elsie Carroll? Revenge on George Carroll for something? But, apart from his apparently not knowing George Carroll except by sight, it wouldn't exactly be revenge, would it? If you think of Carroll as presumably being glad to have his wife out of the way, wouldn't it be doing him a favour?"

"I know all that," Wexford said. "I've thought of all that. It doesn't change my mind." He got up. "There's more to come, lots more, but I'm tired and I'm sure you are. That's enough for now. Say good-bye to Jenny for me."

"I'll drive you home. I've only had that lager and it was all of three hours ago."

"No, I'll walk, thanks. I'll see you tomorrow."

The mild, clear evening had become a cool night. When the sky was cloudless, it was still possible to see the stars from the outskirts of Kingsmarkham. Brighton was just far enough away and London farther. You could see the stars, see the constellations of Charles's Wain and Orion and Cassiopeia, but less clearly than he had from this same point when he was young. That might, of course, be as much due to the deterioration of his eyesight as to the pollution which misted the sky.

But the air revived him and his tiredness went. He recalled how those sightings of Eric Targo had affected him profoundly. He supposed it was because he wanted justice to be done and hated to see it fail to be done. If he could stop them, the wicked must not be allowed to flourish like the green bay tree. Young as he had been, he had felt much like this when it became clear to him that the blimpish DI Fulford, and therefore Ventura, had made up their minds that George Carroll had killed his wife. It had been George Carroll that Harold Johnson had seen cross the dark garden towards the gate in the wall at seven that evening. George Carroll had a motive and a strong one. He wanted his wife out of the way so that he could marry Tina Malcolm. Dissolving a marriage was difficult in those days, long before no-fault divorce came in, especially when it was a husband trying to part from an innocent wife. She would have had to divorce him, and if she hadn't consented to that, little could be done about it. People remained bound to uncongenial spouses for the greater part of a lifetime. Wexford himself had known an old man who had been living with the woman he loved for thirty years but was unable to marry her because his wife refused him a divorce.

That Tina denied being with George that evening and therefore negated his alibi was neither here nor there. Probably she had said she hadn't seen George because she was afraid of being involved—and this was likely true. Where he might really have been, as far as Wexford could see, Fulford made no efforts to find out.

Wexford could see too that it wouldn't be long before George Carroll was arrested and charged with Elsie Carroll's murder. Then another bombshell was dropped by Tina Malcolm. She came forward of her own accord, revoked her previous statement, and said George had spent the evening with her. That did no good as no one believed her. It probably did harm, for it looked as if Carroll had coerced her, as perhaps he had. On the following day he was charged with the murder of his wife.

It was a day lodged firmly in Wexford's memory for other reasons as well. He saw Targo again, out with his spaniel this time in the high street. He didn't speak and Wexford said nothing to him, but their eyes met and Targo stared. After this, Wexford almost went to Ventura, told him about those glances and that unblinking stare, and suggested the man's movements might be investigated. He almost went. Perhaps it was never quite as close as "almost." His day's work done, as yet unaware that George Carroll was at that moment being charged with murder, he imagined what would happen at the interview. He envisaged Ventura's incredulity, turning to anger, that an underling as low-ranking and as new to the job as he could have the presumption to suggest a solution to a murder case which, as far as he was concerned, had already been solved. If he condescended enough to ask for Wexford's evidence, that in itself unlikely, how would he react when told there was none, that it was all a matter of "feeling," of glances and a *stare*?

No, it couldn't be done. It would be pointless. Apart from possibly damaging his career prospects, he would be set down as "cocky," as "cheeky" and getting above himself, even as showing off. He must forget it, put it out of his head. Strangely enough, that particular question came up again in the evening when he met Alison for a drink in Kingsmarkham's only wine bar. It precipitated their first real row. The following day would be a Friday and they always went out somewhere on a Friday night. A repertory company in Myringham were putting on, for one night, a production of Shaw's *Saint Joan*. Wexford very much wanted to see it, he saw little live theatre then, and he had thought it might also appeal to Alison. Her hostility surprised him. She wanted a film, an Ealing comedy—strange that he remembered so much but he couldn't remember which one.

"But that will be on on Saturday too," he had said, "and in Stowerton next week." There had been so many cinemas then, at least one in every small town.

"Reg," she said, looking hard at him, "isn't it time you

faced up to it? You don't really want to see this highbrow stuff any more than you want to read those books you're always mooning over, Chaucer and Shakespeare and stuff. You're not an egghead, you're a cop. You do it to make an impression, don't you? It's just showing off."

He had always had a short fuse, but he was learning to control it, unplug it in time. "You're wrong there. I read what I enjoy, and when I get a chance to go to the theatre, I try to choose what I shall enjoy."

"Of course you would say that. It's not natural for a man always to have his head in a book."

He asked her, his tone growing cool, what would be natural for a man.

"Well, going to football or playing golf. Playing some sport. I've never known why you don't. One thing's for sure, when we're married you won't have time for books. We'll have a house and there'll be plenty to do. My dad's always painting and decorating, not to mention the gardening."

"I've noticed. That's why we never see him when we go round there. He's always up a ladder or down a trench."

"Better than having his nose in a book. That's useless if you ask me."

"I don't ask, Alison. And I shall go to *Saint Joan* tomorrow. You must do as you like."

"I shall." She got up to leave. "And I shan't go alone."

Finishing his drink, he thought that things had reached a grim stage when a man started hoping the girl he was engaged to would go to the cinema with another man. A football-fan, golf-playing, DIY expert—or hadn't that expression yet been coined?—a gardener who read the *Greyhound Express.* You are turning into an intellectual snob, he told himself, with no grounds for being so.

Next day he had learnt that George Carroll had been charged. It hadn't changed his opinion, but he had still believed that if the police charged a man with murder, the chances were pretty certain that he would be found guilty and condemned to life imprisonment—if no longer to death. That made him shiver a bit. Was it cowardice then that stopped his speaking to Ventura or even Fulford? There was a difference between courage and foolhardiness. If he had had some evidence, a shred of evidence . . . But he had not. Forget it, he thought again. Put it behind you.

It hadn't occurred to him then that Carroll might appeal and on appeal be freed—not on the evidence or lack of it but due to the judge's misdirection of the jury. But that was a long way in the future, after many life-changing things had happened to him. In the present it was *Saint Joan* to which he went alone. Even if he had wanted to take a girl, he didn't really know any girls but Alison. He hadn't developed any critical faculty then and couldn't tell if the production was good, though he had thought that the Maid's (assumed) accent was bit over-the-top and the Dauphin a bit too foolish and effeminate. At the interval he went out to buy himself a beer, and when he returned, making for his seat at the rear of the stalls, he looked across the rows ahead, and there, just taking their seats next to an older woman, were two girls, one fairish and plump, the other dark with fine brown eyes and a perfect figure in her red dress. And he thought, she is the woman for me, that's my type. I didn't know that till now, but she is setting my type for me.

THE ROOM WEXFORD was renting was on the first floor of a house in Queen's Lane. Conditions were primitive by present standards. Using the bathroom was often difficult because he shared it with two other tenants, and he used to go home to his parents' house for baths, taking his washing with him. His mother was the rare owner of a washing machine. He had a gas ring in his room and a kettle in which he heated up enough water to shave with. Shaving was carried out from a bowl on a little table by the window, and one morning as he was splashing water across his face, he saw Targo pass by.

Queen's Lane was the easiest route to the footpath across the meadows which led to the Kingsbrook Bridge. Dog walkers naturally chose it. Wexford thought little more about it, though he did wonder why a man who lived in Stowerton would come all this way to find some open land when he could have reached woods and fields nearer home. But when it happened again next day and again the day after that, always between seven thirty and eight in the morning, he began to suspect some other reason. The second time, Targo paused outside—apparently, giving the dog the chance to sniff round the base of a lamppost and then relieve itself against it—but instead of watching the dog, he turned his eyes upwards and stared at Wexford's window. After that, this happened regularly. In today's parlance, Targo was stalking him.

THE ROUTE HE was now taking home from Burden's house under the stars, under a sky where now the moon, a three-quarters-full oval, had climbed above the trees, passed across Queen's Lane by way of York Passage. The whole place had changed beyond recognition. Not uglified (Wexford used Lewis Carroll's word to himself), because the few small shops had been given eighteenth-century-style fronts, the late-Victorian houses pulled down and handsome new ones built, and trees planted in the pavements. These trees were now big and shady, and it struck Wexford, trying to locate exactly where, on the façade of the chalet-style house which now faced him, his window had been, that as things now were, Targo's spaniel would have had to lift its leg against the trunk of an ash rather than against a lamppost. What had that spaniel been called? He couldn't remember, though he had often heard Targo speak to it as he reached the footpath and let it off the lead. It hardly mattered. Targo didn't always use a name but sometimes a term of endearment. It had been chilling to hear this sinister creature, this murderer, call his dog "honey" and "sweetie." Wexford walked on through the lonely dark. No one was about.

At home, his house was in darkness but for a glow from the front bedroom window. He went upstairs. Dora was sitting up, reading in bed.

"Sylvia says she can get us a gardener," she said, looking up from *The Way of All Flesh*, which she was reading for the third time. "He's the uncle of a friend of hers and he's an old Etonian who's just retired from some government department."

"Do Eton and the Civil Service qualify him to do our garden?"

"Probably not but she says his own garden's lovely, so that's a good recommendation."

"We'll give him a go and I won't send off my ad." Wexford touched the cover of her book. "I might read that again when you've done with it."

His mind was too full of the past for immediate sleep. He lay in the dark and a picture of Targo appeared before his eyes, short, stocky, in those days wearing what looked like the trousers of a shabby old suit with an equally shabby raincoat. Every day when he passed Wexford's window he wore the same scarf, a brown wool thing with a fringe at each end. He walked stiffly, strutted really, and after the first few times he began whistling. The tunes he whistled were old, years and years old, "It's a Long Way to Tipperary," "Pack Up Your Troubles," and "If You Were the Only Girl in the World." Wexford moved his bowl of water and his shaving things to another part of the room, but still something compelled him to watch Targo and the spaniel walk by. The whistling would alert him and he would cross to the window, never moving the curtain.

No Internet in those days, none of the records which were kept today. The electoral register was on paper, kept in post offices and of course police stations. He decided to find out as much as he could about Eric Targo without letting it be known he was searching and, necessarily, without letting it interfere with his work and his duties. Soon he had discovered that Kathleen Targo, who had given birth to a girl, was divorcing her husband. A woman that he had to call on in connection with the robbery of the shop on the corner of Jewel and Oval roads was one of those to whom nothing is irrelevant. He didn't try to stem the tide and soon she had told him, without his asking a single a question about the Targos, that Kathleen had thrown her husband out after he blacked her eye and broke her arm.

"Mind you, he's strong," he remembered her saying. "She had to get help. It took three big strapping fellows from down here to get him out of the place and make sure he never went back."

Those were the days when the police never interfered in a "domestic," when violence towards women was generally regarded as all part of married life and private to the couple in question. Kathleen had apparently taken the law into her own hands while Targo, Wexford discovered, was back living with his widowed mother at 8 Glebe Road. According to what records he could find, Targo had been born in Kingsmarkham, the only child of Albert Targo and his wife, Winifred, a woman who had come from Birmingham. Since he left school at the age of fourteen he had worked for a market gardener in Stowerton, for two years in refuse collection for Kingsmarkham Borough Council, and as soon as he had passed a driving test, become a van driver for a hardware firm.

Inescapable was the feeling that Targo was proud of what he had done, knew that Wexford knew it and was teasing him, defying him to come out with it to his superiors, knowing that without a shred of evidence against him he was safe. Wexford had an aunt who sometimes used the expression "I wouldn't give her the satisfaction," and he steadily ignored the homicidal dog walker, refusing to give him the satisfaction. Ignored him, as far as Targo knew. But Wexford watched him proceeding towards the footpath, knowing that as soon as he reached the grass and trees, he would let the spaniel off the lead, first stroking its sleek golden head. He learnt a lot about Targo in the few days he watched him, the stiff way he walked, strutted really, the cockiness that might have been put on for Wexford's benefit but which Wexford felt was natural to him. Then there was the attention he gave to the dog, stopping once or twice to pat it and say something, "Good boy" or "Honey" perhaps, but Wexford was out of earshot.

After a few weeks Targo ceased to walk his dog that way. He had made his point, whatever that was. About that time a Kingsmarkham woman was murdered by strangling. Her name was Maureen Roberts and there was no doubt her husband was her killer. He was in their house when she died, he made no attempt to defend himself, and on the following day he confessed to the crime. It was very different from the killing of Elsie Carroll. But she had been strangled. The murder weapon was one of her own stockings. The day after Christopher Roberts, her husband, was charged with her murder, Targo reappeared, walking his dog to the Kingsbrook footpath past Wexford's window.

"This time," Wexford said to Burden at lunch next day, "I was looking out of the window. I mean anyone passing could see me. I'd gone to the window to open it. I didn't expect to see Targo because it seemed he had given up exercising his dog that way. But there he was, strutting along, bending down right outside my window to pat the dog on the head, and then looking up right at me. He had a blue-and-white-striped wool scarf wound round and round his neck."

"Chelsea," said Burden.

"Oh, possibly." If Wexford had taken the interest in football advocated by Alison, he would have known about things like that. But he did know that it was the same scarf Targo had been wearing when he went into the Rahmans' house in Glebe Road the other day. "He didn't smile," he went on. "He seldom does, but he stared at me and opened his eyes very wide. I knew he meant me to think he'd killed Maureen Roberts."

"He must be mad."

"At least you're not saying I must be mad."

"No, but I'm tending that way."

"It was a strangling, you see, and he meant to take the strangling of victims as his trademark, whether he did it or not. And in this case he certainly didn't do it. Well, he winked at me and then he walked on, the same walk he had always taken until a few weeks before. When he came to the field and the path, he bent down, stroked the dog's head, and let him off the lead, and that was the last I saw of him for a long time. He moved away from Kingsmarkham to Birmingham, where his mother came from. He had relatives there and soon one very good friend. He started a driving school and I thought I'd seen the last of him.

"I had until a few years later when the stalking began again."

Burden was giving him the sort of look he would have given his wife when she raised once again the subject of Tamima Rahman. It was compounded of those two opposites, patience and exasperation.

"You aren't going to want to hear any more of this, are you?"

"There's more?"

"Oh, yes, lots more, but I'm not suggesting telling you now."

They had left the restaurant and walked across to the Broadbridge botanical gardens. There on a seat along the main central path which led to the arboretum and the sub-tropical house, they sat down and contemplated the artificial lake with its island, its ducks, and its two black swans. A squirrel ran down one tree, sat up on its haunches for a moment on the grass, before running up the trunk of another. A dog began to bark at the foot while the squirrel stared at it with loathing, making angry chattering sounds.

"I've got to go back," Burden said. "It's gone two and I'm due in court at half past when Scott Molloy comes up for perverting the course of justice. See you."

Wexford watched him go, then got up himself. He seldom visited the botanical gardens these days, but he had once been a frequent visitor. They had been designed and built to the specifications of a local philanthropist who had died and left several of his millions to the town on condition they be spent on his dream gardens and called them after him, Samuel V. Broadbridge. A tropical house was to be included on the site, a perfect facsimile of the one on the campus of his alma mater, a fabulously wealthy Californian university, as well as an alpine garden, a miniature Red Rocks (in the Rockies), and a small Yosemite-like ravine.

That was in the late seventies, and before that the acres had been open fields. Wexford had been all prepared to despise the place, but once it began to mature and the fine trees to grow, the magnolias, locusts, cottonwoods, and live oaks, all of which liked the mild south-of-England climate, he had begun to appreciate it. It was different, but difference need not mean worse. He should walk in here more often, he thought. He should walk *anywhere* more often. But where else could he find himself transported to a square mile of the western United States while no more than a mile from his own home?

After all, the open fields hadn't been very attractive, nor had the farm buildings on them. If Samuel V. Broadbridge hadn't stepped in with his dazzling millions, one of the several new housing estates would have been built on those fields. He watched a green woodpecker alight on the lawn, which matched its feathers, and begin pulling prey out of the grass. That was only one of the species of relatively rare birds which Sam V.B. (as he was known quite affectionately round here) had saved from expulsion if not destruction. Of course, there had been a worm in the bud and not the kind of worm the woodpecker would have appreciated. And Targo had been responsible for that too....

What was it Burden had said? "There's absolutely no

motive. Finding a motive's not necessary, but you have to admit it helps. There's no evidence."

All true, and as true of what happened in Sam V.B.'s Gardens twenty years later. His eyes went involuntarily towards the Red Rocks garden, though from here it was out of sight. It was time to go back. But he lingered, sat on a seat by the gate, and gave himself to thinking about Kingsmarkham as it was now and had been then.

No council estates—or social housing as you were supposed to call them. No flats with fitted kitchens and bathrooms but cottages with outside privies huddled together along damp lanes, the like of which you only saw these days as a background to peasant appearances in costume dramas on television. The streets where his own house was were meadows then, and at the end of his road the little wood that some law decreed must remain in spite of the developers had been the haunt of nightingales. The nightingales were all gone now. The high street was longer now than then with new buildings alternating with the Georgian frontages. And the police station was the first of these new buildings, assessed when it first went up as the *dernier cri* of modernity.

The Kingsbrook Precinct was yet to be built, and Samuel V. Broadbridge was still at college in California. The open fields and woods were all the botanical gardens the citizens of Kingsmarkham needed. Apparently they didn't need cars either. Or they hadn't had them. Driving had been a pleasure, not a chore, and a test of one's self-control and staying power. But that was common to the county and the country, not just Kingsmarkham. Such a small place then. No car parks encircling the town for they hadn't been needed. So was it better today? Were things better? The answer was always the same, some better, some worse. He got up and walked back to the police station, a building which had begun to look old and shabby, where the lifts went wrong and there wasn't an automatic door in the place.

He meant to leave early for home. A grandson was coming round to teach him how to use his CD Walkman. Do it for him more likely, Wexford chided himself, thinking too that he was certainly the only music lover his grandson had ever encountered whose CDs were all of Purcell and Handel.

5

A STRIKING-LOOKING WOMAN with blue-green eyes, almost fanatically devoted to her job as a history teacher, Jenny Burden was a lot like Burden's first wife in appearance if not in character. Wexford found this rather satisfying. He was a great believer that men and women had a "type" they adhered to in changing partners. Jean, who had been married to Burden when he first came to Kingsmarkham and who had lived with him at 36 Glebe Road, Wexford first met when their children were small. She had died young of cancer, and her widower had been devastated, to use a cliché word which no one used in that sense then. Within a few years he had married this pretty young woman with golden brown hair who, seen from a distance, might have been Jean's twin; close-to, and when she spoke, the illusion was broken.

Wexford was thinking of his own type, hourglass figure, dark hair, invitingly pretty rather than beautiful, the kind of woman of which his wife was the quintessence, when two things happened within moments of each other. Firstly, Hannah Goldsmith came into his office. Then, a call announced the arrival of Jenny Burden for her appointment, which he had forgotten all about. Hannah gave him a rundown on her activities with the small Moslem community in Kings-markham. As a detective sergeant, she had more or less appointed herself the ethnic minorities officer, something to which Wexford had no objection. She made a principle of being intensely antiracist, political correctness personified, a role which sometimes tied her in knots.

While she was telling him of her concerns at the possibility of forced marriages taking place locally, the call came. "I think I've a job for you coming up in the lift at this moment, Hannah."

Hannah turned round as Jenny came in. "We've met before."

"Yes, of course." Jenny shook hands. "At some school function, wasn't it?"

"Jenny, I'm going to ask you to talk to Hannah about this problem of yours. She'll be a lot better than I can be to deal with it." If there is a problem, he thought, but he didn't say it aloud. "Hannah knows all the Moslem families in Kings-markham. She's also one of the few people I know who has actually read the Quran."

Wexford remembered all too well a period of time, some years before, when Hannah had electrified (and embarrassed) his morning roundup-of-tasks meetings by breaking any short silences there might be with quotations she thought appropriate from this holy book. Smiling with relief, doing his best not to show too much haste, he sent Hannah away with Jenny in tow and settled down to the mountain of paperwork which was just one day's accumulation.

HANNAH SHARED OFFICE space with DC Damon Coleman and DC Lynn Fancourt. Both were there at their computers. "Let's go up to the canteen," Hannah said, "and we can talk over a coffee. Or a cup of tea, which is marginally better. School not back yet?"

"We start on Thursday." Jenny had never before been in the police canteen, though she had heard her husband condemn the standard of its cooking, the service, and its dismal appearance. "I hope," she said in the sort of meek tone she would never have used to a man, "you won't think I'm wasting your time."

"Oh, God, no," Hannah said, returning with two cups of coffee on a tray and two chocolate biscuits. "I don't mind an excuse to come up here and have a break. I expect you eat biscuits, don't you? You're like me and don't have to worry about your weight."

Jenny smiled. "I'll go ahead then, shall I? A bit more has happened since I first talked to Reg—I mean Mr. Wexford—about it. The girl's called Tamima Rahman—"

"I know the Rahmans," Hannah interrupted. "House in Glebe Road. They've done absolute wonders with that house. Extended it, had a new kitchen, and added another bathroom. And Yasmin Rahman keeps it spotless. I just wish some of these people who condemn Moslems out of hand could see it."

"Yes, well, Tamima was in my class at school. She was expected to do very well in her GCSEs. And she did. Very well. She told me immediately she got her results, even before I saw them for myself. Then, about a week after that, I met her in the street. I had the impression she tried to avoid me. She saw me coming and turned to look into a shop window. But I spoke to her and of course she had to turn round. We talked about her results and I told her how well she had done, I was very pleased with her. Then I asked her if her parents had applied to sixth-form colleges—you know what they are?"

"Sure. They're really what used to be called the sixth form in schools only they're a separate building. Kids go there from sixteen to eighteen, prior to doing their A Levels. Right?"

Like experts in any field, Jenny was unwilling to take anyone else's estimate of that discipline without adding minor corrections. "Well, more or less. They take their AS Levels at the end of the first year. I was hoping Tamima would decide to do history—that's my subject—English and Spanish to AS and then go on to A's. Of the sixth-form colleges available, I knew Carisbrooke was her favourite. But she said no, she wouldn't be going back to school next week. I thought she'd misunderstood me. I said of course she wouldn't be going back to *our* school, I meant had she applied to Carisbrooke because I thought she'd a very good chance of getting there with her exam results.

"You know how they say people can give you a stony look? Well, that was exactly the way she looked at me—stonily. I meant I'd be leaving school for good, she said. Any sort of school. That's a great pity, Tamima, I said. She looked down and muttered that she didn't want to talk about it."

"You think this is her family's doing? Her dad's?"

Just as she disliked children being called kids, so Jenny disapproved of the current trend to call parents "mums" and "dads," but she had to let it pass. "I'd heard her father was so progressive. He's got a degree himself, hasn't he? Why would he stop her going on to do A Levels? It's not going to cost him anything. There's no reason to think he's against education for women, is there?"

Hannah almost gushed in her defence of Tamima's father. "Oh, no, Mohammed Rahman is a lovely man. He's a social worker with Myringham Social Services, and—a coincidence, I suppose—he has a special responsibility for teenagers in the borough. Of course her going to a sixth-form college will cost him more than if she leaves and gets a job. That way she'd bring money into the household, but I can't believe he'd let that weigh with him."

"She's got a boyfriend," said Jenny, making a face at her coffee, "but he's half Pakistani. Would Mr. Rahman object to that?"

"We don't know that he does." As often happened, Hannah was now torn between militant feminism and antiracism. But the Quran was not the only guide to Moslem ways she had read, and she was never backward in showing off her knowledge. "He isn't a relative, though, is he? The Rahmans may favour cousin-marriage. He wouldn't be the right man for her because his parents came from Karachi, say, or Islamabad. They might want a family member for her."

"Not at all a healthy thing," said Jenny briskly.

Hannah was trapped again. "The marriage of first cousins sometimes seems to result in children with disabilities, though it's a very controversial subject."

"It's a well-known fact," Jenny said sharply.

Hannah ignored this. "I can't quite see how this can be a police matter. The school-leaving age is sixteen and she's sixteen. No one's breaking any laws. There's nothing to show the Rahmans are arranging a marriage for her, and even if they were, while forced marriage is against the law, arranged marriage isn't."

"Do you think I should go and see them? The Rahmans, I mean. Talk to the parents?"

Hannah didn't care for this suggestion. It was all right for her to go as a police officer, but she saw a teacher's visit as on a par with a social worker's snooping or an old-time lady bountiful's condescending to a peasant family. "So long as you remember they're intelligent people, educated people—well, Mohammed Rahman and his sons are. I hope you don't mind me saying this, but Mohammed wouldn't take kindly to being lectured."

Mildly for her, Jenny said, "I won't lecture him. I'll only say it's such a waste a bright girl like Tamima isn't to go on to higher education. I mean, what's she going to do with her life? Work in some dead-end job until she can be a full-time housewife like her mother?"

The position of women in Islam was in conflict with Hannah's feminist views, and this gave her a hard time. Still she couldn't let that pass. She gave Jenny a pleasant smile. "In the case of Tamima's mum I'm sure it's her choice to be a housewife. She's a very excellent one and absolutely the rock of that family. Can I get you another cup of coffee?"

AFTER KEVIN STYLES, self-styled gang leader, aged twenty and of no fixed address, had been committed for trial on charges of breaking and entering and causing actual bodily harm, Burden went off to meet Wexford for lunch at the Kashmiri restaurant they currently favoured. On his way to the Dal Lake he had had an experience he could hardly wait to tell Wexford about. The chief inspector was already there, sitting at a table reading the menu.

"I can't see any difference between this food and Indian at the Indus down the road," he said, looking up. "Of course this may not be authentic Kashmiri. We wouldn't know one way or the other, would we?"

"I've seen him," Burden said, sitting down.

"Seen who?"

"Your stalker."

"How could you know?"

"Well, let's say your description was so detailed, not to mention the white van, that it was pretty obvious. The bushy white hair, piercing blue eyes, his height or lack of it, the way he walks or struts."

"Scarf or no scarf?"

"No scarf. But close-to you can sort of see where the naevus was. When you know there was a naevus, that is. The skin's paler than the rest and smoother."

"You must have been very close-to. Where was this?"

"Outside the police station. Well, outside the court, which is more or less the same thing. The van was parked on a meter, all perfectly as it should be. I saw him put a coin into the meter and then he walked up to our forecourt and stood there, looking up at the windows. I walked over to him. He didn't speak and nor did I. God knows what he was doing."

"And not only God," said Wexford. "He was looking for me."

"What, still?"

"Why not? He doesn't know whether I'm still there or retired or maybe I've died. He wants to find out."

SOON AFTER GEORGE Carroll had been released, Wexford was transferred from Kingsmarkham to a division on the south coast. He thought it was permanent but it turned out to be only temporary, lasting just two years, part of the pre-liminaries to his being made sergeant. It was a time of shifting change; everyone, it seemed to him, moving away.

That George Carroll should move away from Stowerton was no surprise. He might have been acquitted, but not because some startling piece of eleventh-hour evidence revealed him to be beyond-doubt innocent. People were saying he got off on a technicality, just because some old judge who was probably senile had fallen down on the job. Carroll returned home for a while because he had nowhere else to go. In the present climate of social conduct, Wexford thought, his neighbours would at best have catcalled him and daubed abuse on his garden wall, at the more likely worst, smashed his windows and perhaps even stoned him. Then, all those years ago, he was treated with coolness and a few people turned away from him without a word or a nod. His house was put up for sale. Wexford had seen it advertised in an estate agent's window for two thousand five hundred pounds. Its reputation had reduced its price but not, he thought, by more than, say, three hundred pounds. Now that same house would fetch two hundred thousand.

Targo moved too. He waited to see George Carroll come home, be ostracized and excluded, then he and his family disappeared. Or that was the way Wexford had seen it. That was the way it looked. It might, of course, have been only coincidence that when George Carroll returned to Jewel Road after the trial, an estate agent's board appeared outside number 32 advertising it for rent. Wexford had gone down there to look at the empty house and the board himself, though for what purpose he couldn't have said. He enquired of a neighbour and was told the Targo family had moved away, no one knew where, but Kathleen and her children had gone to one destination and Targo to another. Soon after that Wexford himself was leaving.

He said good-bye to Alison and gave a halfhearted promise to come back to Kingsmarkham at weekends when he was able to, fairly certain that he would hardly ever be able to. She was halfhearted too. She had gradually become so since their row over his intellectual pretensions, and he could, to his relief, tell that the matter would be taken out of his hands, that she would soon break off their engagement. Strange that this made him fonder of her. Not fond enough to want them to be as they had been when they first met, but rather with a feeling of what might have been and what a pity it was that it could never come back.

As to the girl in the red dress, it had been only a glimpse he had had of her, not enough to make him go searching Sussex, just enough to make him think that one day he would like to marry a girl like her. Now he had his career to think of, his future. The breach with Alison came in a letter from her, the first letter he ever received in his new home, a room over a tobacconist's shop in Brighton. As he had thought, she had met another man, the one who had taken her to the pictures that night he went to *Saint Joan*. They were getting married almost at once. He wrote back, wished her happiness and to keep the ring, hoping she wouldn't because he could do with the money he would sell it for, but she did keep it. Now, someone had told him, she had several grandchildren and no longer lived in this country.

One day, walking down the high street on his way to interview a man about the disappearance of a sackful of stolen goods, he passed Tina Malcolm. George Carroll's former girlfriend, pushing a baby in a buggy, was with a man who wasn't Carroll. As people were always monotonously telling him, it was a small world, so it wasn't surprising perhaps to see on another occasion Harold and Margaret Johnson, window-shopping in the Brighton lanes. His friends he had left behind in Kingsmarkham, and he had so far made no new ones. Sometimes he went out to the pub in the evenings with DC Roger Phillips, but mostly he stayed in and read. Public libraries were in their heyday then, no nonsense about incorporating coffee shops and what technology there was, but lots and lots of good books. He read them, poetry and plays and novels. Worlds opened for him, and far from distracting him from his duties (as Alison would have suggested), they seemed to make him a better policeman.

COLOURED WAS CONSIDERED the kind and polite way to refer to black or Asian immigrants in those days. Not that there were many of them. Wexford remembered a carpet seller who went from door to door with his wares. He wore a turban and must have been a Sikh, but no one knew about that kind of thing then. A black man who swept the streets was probably from Africa, but no one knew what brought him here or what misfortune made pushing a cart and plying a broom a preferable existence to any other he might find. After he hadn't been seen for several weeks Wexford heard that he had died, had been found dead of natural causes in the tiny, squalid room he rented not far from where Targo had lived.

Years and years had passed before more immigrants came, and now it was becoming unusual to walk along any Kingsmarkham road without seeing one Indian or Chinese face. The way some people, particularly politicians, talked about the situation, integration versus multiculturalism, it would appear to be simple, a straightforward matter of not being racist. But Wexford's experience had taught him what deep waters one struggles to swim in when plunging into the traditions of another culture. He had been told he was too sensitive to these issues and perhaps he was. Oversensitivity was likely to be Hannah's problem too, notably her propensity to bend over backwards to avoid uttering the slightest word that might be construed as criticism of some nasty (Wexford's word) custom. He had even heard her taking great care not to condemn, in a Chinese restaurateur's presence, foot-binding, which had ceased to be performed in China some forty years before the man was born. Useless to tell her that the restaurateur, who was no more than thirty, might not even know that women of his great-grandmother's generation had had their feet deliberately distorted and crippled from childhood.

She walked in now. Anyone ignorant of her profession might far more easily have taken her for a model or perhaps a popular TV presenter than a police officer. He wondered how acceptable it had been for a middle-aged Moslem such as Mohammed Rahman to be questioned by a young woman in jeans and a rather too low-cut top. Hannah was sensitive only in patches.

"I felt I should call on the Rahmans," she began. "Their house is very nice inside, guv. It's small but they've built a beautiful extension and it's very tastefully decorated. Mr. Rahman was eating his dinner. He'd just got in from work. I must say, it smelt fantastic. I suppose Yasmin Rahman had been preparing it all day, and she didn't sit down with him, just stood behind his chair and attended to him." Wexford waited to see how she would get out of that one. She smiled airily. "Still, it's their tradition, of course, and you couldn't see her as in any way a victim. She seems a strong, even domineering sort of woman. I told Mohammed not to mind me but carry on with his meal, he must be hungry. I didn't think I'd find it awkward asking about Tamima and school and all that, but strangely enough I did."

"Not so strange considering the knots you tie yourself up in. What did you say?"

"Pretended not to know Tamima was leaving—well, had left, said we were a bit concerned that Asian girls with very good GCSEs weren't going on to higher education as they should be. He gave me a sceptical sort of look, guv—he's no fool—and I remembered a bit late in the day that he's a social worker. 'Leaving school is Tamima's own choice,' he said. 'Maybe she will resume her education later, who knows? But children have their own way these days, don't they, Miss . . . ?' I asked him to call me Hannah. His wife hadn't said a word and I thought she might have no English when suddenly she spoke and very fluently. Not all girls were intellectuals, she said, and she actually used that word. Some were homemakers as she had been and as Tamima was. She didn't want a career. It was only interfering people like her teacher, that Mrs. Burden, who wanted it for her, and she *would*, having a career herself. Maybe *she* needed to earn money but Tamima would not, her husband would do that."

Wexford nearly laughed. "You must have found yourself torn in two, Hannah, what with your adherence to militant feminism and your well-known defence of the multicultural society."

To his delight, Hannah really did laugh, if in rather a shamefaced way. "You've got to admit it's hard, guv. While Yasmin was going on about the virtues of being a housewife, Tamima came in. Yasmin said something to her in Urdu, I suppose it was, and whatever it was, she looked mutinous—well, resentful. I couldn't help wondering if it had been something about the boyfriend they don't approve of. . . ."

"Come on, Hannah, that's pure guesswork, or else your Urdu's come on a lot."

"OK, you're right, of course. I couldn't say anything to Tamima in her parents' presence, though I will. As soon as the chance comes along, I will. Anyway, one of the brothers arrived and Yasmin started busying herself getting his food—I noticed she didn't get Tamima's, suppose she had to wait till the men were done. Oh, I know, but you can't excuse everything in every culture. So I left. It wasn't exactly satisfactory, was it, guv?"

He was preoccupied because he had been thinking, before she came in, of times long past. He asked himself how astonished he would have been if, when he was young, some soothsayer had told him forced marriage would one day be an issue in England. The answer was simple—he wouldn't have believed it.

But Hannah's visit hadn't been exactly satisfactory. It hadn't been satisfactory at all. It seemed to him that she and Jenny had manufactured a serious problem out of nothing. A girl had chosen to leave school at sixteen as the law said she could. No doubt, she wanted to earn some money, the way young people did. That same girl had been seen walking with a schoolmate who happened to be male. Out of this, those two had composed a tragic romance. The girl was in love with a boy but snatched away from him into a forced marriage with a cousin. Perhaps she resisted, ran away with the boy, the result of which was that the two of them were murdered in horrible circumstances by one of the girl's brothers. It was a good thing neither of them knew of his sighting of Eric Targo, otherwise they would have hauled him into the plot, as the hired assassin employed by the brother.

Wexford believed none of it. It was more than ever a pleasure to go home now that work had begun on his garden. Andy Norton had done two afternoons' work on the flowerbeds and twice mowed the lawn. No one had got around to pruning the roses the requisite six weeks prior to blooming, so this year they were a failure. But red and yellow begonias were out in the tubs, and purple and red salvias in the borders, now freed from weeds. Dora told him the names, otherwise he would have had no idea. It was enough for him to look, admire, and be soothed. To forget for half an hour Targo the stalker, the murderer, the dog lover with the birthmark. The birthmark which was now gone. He'd like to know, he thought, when that naevus was removed and why, considering, to say the least, the man was no longer young.

6

HE WAS TO be best man at Roger Phillips's wedding. It was a sign, Wexford thought, of the almost friendless state the man found himself in that Roger, who had known him for less than a year, should have no one closer available for this "best friend" role. And he wasn't much better himself. He would have been lonely in Brighton if there had been less work to do and fewer books to read. And if he hadn't met Helen Rushford. He had been taking her out once or twice a week for the past three months.

Couples saved for years to give themselves a luxury wedding. He thought now of his younger daughter's fabulous feast, the marquee, the champagne and flowers, the dinner for two hundred. It had been different in the days when Phillips got married, a small affair paid for by the bride's father, the reception in a church hall, beer and lemonade to drink. No one drank wine then, sherry maybe and port but none of what they would have called table wines. No gift lists deposited at a West End department store. No presents picked out and ordered on the Internet. Guests gave toast racks, tea trays, or modest cheques. Wexford asked Helen what she thought he should give and she suggested bed linen, a sensible, practical gift. She was a sensible, practical girl and he took her to the wedding with him.

He had handed the ring to the bridegroom and was turning round to take his seat in the front pew when a glance at the congregation on the other side nearly made him drop the little box the ring had been in. Sitting in a pew about halfway down was the girl in the red dress. Or a girl who looked a lot like her, a twin if not quite the same girl. And, no, it wasn't the same girl. But even prettier than the one in the red dress. The quintessence of his type, the type he now knew was his. Not a red dress but a pale pink suit with a tight top and full skirt and matching hat. Women habitually wore hats then and no woman would have gone to a wedding without a hat. Hers looked as if it were made of pale pink mist in which a rose half-hid itself.

I shall speak to her as soon as we get out of here, Wexford said to himself. I'll start some sort of conversation with her at the reception. I shall think of something to say. Helen forgotten, he tried to think of what that something might be while the inimitable words of the Book of Common Prayer marriage service passed over him unheard and the congregation rose to sing "Praise, My Soul, the King of Heaven." It didn't occur to him then that pretty as she might be, well dressed and elegant, she might be even less similar to himself in temperament, even less congenial, than Alison had proved to be. His mind was never crossed by the thought as he sang a hymn in that church that she might be anything other than as charming as she looked.

In the event he never got to speak to her. When the bride and groom emerged from the vestry, they soon began the procession down the aisle followed by the four bridesmaids, her parents, and his parents. Wexford found himself paired up with a girl who seemed to be Roger Phillips's sister, and though he saw the girl in the pink hat as he passed her pew, she was whispering to an older woman who had sat beside her and he could do no more than cast her an imploring glance. Outside the photographs began—in a bitter east wind and spitting rain—and no groups included the girl in pink. She had gone, and the people she was with had gone. He would see her at the reception, but with even more people there than at the church, he only caught sight of her in the distance. Seeking her out was almost impossible with Helen on his arm. Besides, he had his speech to make and other speeches to listen to. But he managed to make his enquiries while Helen and a bevy of girls had accompanied Pauline to the room set aside for her to change into her "going away" clothes.

"Oh, that girl," Roger's mother said. "I've never seen her before. She was staying with some old friends of Pauline's parents, but they've gone now. She was a friend of their daughter's but the daughter wasn't well and they asked if they could bring this girl with them. Someone said her name was Medora. Very unusual, I thought."

BYRON, HE THOUGHT. Byron had a character in a poem called Medora. "The Giaour"? And wasn't the daughter of Augusta Leigh, his half sister, that someone or other said was his child, wasn't she called it too? Strange choice for one's own daughter. But beautiful and romantic. Which parent was the Byron reader? He would ask her when they met—in the unlikely event of his ever getting to meet her.

Still, he mustn't be feeble for he knew what faint heart never won. Now for a way, once they came back from their honeymoon, to find out from Roger's new wife the name of her parents' friends and find it out without arousing suspicions. Even if he hadn't been going about with Helen, he would still have disliked the idea of himself and the girl in the rose-pink hat becoming the subject of teasing. He couldn't forget her, and once or twice he dreamed about her. In the cold light of day he told himself what a fool he was, behaving like Dante over Beatrice. This was the twentieth century and he was a *policeman*, for God's sake. Forget her. Don't keep imagining you see her in her pink suit and her rose-pink hat. He argued the case with himself the whole time Roger and Pauline were away and, when they returned, tried to discover the name of Pauline's parents' friends by a circuitous route, asking Roger to ask his wife if this couple were the Derwents his mother used to know in Coulsden. He said he thought he recognised them from years back.

Of course this turned out to be the least pressing matter on Roger's mind. He had to be reminded twice. "I hope you weren't expecting these people to be your long-lost aunt and uncle about to leave you a fortune," he said, passing Wexford a slip of paper. "As you see, they're not called Derwent, they're called Moffat, and Pauline's got no idea where they live."

"I think someone said the girl with them wasn't their daughter."

"So that's it, is it?" Roger gave a crow of triumph. "I might have known."

Wexford had said there was nothing to know and resolved never to speak of it to Roger again. The name Moffat was written on the paper. There must be hundreds of Moffats in the country, perhaps not all that many on the south coast, and Pauline's parents, Roger had told him, had moved to Brighton from Pomfret. So should he start on the East Sussex phone book? How much easier it would have been today, he reflected, when anyone could be run to earth via the Internet. Or could be if you knew how to do it or someone working for you did. For all his resolution not to think of the girl in the pink hat as any more than his type, he was hooked on that type now and on her as its representative. . . .

"Reg." Burden's voice broke rather harshly into Wexford's reverie. "Are you going to sit there all night?"

He shook himself, blinked. "Sorry. I was thinking about the past."

"It's usually pleasanter than the present. I thought we might have a drink somewhere. It's gone seven and you said Dora was out. I finished that photocopy you gave me. It made me want to read more and I got Chambers's book out of the library. But your photocopy says it all and there's no more. He may call it *Unsolved Crimes and Some Solutions*, but he doesn't offer many solutions and none in the Carroll case."

They went into the Dragon rather than the Olive and Dove and found a quiet corner away from the crowd, who had gone into the little room which used to be called the Saloon Bar to watch a football match.

"Claret or burgundy?"

"Doesn't matter," Wexford said. "Their red wine all tastes the same."

His thoughts went back to those Burden's entry had interrupted. He had taken a big step from dreaming of the girl in the pink hat to actually hunting for her. He told himself that he had already done the preliminary work—he was already thinking in policeman mode—and now all he had to do was perform a few practical actions, starting with the electoral register for the Coulsden district. You could go into a post office in those days, stand at the counter, and look down the street numbers for the name you wanted. It was the Internet now, more difficult, he thought, more confusing. But to start on this while he was going about with Helen, taking her to the cinema, out for meals, for walks and a picnic in the countryside, kissing her good-night—though no more than that—to do all this while she regarded him as her boyfriend, that seemed wrong to him. That seemed dishonourable. He told her he thought they should stop seeing each other. The look on her face appalled him, the tears that came into her eyes. She was five years younger than he and suddenly she looked very young, a child starting to cry. He told her he was too old for her, that she should find someone nearer her own age, and he sugared the unpalatable medicine by adding that she was so lovely she was wasting herself on him.

"But I love you," she said. "You're everything I want."

Had any other woman ever said that to him? Had Dora, his wife? He thought not, but he had broken with Helen just the same and he had never seen her again. Never seen her but occasionally heard of her. She lived in the village of Stoke Stringfield now with her husband and grown-up children, the village next to Stringfield where Targo had Wymondham Lodge. He knew of her and knew her married name was Conway. You should have been ashamed, he told himself, ashamed of treating the poor girl like that and even more of romantic fantasies which were bound to have a disastrous outcome.

He shook himself back into the present. "You have to remember that there *was* a solution," he said to Burden when their drinks came. "Arresting and charging George Carroll with the murder of his wife was the solution. And it didn't cease to be the solution—that is in Fulford's and Ventura's and a lot of other people's eyes—when Carroll got off because the judge gave some direction to the jury he shouldn't have. The difference between them and me was that I had never believed Carroll guilty and believed him neither more nor less guilty after he was acquitted, whereas Fulford and Ventura were pretty sure he was guilty and absolutely believed he was guilty after he was convicted. His acquittal made no difference to their belief, but they were both very angry. That expression *hopping mad* describes them well. Ventura was positively jumping up and down with rage.

"He kept saying over and over, 'This villain is to go free because some old fool in a wig doesn't know his job!'"

"So there were no other suspects?"

"Only in my mind. Targo was always there. While I was living in Hove, I thought a lot about him and the wife he'd beaten up and the little boy Alan and the new baby. I knew they'd left Jewel Road and then they'd divorced, but I wondered if he was paying her maintenance and the child support as he should have been. One day I bumped into Tina Malcolm, walking along with a baby and some man she may have married. Probably had as people rather shied away from having babies without benefit of wedlock in those days—as you'll remember. She didn't recognise me or didn't appear to. I used to wonder what she must have felt when her lover came up in court on a murder charge."

"You mean he really was with her that night?"

"Oh, yes, I think so, don't you? He was with her, and when he heard she had denied what he said—betrayed him, you might say, never mind the revocation he wouldn't have known about anyway—I imagine his world went to pieces. Perhaps he had loved her. Who knows?"

"You reckon he'd have got off the first time if she'd said he was with her?"

"I suppose so. It was an absolute alibi if she'd said he was with her for three hours. You see, although on Ventura's orders I questioned those neighbours who were at home, no one went back later and questioned the ones who hadn't been at home earlier. One of them might have seen Carroll go in there. But Ventura wasn't interested. Once Tina had said Carroll wasn't with her, that only confirmed what he'd made up his mind to, that Carroll was guilty. But they were never asked, not after she denied it. Carroll couldn't have been in two places at once, and he was never in sixteen Jewel Road after six thirty p.m."

"Chambers says Carroll went up north somewhere. No one seemed to know what he did for a living, but he fell ill and died of pancreatic cancer about a year after his acquittal. What happened to Targo?"

Wexford shrugged. "He started a driving school in Birmingham. He'd met a woman there who had quite a lot of money. Her name was Tracy something. She was very young then, she'd been left a lot of money by her father, and she had a big house in Edgbaston. But he never married her and he came back here when his mother died and he inherited her little house in Glebe Road."

"How do you know all this?"

"I made it my business to know. Just as I believe he made it his business to know about me. You see, if I was obsessed with him, as you'll say I was, he was obsessed with me. Oh, I don't mean in any sort of homosexual way, I mean he got it into his head that it would be—well, *fun*, to have a policeman in a way in his power, someone who knew what he'd done and, incidentally, would do in the future, but who could do nothing about it. But then I never suspected, for instance, that he might be a psychopath. I never considered he might be a serial killer and Elsie Carroll only the first of his victims *or an early one.*"

Burden began to expostulate, as he had done on the previous occasion this had been discussed. "But you'd no evidence. Just a look and a man being fond of his dog. You'd *nothing*."

Wexford shook his head. "I had the stalking. It started again. I'd just got married and we were living in one of those houses near the Kingsbrook. You remember."

"Sure I do. There was a meadow at the end of your garden that ran down to the river." Burden added rather sadly, "It's all built on now."

"Well, people have to have places to live. Targo began exercising his dog down there. It was the same dog, the golden spaniel, and it must have been very old by then. There were a good many ways of getting into that meadow, one of them being the Kingsbrook towpath and another a gate to a path off the high street, but he chose to pass my house and take the footpath that ran down to right of it. I got used to seeing him and I didn't like it."

"What, just because he was walking his dog?"

"At that time, Mike, he was living—alone, I think—in his mother's old house at eight Glebe Road. To have come into the meadow by any of a dozen entry points would have been easier than walking uphill to my house and using that footpath."

"What did he do when he saw you?"

"Well, of course, he seldom did see me. It was summer when this started and very early in the morning. I'd see him from my bedroom window just after I'd got up. Sometimes he'd pause and look up at my windows the way he did when I had that single room. He always had a scarf tied round his neck. He always stared. Once and only once I was getting into my car. It was later because autumn had come. He said good morning and I said good morning and after that the

71

stalking stopped. He didn't stay long. He sold the place he'd inherited and went back to Birmingham."

"If it was stalking," said Burden, "you'd nothing to go on for calling him a psychopath."

"I had the man who sneaked across the Carrolls' garden at seven o'clock, the short man, the man who lived so near the Carrolls that he could have left his sleeping child, done the deed, and been back home in ten minutes."

"It's a bit thin, isn't it, for calling someone a psychopath and a serial killer? Just that one murder and that of a woman he'd never even spoken to?"

"Ah, but there were his fantasy murders. I mean the killings he wanted me to think he'd done. Yes, I'm serious. Maureen Roberts, for a start. The next real one—as far as I know—was years later after he'd done rather well for himself—inherited his mother's place, had money from that Tracy—bought a house and set himself up running a boarding kennel. You'll remember the case. Well, I know you do. You mentioned it the other day, that poor chap who was strangled in the botanical gardens. Billy Kenyon. Remember?"

"You mean you think Targo was responsible for *that*?"

"More than 'think,' Mike. I'm sure."

"Are you going to tell me?"

"Maybe I'll wait till you ask."

7

S HE WAS BEHIND the counter at the checkout.

"And it wasn't even Tesco," Burden said, as if the size or status of the supermarket where Tamima Rahman was working made any significant difference. "It was one of those Indian places where you can buy everything you can think of in tins and they sell halal meat. They call them corner shops, only it's not on a corner. Just one checkout and she was at it."

"There's nothing we can do, Mike," Wexford said. "We couldn't stop her leaving school, we couldn't make the Rahmans apply to a sixth-form college, and we can't ban the child from working. She's over sixteen."

"But such work. It wouldn't be so bad if it was some sort of office job or something which involved training."

"What a snob you are. I suppose the proprietor's a family friend. He offered the job and she was glad to take it. It may be only temporary."

"Jenny says she's going to this place—it's called the Raj Emporium—and she's going to ask her. She could hardly believe it when I told her."

Jenny must do as she likes, Wexford thought. If she wants to make private enquiries, let her, but I'm having no police interference. She is determined to stick to her romance, it's her own Romeo and Juliet, and she's hanging on to it. I never would have thought her so foolish. Three weeks passed before he heard any more, and by that time it had largely passed from his mind. A boy named Kieran Upritchard had been stabbed in the street, and the perpetrator, Neil Dusan, a Molloy gang member, was in custody while the boy lingered between life and death. A five-year-old had disappeared and turned up with an aunt in Macclesfield, but not before everyone in Wexford's team had abandoned their other work to go out hunting for him. A petrol-station owner had installed spikes to spring up from the tarmac if a customer left without paying for his fuel. One driver had called the police, the second had accepted the damage to his car and paid up, but the third had pulled a gun on the owner, who was now in hospital with serious if not life-threatening injuries. Wexford had no time to concern himself with Tamima Rahman, who had committed no offence, had nothing illegal done to her, and made no complaints.

But meanwhile Jenny Burden had been several times to the Raj Emporium and extracted information from Tamima. Though the corner shop was busy in the evenings, for long hours only the occasional shopper visited the place, and few who did weren't immigrants or the children of immigrants. Jenny wasn't quite the only white customer. On one occasion a youngish man with brown hair and blue eyes was in there, filling his wire basket with a selection of spices, his eyes lingering too long on the pretty Asian girl at the checkout. Tamima lost patience with Jenny's visits, but the proprietor, apparently her father's brother, was too good a businessman to tolerate her attempts to drive her former teacher away. His checkout girl got a severe dressing down in Jenny's presence.

Wexford found her giving Dora an indignant report of what had happened when he got home one evening.

"Her excuse is that she needs the money. Apparently she's not satisfied with the pocket money she gets from her father. She insists it's temporary, but she has no idea what other work is being arranged for her. If any is. It wasn't worth doing anything better than working for 'uncle,' she says, because her mother is taking her to Pakistan on holiday. They'll be away at least a month, staying with relatives, and she's looking forward to it. Why not look on this as a kind of gap year, I said, and get your parents to apply to Carisbrooke for next October. She didn't answer for a bit and then she said that wouldn't be possible. I asked her if she was still seeing her boyfriend."

"That was a bit much, Jenny," Wexford said. "It wasn't exactly your business, was it?"

"You wouldn't say that if she were a white girl. You've got inverted race prejudice, you know. Caught it off Hannah Goldsmith, I suspect. I know the boy, he's a nice boy. His name's Rashid Hanif. He's going on to sixth-form college, but *he'd* be encouraged to. He's male."

"Well, is she seeing him?"

"She says she hasn't a boyfriend, but I saw them together in the Kingsbrook Centre."

The place was run-down now. Once a state-of-the-art pattern for all small shopping malls, it had gradually become rather shabby, its shops down-market high-street chains mostly selling cheap clothes produced in Southeast Asian sweatshops. It was rather sinister too, drug dealers operating in what had once been elegant passages leading into café gardens and which now stank of marijuana and urine. For Wexford it was a perpetual headache. His hope was that a promise (or threat) would at last be carried out, in spite of relentless opposition, and the place be demolished—even if demolition meant yet another supermarket and multistory car park taking its place.

"It's a dump," Dora said. "What on earth were they doing there?"

Jenny shrugged. "How about hiding from her parents? Respectable Moslems won't go in there. They say it's dirty and it is. They prefer to buy from their own. Tamima and Rashid could wander about the place, maybe have cups of coffee in one of those cafés, sit on the seats by that so-called fountain that hasn't worked for months."

Wexford fetched her and Dora glasses of white wine and a large red for himself. He helped himself to a handful of cashews before Dora snatched away the nut bowl. "Jenny," he said, "whatever is going on, there is nothing to be done about it. There may come a day when higher education is as compulsory for sixteen-year-olds as primary school is today for five-year-olds. It may come, but it's a long way off yet. The time may come when it is an offence for a girl with seven GCSEs to work on a supermarket checkout, but I doubt it. It's more likely that parents may be one day prohibited from arranging a marriage between their daughter and her first cousin, but if there is no coercion applied, I doubt that too.

"Have the Rahmans locked Tamima up? Have they compelled her to work for her uncle? Are they forcing her to go on holiday to Pakistan? No to all those. I know you believe that her mother is taking her to Pakistan because when they get there she'll be made to meet a cousin who may be twenty or thirty or forty years older than she or hideous or unable to speak English, an illiterate peasant maybe, and forced into marriage with him. That what's in your mind, isn't it? Forced marriage?"

"If you put it like that, Reg, yes, it is. I just don't think you know what lengths some of these people will go to in order to force marriage on a girl. I heard of one case where the parents tortured their daughter into consenting and another where a mother threatened a girl with being raped by her stepfather."

Wexford was relieved when Jenny went. He wanted to talk to Dora about the gardener.

"It's true about him being an old Etonian, but as far as I'm concerned, that only means he speaks properly. You get so tired of people who can't speak their own language. Balliol as well as Eton, I think. He comes in that ancient Morris Minor he drives and gets straight on with things. I make us a cup of tea at four, but he doesn't linger. He drinks it, refuses a second, and gets back to work."

"So he's a treasure?"

"He really is, darling."

She went back to the book she had been reading before Jenny came. He thought about the past. Was he, already at his age, beginning to hark back there more than living in the present? It was Dora's saying she got tired of people being unable to speak their own language properly that set him off, that fired this train of thought.

FANCY-FREE, WHICH WAS not quite the way he put it to himself, guilty over Helen, he had found Moffat, Edward P.; Moffat, Josephine; and Moffat, Elizabeth M., all living at a house numbered 21 in a street which sounded rather posh. But now he had the address, he didn't know what to do with it. Of course he looked in the phone book and found the Moffats' number, but he had no idea what to do with that either. You can't write a letter to Edward Moffat, Esq.— people addressed letters like that then—and ask him for the full name and home address of a Miss Medora something who happened to take your fancy while you were being a best man. You can't phone Mrs. Elizabeth Moffat, tell her you'd done a sort of Dante and Beatrice thing and fallen in love with a girl she'd brought to Roger Phillips's wedding.

But perhaps you could go to their house with some story, some ploy. You could invent some tale—after all, hadn't you a fertile imagination, fed with literature and romance? Whatever the ploy was, it must have nothing to do with his life and his work as a police officer. That was out, utterly banned. He would spend some thought time, he decided, on a careful plan, do nothing impetuous, though of all things he wanted to do it as soon as he could think of it. He was greedy for a sight of her. But before he had reached that point, he had been moved back to Kingsmarkham and promoted.

It was his home, his parents were there and a lot of old friends. It also had the advantage of being nearer to Coulsden. Three months had passed since Roger Phillips's wedding— the event that in his mind he called "the fateful wedding" because that was where he had seen her—but he thought that not too long to carry out his plan. When he presented himself at the Moffats' door, it would seem more casual, more a "just passing" situation, than if he had turned up with the little book on the following day.

It never occurred to him beforehand that a phone call would appear to them a far more natural way of setting about things. But because there was necessarily a delay in putting his plan into action, he did ask himself if he wasn't assuming too much, taking too much for granted, almost committing himself to something from which there might be no going back. Suppose she turned out to be cold and scornful or, worse, laughed at him. Having good taste in clothes and walking like a queen meant no more than that she took pride in her appearance. It might mean worse, that she was vain and narcissistic. He would never know if he didn't try.

In what was then Kingsmarkham's only bookshop, he bought a little book, *Poems* by Anne Finch, Countess of Winchilsea. She was a poet before women were ever allowed to be poets. He read all the verse in the slim volume because he read everything which came his way and also to give the book a slightly worn appearance. Its cover was a dark red suede, and he rubbed at the suede a bit with his fingertips to mark it. This was for the Moffats' benefit, to make his story more convincing. After all, she, the unknown Medora, was hardly likely to be persuaded that she had left it behind in a pew in a seaside town church, a book of verse she had never before seen.

In the event his effort, if not a total failure, was a bit of a damp squib. It crackled for a split second, then fizzled out. Mrs. Moffat opened the front door to him and listened in puzzlement to his excuses for being there. At first she hardly seemed to know whom he meant by Medora, then she spoke. He expected patrician accents and got what they called now but didn't call then, estuary English.

"Oh, yes, my daughter's pal." No explanation was forthcoming as to why she was staying in this house or why she came to the wedding. "She lives in Cornwall. I haven't got the address but I reckon Josie could have. She's away right now, Josie, I mean." Mrs. Moffat looked suspiciously at the book. "Are you sure it was her left it behind?"

"Quite sure," he lied. "I saw it in her hand."

"Well, leave it with me. I'll see what Josie says."

He had no choice. But he knew enough of people and human nature by that time to be pretty sure of the little book's fate. It would lie about in that house for a few weeks. The daughter might come home, glance at it, say, "What am I supposed to do with it?" and lay it down again until a cleaning lady, tidying up, stuffed it into a bookcase between a Dennis Wheatley and a Vicki Baum.

In the fiction he read so voraciously a character like himself might have got somewhere, but not in life. He quelled his disappointment by thinking how grim it would have been had he met her and she turned out to be all those things he had considered but dismissed, vulgar and vain and empty-headed so that a book of verses would only evoke a "I've left school, thanks very much." He had to forget her and get on with his work. It shouldn't be too difficult to forget someone you had never met, whatever the song said, and he repeated to himself, "She was a lady sweet and kind, ne'er a face so pleased my mind. I did but see her passing by, and yet I love her till I die." Well, of course he didn't. What nonsense. Never go back, he thought, otherwise he might have contacted Helen. . . . But he had a flat in Kingsmarkham now, a quarter of a big house, and the girl who lived in the next flat on the same floor was attractive and unattached. . . . Next time they met on the stairs he'd ask her in for coffee.

Meanwhile, there had been a murder in Pomfret and he was busy night and day questioning suspects. It was his first murder since Elsie Carroll, and though Targo was long gone, it was the thickset, sturdy little man, the stalker with the spaniel, whose image came into his mind. Impossible, of course. Lilian Gray had been murdered by her husband. He had long since learnt that most people who meet a violent death have been dealt it by one of their nearest and dearest. The exception was a Mrs. Parsons who had died in strange circumstances, killed by an old schoolfriend who was in love with her.

"You were here by then, Mike," he said to Burden. "Do you remember the case?"

"I'll never forget it. People were still shocked by lesbianism then. I'm sorry to say I was a bit myself. You weren't, you took it all in your stride."

"She wasn't really a lesbian, was she? Just a poor woman puzzled by her desire for another woman."

"It's a long time ago," said Burden.

He said nothing about wanting to hear more of Targo. Perhaps, Wexford thought, he never would. There had been few unsolved crimes in those years and no repetitions of the Carroll case with a man enduring a trial, a conviction, and an appeal only to be ostracised for what Wexford was certain someone else had done.

By that time he had found the girl who was the quintessence of his type, married her, and their children had been born. But he said nothing about that to Burden, that was his private thing, to be kept even from his best friends.

8

THE MOFFATS' DAUGHTER phoned him. It was the last thing he expected. "This is Josephine Moffat. You came to our house and brought a book for Medora."

She sounded nice and not much like her mother.

"We met when I was on holiday down in Cornwall with my parents," she said. "I don't see her very often because she lives so far away and mostly we just write. But she did come up to stay when we were going to that wedding, only I couldn't on account of I got flu." Cornwall was thought of as far away then. The world had shrunk. "I sent her the book."

Now she would tell him Anne Finch's poems weren't Medora's. He had made a mistake. But, no.

"She was named after someone in a poem herself. She says she'd like to meet you, but I told her you were a policeman in Sussex."

He hardly recognised his own voice, it was so shy and hesitant. "Would you give me her address? I don't even know her surname."

"Don't you? How funny." Suddenly the voice was coarser and less ladylike. "It's Holland and she lives at fourteen Denys

Road, Port Ezra, Cornwall." She gave him a phone number he wondered if he would dare to use.

No postcodes then. Just the town or village and the county. Writing that letter was difficult but he did it, suggesting he might call and see her when he had a week's holiday in August. No answer came and he was deterred for a while. Then Ventura sent him to Cornwall to interview a man the Cornish police were holding on suspicion of his being involved in a bank robbery in Kingsmarkham. William Raw was taking refuge with his mother in St. Austell when he was arrested, and Wexford, with the interview fixed for the following morning, would have a free late afternoon and evening. Port Ezra was no more than seven miles away along the coast towards Plymouth.

It was now or never. This was a long-distance call, costly and not to be made lightly. He could have done it from the police station, but too many of his colleagues did that sort of thing and he wasn't going to. Presumably, she lived with her parents. Most young girls did then and most young men too. But it was she who answered, her voice not quite what he had hoped for. What kind of a snob was he that he was daunted by a Cornish burr?

"I'd like to meet you," she said. "Could you come about six? Mum and Dad will be home by then."

Meeting her parents wasn't part of his plan, but he made enthusiastic noises and said he would like to take her out to dinner. Was there a restaurant nearby?

"Not in Port Ezra." She giggled. "There's the Pomeroy Arms, but that's just for drink." It was long before the days when pubs did food. "You could have supper here with us."

He said he'd be with her by six. That giggle was another point against her, but he castigated himself for his rigidity.

Port Ezra was a strange name, he said to his landlady before he left the boardinghouse where he and DC Bryson were staying. Not so strange for Cornwall, she said, where they had Cairo and Indian Queens, transliterations from the old Cornish language. The nearest English equivalent to Medora's hometown was Port Ezra, so that was how it was known.

He and Bryson had come to St. Austell by train. They had no car at their disposal. Wexford took the bus that followed the coast road to Port Ezra and beyond. It was less a town than a village, with two shops and a pub, a dour gray church, white cottages with fuchsia hedges in full red and purple blossom, newish bungalows in its half dozen streets leading off the cliff road, and a magnificent view of dark blue sea pierced by jagged black rocks like a thousand islands. Number 14 Denys Road was one of the bungalows. The small car called the Mini had been on sale in Britain for a year or two, in just two colours at first, pale blue and red and the Hollands had a red one standing on their driveway. Now he was outside the house, Wexford hadn't the least idea as to what he would say. "I did but see her passing by, and yet I love her till I die" would hardly serve as an opening move with her mother or father.

But it was she herself who opened the door.

"So here you are then," she said in a broad Cornish accent, a burr as thick as a television actor might have with a part in *Jamaica Inn*. "I never thought you'd actually come."

He had to remind himself that he had a Sussex accent. For years he had thought he spoke the Queen's English, pure BBC, and then he had heard a recording made of his own voice and been disillusioned.

"Anyway, come on in," she said.

She was wearing dark green trousers that they called slacks then and a low-cut, green, floral blouse. The clothes didn't suit the girl he had previously seen in tight-waisted, full-skirted pink. His mother would have thought that blouse daring and even close on indecent. But her skin was perfect and her dark hair as glossy as satin. By this time he had been in dozens of strangers' living rooms, and nothing was out of the ordinary in this one from the flying china mallards on the wall to the beige, uncut-moquette, three-piece suite. Perhaps there were rather more framed photographs than usual. And which parent owned the *Complete Works of Byron* sitting among the cookery books and the Dennis Wheatleys? It comforted him to see it there, almost as if a sympathetic old friend were sitting in on their meeting.

"You're a cop, Josie says." She smiled invitingly

"Yes. A detective sergeant."

Her perfume was musky and suitable for a woman twice her age. He sat down in one of the armchairs, but when she patted the sofa cushion beside hers, he moved to sit next to her.

"Fancy you seeing me and wanting to take me out. That's very romantic." Now her face was quite close to his, he could see how heavy was her makeup. Had it been like that in the church but he not near enough to notice? Where were the parents? Not home yet? In another part of the house? "I never lost that book, you know. That was just a way of getting to meet me, wasn't it?"

He nodded. Her rather aggressive tone disconcerted him.

"Poems by a woman written hundreds of years ago. Not exactly my cup of tea."

"Whose is the Byron then?" he had asked.

"Oh, that. My dad's. He's a bit of an egghead, or used to

be. Shall we have a drink? We've got sherry, Bristol Cream or Dry Fly?"

"Should we wait for your mother and father?" He was still anxious to do everything right. She must be nervous and that would account for the way she spoke and the words she used. "They'll be home soon, won't they?"

"I don't know why you're bothered about them. I thought you'd like to be alone with me."

Her face was very near to his now, the mouth half-open. He edged backwards along the sofa, conscious of how this must look. It was no use any longer telling himself her behaviour was due to nerves. Then he heard a footstep overhead. So someone was in the house, those parents or someone else? You're a cop, she had said, and being a cop stood him in good stead now. But instead of standing up, leaving without ceremony, he turned back to face her, and as he did so, she took him by the shoulders and pulled him down on top of her. At some point she must have ripped the green blouse because he saw her naked breasts and, in spite of himself, was excited by them.

It hardly mattered because she screamed, a shattering sound from strong young lungs. There was a pounding on the stairs, the door burst open, and a man came in. Not her father, but a young man about his own age. He was big, burly, and red-faced.

"What's going on here? Get off her."

"With pleasure," Wexford said, extricating himself.

"He assaulted me," the girl said. "Jumped on me and tore my blouse."

She was holding the two sides of it together. "Look at that, Jim. That's what he did."

"You're going to pay for this," Jim said.

Wexford stood up. "And who are you?"

"He's my fiancé."

"I see. I'd strongly advise you not to marry her," Wexford said to the man, "not unless you fancy visiting your wife in prison."

He expected this to have an inflammatory effect, but instead a shifty look crossed Jim's face. "Let's talk about this. There's no need to take it further. I mean, I was going to call the police. . . ." He stopped when Wexford began to laugh. "All right, all right. Only we'll need paying. Or Meddy will. Her blouse is ruined for one thing, and you've frightened her. We'll say fifty quid and we'll forget about it."

It was an old trick. Wexford had been told about it but never personally come across it before. Usually, he understood, the players in the game were a prostitute, her pimp, and a client. Perhaps the situation wasn't that different. "Forget about it, is right. For one thing I don't carry fifty pounds about on me." It was a large sum then. Laughable as the price for a blouse which might have cost two pounds. "And even if I did, I'd not hand it over to a thug like you when I've done nothing."

The two of them, Medora still clutching her blouse, had moved over to bar the door. The man called Jim pressed himself against it with arms outspread. The girl stood next to him, glowering at Wexford.

"Open the door," he said.

"Make me."

"All right, I will."

As he grabbed Jim's left arm to pull him away, the other arm came up and struck him a glancing slap across the face. That was it. Wexford was young and strong and could pull a hefty punch. He took a step back and struck the other man a blow to his jaw. It wasn't all that hard, not half as hard as he could have made it, but Jim's knees buckled and he fell to the floor. Medora was screaming, real, heartfelt, terrified screams, quite different from the sounds she made when claiming to be raped.

"Stop that noise," Wexford said. "He's not hurt." Jim was struggling to sit up. "Well, not much hurt."

"You've busted my jaw," said Jim. Wexford knew he couldn't have if the man could speak. "You've not heard the last of this."

Wexford gave him a poke in the thigh with the toe of his shoe. "Good night," he said, and let himself out the front door. Down the garden path, past the parked Mini. Jim's car? Out into the street, pulling the gate shut behind him. No one tried to stop him. He was quite sure he would hear no more about it and was in no doubt he had done the right thing in hitting Jim, but he still felt all kinds of a fool. A fool for going there, a fool for not walking out when she said he'd like to be alone with her, and most of all a fool for letting himself become obsessed with a girl he had never even spoken to just because she was pretty, wore a rose-pink hat, and had a romantic name. Walking up Denys Road towards the beach and the bus stop, he resolved that he would never again let an obsession master him, not realizing then that the peculiarities of our psyches are not so easily conquered and subdued. In those days, if he decided on something, he was certain he would keep to it, for he was full of self-confidence. This particular resolution was doomed to failure from the start, and even today Burden often cautioned him about another fixation. Hadn't he, after all, been obsessed for half his life with Eric Targo?

The buses from Port Ezra to St. Austell were infrequent,

and he had walked for nearly two miles in sight of the sea before his reaching a bus stop coincided with the arrival of the bus. He had enjoyed walking in those days, walking fast and vigorously, in contrast to today when it was done purely for exercise and to offset the results of red wine and cashews. In St. Austell he found a pub and asked for a half of bitter. He took his drink to a table in the corner because he wanted to be alone to think. But when he was sitting down, he realized that there was nothing to think about, he had done all the cogitation and recriminating that was necessary.

"Tomorrow to fresh woods and pastures new," or in other words to interview William Raw and take him back to Kingsmarkham. He looked forward to another ride on the Cornish Riviera back to Paddington.

HIS EXPERIENCE PUT him off Cornwall. Medora Holland and her boyfriend had tainted the county for him, and when his mother wanted him to go on holiday to Newquay with her, he contemplated a flat refusal. But his father had died six months before, her sister—the aunt who said she wouldn't give someone or other the satisfaction—six weeks before, and his mother seemed puzzled, forlorn, and lost. Anywhere else, he said at first. Lyme Regis was supposed to be nice (and he could see where Jane Austen's Louisa Musgrove jumped off the Cobb) or how about Teignmouth, where Keats had written about going over the hill and over the mead to Dawlish? Ultimately, he couldn't refuse her. Newquay on the north coast was quite a long way from Port Ezra on the south.

It was the first time in his life he had stayed in a hotel. Up till then it had been boardinghouses, which later on became B and Bs. The hotel wasn't big and not at all grand, but it had a dining room with separate tables, and at one of them, not on their first evening but on their second, sat a middle-aged man and woman with their son and daughter. Wexford could tell they were the couple's children because the boy looked exactly like the man and the girl very much like her mother. Doing Latin at school, he had come across the phrase *mater pulchra, filia pulchrior.*

He said it aloud, not really intending to.

"What does that mean, dear?" his mother asked.

He laughed. "Beautiful mother, more beautiful daughter."

"Oh, yes. They are good-looking, aren't they? The girl is lovely. But I would never have thought dark hair and blue eyes your type."

She was thinking of Alison, the last girlfriend of his he had thought it prudent for her to know about. "Exactly my type," he said, then, as they were leaving the dining room, he heard her mother call her Dora. That was enough to put him off for the night and half a day. The book he had brought with him to read was *David Copperfield.* He was about halfway through it when he came upon a highly relevant sentence. "'Dora,' I thought. 'What a beautiful name.'" He had laughed, had his own version: "What an ugly name." He dreamed about Medora that night and her hateful embrace. Next day, while they were having lunch at a restaurant by the sea, his mother told him she'd invited the couple, the boy, and Dora to have a drink with them that evening.

How decorous it all was! How different from how it would be today, even if you could imagine people of their age—in their twenties—going on holiday with their parents. Even then he found it deeply dull and pedestrian. In the unlikely event of this Dora—horrible name—being the girl for him, would he want to meet her, his fate, his future, in company with his mother, her mother and father, and her brother, over Dry Fly sherry in a hotel bar in Newquay? Who knew then that Newquay would one day become fashionable as a surfing resort and rival Ibiza as a venue for young people's raves and binge drinking?

She had a pretty voice as well as a beautiful face and figure. She was witty and sharp. He fell in love three days later, forgot the awfulness of the name and came to love it, took her away from her family and abandoned his mother to the—acceptable and perhaps preferred—company of Dora's mother and father. It is said that we all have a peak experience, one day that is to be the best of our lives. Perhaps his was the fifth day since his meeting with Dora, when they were walking by the sea. When he told her he loved her, she lifted her face to his and said she loved him too.

To meet your future wife in a hotel where you are on holiday with your mother and she on holiday with her parents seems the reverse of romantic. He was learning that romance has little to do with location or the exotic or glamourous circumstances, and everything to do with feelings. And learning too that you like a name because you love the person who is called by it.

9

ALL THE TIME he was engaged Wexford thought how wonderful it would be if Dora were living in his flat with him. She was often there, of course she was, but she always went home to Hastings where her parents lived. It became an obsession with him to long for her when he was alone, to imagine her letting herself in with her own key, making a phone call to a friend on his phone, running a bath and walking about the flat in his dressing gown. Because of this, because he wanted to see a dream made reality, they went back to Kingsbrook Court after their wedding—a small quiet affair—before going away on their honeymoon. And the real thing was better than the imagined cameos.

His expected promotion had come. This meant they could afford to take out a mortgage on a house and they had just moved in when their first daughter was born. It also meant more responsibility, longer hours and more travelling. Dora bore the evenings he was late, the evenings he had promised to take her out until work got in the way, the nights when it was his turn to get up for the baby but in the event was too tired even for her crying to wake him. She bore them with some resentment and he took her resentment patiently because it meant she loved him and wanted his company.

He was happy and doing well. Another baby was on the way. He hadn't forgotten Targo and the man was always at the back of his mind, sometimes at the forefront. When Targo had sold his mother's house and was back in Birmingham, sometimes with Tracy Thompson and sometimes alone, later while he was in Coventry, Wexford had interested himself in the murders that took place in those particular areas of the Midlands. Several were of women who had plainly been killed by husbands or live-in partners. There were the inevitable child murders, most of them also associated with sexual abuse. Only one case was a strangling. The woman was a prostitute called Shirley Palmer, eighteen years old, and the suspect had previously been convicted of a serious assault on a woman in Stowerton, for which he had served a prison sentence. This gave Wexford a reason to go up to Coventry and sit in on the questioning.

To the investigating officers, and to a lesser extent to Wexford, it was clear that Thomas Joseph Mullan was guilty, but Targo was always in his mind. Targo had killed once and would kill again. He was living nearby. He had strangled Elsie Carroll, or Wexford firmly believed he had, and that he had no apparent connection with the victim was in line with his part in the Carroll case. But this very fact made it impossible for Wexford to suggest to Detective Inspector Tillman that it might be worth questioning him or at least checking if Targo had an alibi. He could imagine the conversation.

"He stared at you? You think he stalked you?"

"I'm sure he did. On three separate occasions. There's no doubt about it."

"And this goes to show he killed this woman he didn't know? You've no evidence, have you?"

It was impossible. He was starting to see that he could confide in no one, could tell no one that he believed Targo to be a murderer, and expect not to be met with incredulity. Of course he hadn't tried. He tried no one until he began telling the story to Burden all those years later.

At last, late in the evening, Mullan was charged with murder, and Wexford went back to the hotel where he was staying the night. He phoned Dora to ask how she was and how his little girls were. Sheila had had a temperature when he left. Dora said she was fine now, both of them were fast asleep. In those days no one said, "I love you," as an invariable concomitant of a phone call to one's wife, and no one said, "Lots of love," when terminating a conversation.

"I miss you," Wexford said, and she said, "I miss you too and I haven't got all the excitement of a wet night in Coventry."

After that he went downstairs to the bar and asked for a glass of red wine. People were just starting to drink wine instead of beer or spirits.

"Claret or burgundy, sir?"

"Oh, claret," said Wexford, who didn't much care.

He was thin then and had no need to worry about his weight, so he carried a dish of nuts and a bag of crisps to a table along with his wine. It wasn't the kind of place where the barman waited on you. The room was half-empty. He sat down in a scuffed leather armchair. The only difference between this bar and one in a pub was that you sat in armchairs.

He helped himself to a handful of peanuts—no one seemed to have discovered cashews then—lifted the glass to his lips, drank, set it down, and looked about him, as he always did in these circumstances, at the clientele. There was a group of four salesmen, then still called commercial travellers, three middle-aged couples he could tell were married because they didn't speak to each other—he made a mental resolution never to let himself and Dora get that way, never let them be identified as married by their silent indifference—and an over-made-up blond woman sitting alone. Such was the state of things in those days that if this had been a pub, it was doubtful if a woman on her own would have been served. He thought, by the look she gave him and a certain desperation in her eyes, that she would have liked to pick him up. He looked sharply away and saw, seated at a table in the far corner, also alone, Targo.

It gave him a bit of a shock. The last time he had seen him was some years before when he had passed Wexford's house on his way to the river and the water meadows, paused and stared up at his windows. And repeated that behaviour day after day. He had no dog with him in here. Targo was drinking something which might have been lager or pale ale. He was better dressed than in former days—or more showily dressed—in black jeans and a brown leather jacket. His shirt was black, he wore a black-and-white-chequered tie, and his yellowish brown hair, which had been clipped quite short in the stalking days, had been allowed to grow long, had developed a slight curl and reached to his shirt collar. But he still wore the scarf. It was black, brown, and white stripes this time. The naevus was still there.

If gazing at someone will force him to look up and meet your eyes, Wexford's stare had this effect on Targo. Or maybe it didn't. Maybe the man had been sitting there waiting for him to come into the bar, was aware of every move he made and had calculated when he would arrive. It might even be that Targo was more aware of Wexford's movements than Wexford of Targo's.

They looked at each other. Targo stared. Staring at someone is usually a sign of recognition, but of course Targo undoubtedly recognised him. Once, years before, having his photograph taken for some identification requirement, the photographer had complained that Wexford blinked too much, but trying to hold his eyelids still only made things worse. Targo seemed to have no problem. Had he practised, even studied how to do it? As Wexford wondered, the man's gaze fell. He walked out of the bar, leaving his glass half-full.

Wexford started to go after him but stopped at the door and turned back. Go after him for what purpose? He already knew where the man lived, and he knew from the notes Tillman had provided that Targo hadn't been among Shirley Palmer's regulars, that Targo's name wasn't mentioned at all. No one answering Targo's description had been seen in the neighbourhood of her beat either on the night she was killed or in previous days and weeks. How excited Wexford would have been if it had! Then he could have talked to Tillman about Elsie Carroll and the stalking, even about his conviction that Targo wanted him to believe he had killed murder victims where it was physically impossible he had been the perpetrator. As things were, Wexford could do nothing unless it was less a matter of doing anything but more of being able to confirm, now absolutely for sure, that Targo was pitting his wits against Wexford's. He was challenging him, saying in effect, you can do nothing but I can kill where I like or not kill, only make you believe I kill hecatombs of victims until you begin to doubt if I've killed anyone at all.

Something had been different about Targo, and for a

while Wexford had pondered what it was. Then he realised. No dog had been with him. He asked the barman if dogs were allowed.

"Oh, no, sir. We can't have dogs in here. There's a notice outside saying so."

There was—outside the street door by which Targo had left and had no doubt entered.

When Burden came to Kingsmarkham and as they got to know each other well, becoming friends as well as colleagues, Wexford thought that here was someone he could tell. But something stopped him. It was a while since Coventry and that sighting—you couldn't call it a meeting—of Targo in that hotel bar. He had never seen him again. He even sometimes thought that he must let it go, not that he had been wrong or mistaken, but, that justice could not always prevail and that some people, many perhaps, had committed terrible crimes for which they would never be punished. If Targo was one of them, so be it. The man began to take on the aspect of a character in a recurring dream, someone who has no existence in life but only in the dream, where he is vivid enough and haunting enough. Wexford did actually dream about him or had dreams in which he fleetingly appeared but never spoke, and he understood that the reason for this might be because Targo himself, the real Targo, though they had encountered each other on several occasions, had only once had a conversation with him, and only once passed the time of day. But Wexford knew where he lived, back in Birmingham now, and with a woman who was not his second wife. He appeared not to have married again. The driving school was a success, had expanded, and now he sold second-hand motor vehicles. He had also bought up several small slum properties for rent.

The illness Wexford had in the seventies, a thrombosis behind the eye, took him to London to convalesce. He stayed with his nephew, a detective superintendent in the Met called Howard Fortune, who lived with his wife, Denise, in Chelsea. Wexford hadn't expected to miss Dora specially, he certainly wouldn't get into the business he deplored in other men of phoning his wife every evening. That was what he thought.

The reality was that he slept badly. He hated sleeping alone. These days he sometimes thought how incredulous young people of the present would be if they knew that, in spite of his relationships with several girlfriends, he had never slept a whole night in bed with a woman until he was married. Yet, after saying good-night to those girls at some late hour, he had slept heavily until his alarm went off. In London, after his broken night, he phoned Dora in the morning and then went for long walks—doctor's orders—in the neighbourhood, often wondering if he might encounter Targo on one of them.

Targo was still living in Birmingham, but it wasn't outside possibility that he might come to London and look for him if he knew Wexford was there. And one day, in the King's Road, he saw a man ahead of him whose back, whose height or lack of height, whose walk, were all Targo's, but when he turned his head, showing where the birthmark should have been but wasn't, Wexford saw an aquiline face, a pointed chin, and dark eyes.

IT WAS AS he had begun to think. Targo had grown older, had given up the wits-pitting and the challenge and lost all interest. It began to seem likely that Elsie Carroll, who had been his victim for some unknown reason, was also his only victim, and there had been no hideous murder spree.

For all that, Wexford thought of telling his story to his nephew. He was close to doing so some evenings when Denise had gone to bed early and he and Howard were alone, having a late drink in Howard's study. But the moment passed and he no more told him than he told Burden. His health improved, he went back to Kingsmarkham, and there he encountered Targo's wife—or the woman who had once been his wife.

It was in the then newly built Kingsbrook Precinct, later called the Kingsbrook Centre. Kathleen Targo was window-shopping, pushing a child of about three in a buggy. Two days before Christmas it had been, and Wexford, as usual, was doing his last-minute Christmas shopping. He recognised Kathleen, noting how much healthier and happier she looked, though many years had passed, but was surprised when she recognised him and spoke to him in the sort of friendly way he would never have associated with her.

"It's DC Wexford, isn't it? Remember me?"

He didn't correct her, though he was a detective inspector by then. "Mrs. Targo."

"I was once." She laughed. "Good riddance to bad rubbish."

"And this must be the baby you were expecting."

As soon as he said it, he realised that was impossible.

"No, that was Joanne. She's seventeen now. I got married again, I'm Mrs. Varney now, and this is Philippa. We've been living here since she was born. It's a wonder we haven't met before."

She was a different woman, happy, placid. He remembered her as painfully thin apart from the swinging mound of pregnancy, but now she had "filled out," as they said, had "middle-aged spread," as they also said. He had lost touch with Targo's whereabouts recently, and he could ask where her ex-husband now was. Her answer surprised him and he felt a quickening of his pulse.

"Living in Myringham," she said, turning up her nose, "with some woman. I don't know what she's called and I don't want to. Alan and Joanne see him, and that's how I get to know how he's doing. Not that I care. He was in Glebe Road for a bit after our marriage broke up, then it was Birmingham for years. But he's done well for himself, and he's got quite a big house. You never got anyone for poor Elsie Carroll, did you?"

Why did she ask? Like that, then, such a non sequitur. Because she *knew*? He would have loved to spend the rest of the day with her, take her and Philippa into one of the smart, little cafés that were then a feature of the Kingsbrook Centre, sit them down, order coffee and cakes and talk to her about Targo. Or, rather, get her to talk to him about Targo. But that was impossible. She would likely say no, be astonished at such a request. It was Christmas and she had a family, she'd be busy. And once again he came up against the barrier—he had no reason to suspect her first husband of anything.

"I must get on," she was saying. "Nice to see you. Eric's got four dogs, Joanne says. That old spaniel lived to be seventeen but it's dead now, and he's got more dogs and three cats and a couple of snakes. You wouldn't credit it, would you?" She hesitated. "He always did like animals more than people. Well, he didn't like people at all. That was the trouble." She laughed, the merry, carefree laugh of a contented woman.

He had said good-bye to her and gone into the perfume

shop to buy scent for his wife and his elder daughter. The one he tried—that he couldn't help trying because the assistant sprayed it on his wrist—reminded him of the perfume the girl in the pink hat had used. Medora. All that way across the years, it reminded him. He laughed, shaking his head, and bought a different kind. Was there any point in finding out Targo's precise address? No harm in knowing, he thought.

DORA WAS SAYING, "Andy Norton knows a plant from a weed. That makes a change from some of them."

Always interested in people, Wexford asked her what Norton had done in the Civil Service before his retirement. "He was in some government department, apparently. Social Security, I think it was, only they called it something else then."

"Well, on the subject of pensions, he must have a good one. Why's he doing our gardening?"

"He gets bored at home, I gather. And he likes to be out in the fresh air."

It was a surprise when Burden arrived. He looked a little abashed, which was unusual for him. "Not in the firm's time, you see," he said.

"If you're saying what I think you are," Wexford said, "one day this is going to be the firm's business."

"I've been in Sam V.B.'s Gardens. We got a call that someone had been stabbed, but it was a false alarm or a hoax. But it reminded me of Billy Kenyon and what you said about Targo. Not," Burden added, "that I believe it. Not any of it."

"But you want to hear?"

"I want to hear."

Wexford smiled. He sat him down in an armchair, fetched wine and crisps. They had run out of nuts. When he had told

Burden about the meeting with Kathleen Varney, he said, "It was true that Targo was living in Myringham. In Hastings Avenue and in a much better house than the one in Jewel Road. It looked as if he and Kathleen were both doing well for themselves. But she wasn't quite right in one respect. He had all those pet animals but he was also running a boarding kennels for dogs."

"At his home?"

"It had been a kennel before he took it on. Bought the place, rented it, I don't know. I went over there to have a look at it—and him." The look on Burden's face prompted him to say, "Not in the firm's time, I may add."

"Well, I suppose you thought it was for the firm in a way."

Wexford laughed. "I didn't even have to invent a story. Do you remember that dog Dora and I had? Sheila insisted on looking after it for some boyfriend called Sebastian, brought it home, adored it passionately for two days, fed it, walked it, and then abandoned it to us the way kids do. We were going away—it was when we went to that Greek island—and I was genuinely enquiring what to do with the dog.

"Targo recognised me at once. I had a feeling he knew all about me and was waiting for me to come. Nonsense, of course. He had—has, I suppose—an uncanny habit of absolutely meeting your eyes. When he talks to you, he holds your gaze in an almost hypnotic way. That was the way he looked at me when I asked him about boarding Sebastian's dog. 'I remember you,' he said as if he'd never stalked me, as if he'd never stared at me in that hotel bar in Coventry. 'You were on the case when that Mrs. Carroll was murdered down Jewel Road. Must have been nearly twenty years ago.' I tell you, Mike, he knew that I knew."

"What, you mean he knew you knew he'd killed her?"

"Yes."

Burden's tone could hardly have been more sceptical. "A lot to read in a meeting of eyes."

"He didn't care. He liked it. He knew I couldn't do anything. The house was full of his pets and it smelt of them. Have you ever smelt a marrow bone that's been lying around for a fortnight and every so often been chewed by a dog? Well, that's what the place smelt like. He had a snake and I can't say I was too keen on that. It wasn't in a cage or anything. Just lying curled up on a shelf next to a couple of books and a potted plant. One of the books was the *Bumper Book of Dogs*. Kathleen had said he was living with a woman, and he was, the one called Adele he eventually married, but she wasn't around. There was a building outside in the grounds. They really were grounds, a couple of acres, I should think, and the building was a kind of glorified shed or stables. He took me out there. Everything was very neat and trim. *Shipshape* was the word he used for it. 'Shipshape enough for you?' he said. There were about a dozen dogs in separate pens, and of course they all came up to the wire, looking pathetic and whining and wagging their tails. The smell was there too but somewhat modified by the fresh air.

"'I do this because I love animals,' he said. 'It's not my main source of income. I'm in business.' I didn't ask what business because I could see he expected me to ask. Something to do with cars or slum cottages, I expect. 'Some of these boarding kennels are a disgrace. I like to think I run a luxury hotel for dogs.' Well, I didn't comment on that. He showed me a pen where there was a mother dog with five puppies, all mongrels but very appealing. You needn't look like that as if I'm going soft on you. I assure you this is relevant."

"OK. I believe you. Thousands wouldn't."

"We went back into the house and he handed me a brochure setting out their terms. It was very expensive. I wasn't going to commit myself, though I stood there reading it, or pretending to read it, while I sort of sized up the place. Then he did something rather nasty. It was obviously intended to tease or possibly frighten me."

"What do you mean?"

"The snake was apparently asleep but he took it down from the shelf and draped it round his neck with its head right up against his face. Right up against the scarf he was wearing. He was fondling it like you might a kitten. He came up very close to me and I was determined not to flinch, but it took a hell of a lot of self-control on my part to stay standing there and trying to look—well, unfazed. 'What do you think, Mr. Wexford?' he said. I don't know how calm I was. I hope I didn't tremble but I'm not sure. I just said, 'Thanks very much. I'll let you know' or 'I'll be in touch,' something like that, and I got out of there. When he'd closed the door after me, I could hear him laughing."

"Did you let him board the dog?"

"You must be joking. As it happened, the poor little beast died, got distemper. Had its injections too early or too late or something. I didn't speak to Targo again, didn't see him again, not until Billy Kenyon was killed. That must have been two or three years later."

"Where was I? I mean, I remember the case but not being involved in it."

"You were away doing that course. The forensics thing in Dover."

"Of course I was. Are you going to tell me why that sentimental bit about the mother dog and the appealing puppies was relevant?"

"When he took in a pregnant bitch no one wanted—and he did a lot of that—Targo made a point of finding good homes for the puppies. Well, the good home he found for one of those puppies I saw was on the Muriel Campden estate with Eileen Kenyon, Billy's mother."

10

KINGSMARKHAM'S BOTANICAL GARDENS, seven acres of them between Queen Street and Sussex Avenue, were still well-maintained but had long been reduced in size to no more than half that by one of the lawns becoming a children's playground with swings and climbing frames and the tropical house turned into a coffee bar and brasserie. The picnic area had taken over most of the rose garden, and Red Rocks fallen into disuse. It had not always been so. Once the place was looked after by a superintendent and deputy and five gardeners who took pride in their work. Visitors on their way to a day out at Leeds Castle or Sissinghurst would make a detour to take a look at Kingsmarkham's rock gardens in the spring or its prize blooms in the orchid house.

Those were the days when the botanical gardens were both a refuge and a pleasure ground for Billy Kenyon, a place to hide in and a place to enjoy, especially when the flowers were out. If he was capable of enjoyment. He was certainly capable of fear when his contemporaries shouted after him, and he seemed never to get used to bullying and catcalls. What was wrong with Billy so that he never spoke, had never spoken, but still was able to look after himself? Harsh terms for someone like him were used in those days, *mentally deficient, very low IQ*, even *moron*. But how could anyone be those things when he valued plants and flowers the way Billy did? When he learnt the names of plants and could write them all down if not utter them?

Today I think we'd call him autistic, Wexford thought. He would go to a special school for people with "learning difficulties"—at least, I hope he would. His IQ might not have been low at all but quite high as was often true of those with the Asperger's type of autism. The neighbours' children on the Muriel Campden estate where he lived with his mother called him "loony," and it was said that Eileen Kenyon did nothing to defend her son. He had left school at fifteen, the then school-leaving age, though he had seldom attended, and that was something else which Eileen failed to concern herself about. Even in his school days Billy had spent more time in the gardens than he had in class. The superintendent, George Clark, and deputy superintendent and the staff all knew him for a harmless innocent. On wet days they would let him sit on a chair in the temperate house, and the deputy superintendent, Denis Glaspell, often invited him into the big brick shed where the staff assembled on their tea breaks. Glaspell gave him a notebook and asked him to write down the Latin names of all the plants in, say, the rock garden, and Billy would do so, never making an error in identification or a spelling mistake. It was a pity, Wexford thought, when he was investigating the murder, that his teachers had never witnessed this. But would they have done anything if they had? Would they have had the time?

Billy was seventeen when he died. On the day of his death, in the hot summer of 1976, he left his mother's house in Leighton Close at nine in the morning, having made himself sandwiches of Mothers Pride and presliced cheese. These with an overripe banana, which was the only item of fruit to be found, would be his lunch and mean he need not return till the gardens closed. His friend Denis Glaspell would give him a cup of tea. The dog came up to him, whining to be fed, but Billy left feeding him to his mother. The neighbours said she loved the dog much more than she loved him, but if he knew this, he gave no sign of it.

He had left her in bed with her lover, Bruce Mellor. How much of their relationship Billy understood no one seemed to know. But Billy's powers of comprehension were far greater than the people close to him believed, and when Bruce said, and said frequently, that he'd like to live with or even marry Eileen Kenyon but he wasn't taking on a loony, not he, Billy no doubt had a good idea of what he meant. Bruce didn't mind the dog, he liked the dog. Eileen too was in the habit of telling the neighbours that it was "unfair on her" that she was "lumbered" with Billy and it stopped her leading what she called a normal life. She'd like to get married before it was "too late."

IT WAS THE middle of June. The best of the flowers were past, they came in May, and the late-summer blooms had yet to blossom, but roses were still out and Billy made first for the rose garden. All the roses had their names in front of them on green metal tags pegged into the soil, and Billy did his best to memorise the names, Rose Gaujard, Peace, Étoile d'Hollande, but when he forgot, he checked with the green tag and wrote the name down in his notebook. One of the gardeners came along at about eleven—not that Billy wore a watch or had much idea of time—and told him Denis

THE MONSTER IN THE BOX

Glaspell had a cup of tea for him in the big shed they called the "office." Billy went along to the office, drank his tea, and sat listening while the gardeners talked about football and snooker and what had been on TV the night before. He had another cup of tea in the office at three in the afternoon, by which time he had eaten his sandwiches and his banana. Another thing about Billy which endeared him to Denis Glaspell was his habit of taking his litter home with him or at least placing it in one of the wastebins. Too many visitors just dropped their food wrappings and fruit peel where they had been eating.

Denis noticed the plastic bag and the banana skin when Billy opened his backpack to put away his notebook.

"Let me dispose of that for you, Billy," he said, and Billy handed over the two items of rubbish without a smile and of course without a word. Denis had never seen him smile.

No one was quite sure where Billy had been after that. One of the gardeners had seen him in the hothouse, but he hadn't stayed long. It was hot outside, though at about five the sky clouded over and it began to rain a freak shower in a dry summer. Heavy rain always emptied the gardens, and it did so that day, but lasted only half an hour before fading to a mist. There was no reason for any of the staff to keep a special eye on Billy Kenyon. He was their most frequent visitor, was entirely harmless, and had an almost reverential attitude to the place. So it was never to be known who was the last person to have seen him, apart from his murderer.

George Clark, the superintendent, went round locking the gates at nine. It was still light, though going on dusk. George did as he always did and walked round the gardens, making sure that no one was left inside—occasionally a street sleeper would try to spend the night in there—and checking on the various designated areas that no damage had been done during the day. In Red Rocks he found Billy Kenyon's body, lying spread-eagle across the russet-coloured, flat stones, one hand trailing in the water of a small pond, the other resting on his notebook. George felt for a pulse, laid his own face against the place where he thought the boy's heart must be. Then he looked more closely at his neck and the weals round it, at his face where the eyes protruded, and knew for certain that he was dead, guessed he had been strangled. A leather belt, obviously the murder weapon, lay across his forehead, where it had seemingly been draped.

No mobile phones then. George went back to his office and phoned the police, first taking a small swig from the miniature of brandy he kept there for emergencies. The little bottle was full because there had been no emergencies till now.

"If this death had happened today," Wexford said, "the press would have made much of Billy's notebook with the names of the flowers in it. They'd have called him 'the dumb genius' and the 'boy wonder failed by the education system.' There was nothing like that then. I don't remember anything in the papers about Billy being other than a normal teenager. His mother and the man who wouldn't marry her while that meant taking on Billy—they didn't appear on television saying how Billy lit up their lives or what a saint he was. People didn't do that then. Nor did the press refer to Eileen Kenyon's on-and-off lover as Billy's stepfather the way they would now."

"You're saying things were better then?" Burden raised his eyebrows.

"Yes and no. In some ways and in some ways not. I expect that's true whenever you contrast one period of time with another period of time. We have far more sophisticated forensic methods these days, as you know. If we haven't yet perfected tracing perpetrators by means of DNA, we're fast getting there. The mobile phone makes communication a whole lot easier. Parents ought to be able to keep a closer eye on where their children are—but do they? I don't know.

"To get back to Billy. He had been strangled with a leather belt. Those belts were on sale in the Saturday market, but they were on sale in Pomfret market too and in Myringham market. Tracing it was impossible and there were no prints on it, though it could have taken prints. Our principal suspect was Bruce Mellor, the lover. But Eileen Kenyon ran him a close second."

"Because Bruce Mellor wouldn't marry her while Billy was alive?"

"That's right. Neither of them had jobs and they were living on what in those days was called 'assistance.' They were both at home between five and eight p.m., which according to the pathologist was when Billy died. Mellor took the dog out in the morning, returning after about an hour, and neither of them went out again. For the relevant time they alibied each other. But a next-door neighbour—I don't remember her name, Lucas or Lewis, I think—told me she had seen Bruce Mellor leave the house without the dog, this time at about six. This he denied, she had been mistaken, and Eileen denied it too.

"I asked her if she wasn't concerned when Billy hadn't come home by ten. As you know, the garden closes at nine in summer. It still closes at nine, what's left of it. Eileen said he was seventeen and able to look after himself. Besides, the body had been found by then and she had been informed by ten thirty.

"If Bruce Mellor had gone into the botanical gardens, no one remembered seeing him. If the neighbour's evidence was true and he had left the house next door at six, he would have reached the gardens by about twenty past, by which time the rain had slackened and become a drizzle. Most visitors would have gone by then, so if Mellor had entered by either gate, it wasn't surprising that no one had seen him. He would have been hard to ignore for he was exceptionally tall and thin and wore his yellow hair long—it was an unusual tawny colour—and either loose or tied back with an elastic band. Glaspell and his immediate superior, George Clark, who found the body, and all the gardeners were closely questioned. None of them admitted to seeing Mellor. They were all, to a lesser degree, suspects, but not for long. They had alibis a lot more sound than Mellor's or Eileen's."

Burden had a question. "Since you're going to say that you suspect Targo of this murder, how do you account for none of them seeing *him*? Or didn't you suspect him at that time?"

"I didn't because I couldn't find the connection. The link between Targo and Elsie Carroll was tenuous enough but at least he lived in the same street. When Billy Kenyon was killed, Targo was living miles away in Myringham in a big house in two acres of land and had at least one prosperous business going. Eileen Kenyon lived on what she called 'the dole' on a council estate with a mentally incapacitated son. There was no reason even to consider Targo, and, you know, Mike, how you sometimes label me an obsessive—well, I'm not blind to that in myself"—Medora Holland in her torn green blouse flitted across his mind's eye—"and I told myself to stop it, stop even imagining it while I had two quite feasible suspects."

"There was the dog," said Burden.

"Indeed there was the dog. But I didn't know that. When I went to the kennels to ask about boarding it, Targo didn't tell me he'd given a woman called Eileen Kenyon in Kingsmarkham a puppy. Why would he? This was a long time before the murder, no one had ever heard of Eileen Kenyon, and Targo had no possible reason to tell me such a thing."

"I came back," said Burden, "just about the time you gave up on the case. Sorry to put it like that."

"Well, we did give up eventually, only we went on saying we would never give up. We always do say that, no matter how hopeless things look, don't we? We would never rest until we'd brought Billy's murderer to justice et cetera, et cetera. But we knew we had given up. To recap a bit: the only evidence against Bruce Mellor was that he had possibly lied about going out that evening. But Mrs. Lucas—she was called that, not Lewis—may have lied. She and he were at daggers drawn since there'd been some dispute about an all-night party the Lucases had for a son's twenty-first birthday. It may have been spite that made her say she had seen Mellor go out. Mellor alibied Eileen and she alibied him. Both had a motive of sorts, but you know how unimportant motive is in getting up a sound case. It was one of our few unsolved murders."

"When did you find out about the dog?"

"You mean that the dog came from Targo's place? Not until after we gave up. We questioned Mellor and Eileen exhaustively. I don't remember an interrogation like it—not one that came to nothing, at any rate. They were inarticulate and far from bright, but they stuck to their story, that they had been in all that day.

"No one but Mrs. Lucas claimed to have seen Mellor. Did we ever seriously suspect Eileen? Only perhaps as in cahoots with Mellor, supporting him, alibiing him, lying for him. She never denied wanting to be rid of Billy in order to marry Mellor, but she said she only meant he should be in some sort of home. The trouble was that we had no evidence that Mellor had been in the gardens. No one had seen him, and as I've said, he was a memorable figure. Of course we tried to trace the leather belt with which Billy was strangled. We failed. It might have belonged to Targo, may have been in his possession for years, but it might have come from any of those local markets. You try getting a market stallholder to identify something he's sold. All we did establish was that no shopkeeper in Kingsmarkham, Stowerton, or Myringham had sold such a belt for years."

"But the dog, Reg. What about the dog?"

"OK, I'm coming to that. Any case of strangling—and they were few—brought me back to Targo, as Billy's death did. I couldn't see any possible motive for his killing Billy. But then what motive was there in the case of Elsie Carroll? If it were just that Targo was a psychopath who killed at random, why those two? Why kill people when access is difficult if the place is full of loners, available as victims in the streets by night? Then I met him again.

"He'd told me he had what he called a business. It was a travel agent in Myringham high street, a tiny little place grandly called Transglobe, and its walls were papered with advertisements for exotic places. People had started going to India and China for their holidays, and he was cashing in on a new trend."

"You mean you went there to book a holiday?"

"No, no, of course not. I went in there in connection with someone we suspected of smuggling raw opium out of Hong Kong. Opium! Those were the days."

"I remember him. Berryman he was called. Raymond Berryman. He went down for a long time. So you went in there in all innocence and there was Targo."

"That's right. There he was, sitting at the receipt of custom. No one else there but his dog. Mind you, there wasn't room for anyone else, and when I was in the place, it was crowded. I saw him and it gave me quite a shock, so that for a moment I thought I must be seeing things, confusing him with someone else. I'd never associated him with anything but dogs and driving. He seemed delighted to see me. Unnaturally delighted, I mean. That was one of the rare occasions when I saw him smile. Everyone else had gone and we were alone. He got up and put out his hand, but of course I wasn't going to shake hands with him. The dog was a corgi, and there in that tiny place it had its water bowl on the floor and a dish full of some sort of cooked entrails. Targo said, 'Meet Princess,' but I ignored this command just as I'd ignored his hand. He didn't appear offended. I asked him a few questions about our opium-running suspect and he answered them. Truthfully, I'm sure.

"He was looking more prosperous than I'd ever seen him. Very nice suit, expensive shoes I could just see under the desk, an Omega watch. A scarf, of course, but not a woolen one. His was more like a sort of cravat, gray, black, and pink silk, not quite adequate to cover the birthmark. He was aware of that and he kept fidgeting with it, pushing the edge of it up to his cheek with his fingers, and each time it slipped down again.

"He hadn't put on weight, he was the same sturdy, muscular type, unchanged except that his hair had receded a bit and there was more gray in it than fair. I was about to leave when he said, out of the blue as it seemed to me, 'Funny how these cases fizzle out, isn't it? One week it's all over the papers, and then when you people can't find the culprit, it disappears and we never hear a word about it again.' He fixed me with his staring eyes in that way he has. 'I'm talking about the Billy Kenyon murder, of course.'

" 'I can't discuss that, Mr. Targo,' I said, and I thought *culprit* a funny word to use about a killer, too feeble a word. But of course I wasn't going to leave at that point. My eyes looked into his and he said, 'I knew them, you know, that Mrs. Kenyon and her fancy man.' Another strange, and in this case old-fashioned, word to use. 'No, I didn't know,' I said. 'Oh, yes,' he said. 'That dog she's got, that was one of my puppies. My Dusty's young 'uns. I knew a dog would have a good home with her. Wouldn't like to say the same of anything human.' And he laughed, Mike, he actually laughed. Laughing was something he did more than smiling. I can't quite say my blood ran cold because it never does, but I had an idea what it would feel like.

"I asked him why he called the dog Princess. 'She's a corgi, isn't she? They're royal dogs.' He laughed again and was still laughing when I went, chuckling in an unpleasant way while he stroked the royal dog's head."

"But you did nothing," said Burden.

"I did what I could. I went back to questioning the staff at the gardens. I managed to get hold of a photograph of Targo, showed it to Glaspell and the rest. None of them remembered seeing him on the relevant day or any other. Once more I had nothing to go on, nothing but a laugh and his saying Eileen Kenyon wouldn't be fit to have charge of anything human."

"He had an alibi?"

"I've no doubt he would have fixed one up or *already had*

one fixed up if I'd asked him. He'd married again by then, that woman called Adele. It didn't last long but she would have alibied him. I gave up, in your useful phrase, because I couldn't see a motive. What was in it for Targo? And why? Who benefits from Billy's death? Not Targo. Only Eileen Kenyon. So he did it for Eileen Kenyon's sake? He hardly knew the woman."

"You're sure of that?"

"I'm sure. Come to that, he hardly knew Elsie Carroll. Well, he didn't know her at all except maybe by sight. I talked to Eileen Kenyon and Bruce Mellor about him. That conversation was the only one I had with them when they were transparently honest, not prevaricating or defensive. Eileen had met Targo three times, the first when she went to the boarding kennels because someone had told her he had puppies he'd give away to a suitable owner. The puppies were too young to leave their mother then, but she could choose which one she wanted in advance. Targo had a talk with her about the proper care of a dog and said he'd come and inspect her place after she'd had the puppy two weeks. She came back to fetch the dog when it was eight weeks old, and on that occasion he only spoke a few words to her. His wife attended to Eileen, putting the puppy in the dog carrier she'd brought with her and getting the carrier into Mellor's car.

"Two weeks later he called at the house in Leighton Close, was apparently satisfied with the dog's condition, its sleeping and feeding arrangements, et cetera. He accepted a cup of tea and they chatted for a while, she said. I'd rather not imagine what having a chat with Targo would be like. Billy wasn't present. She didn't tell me what they talked about, she said she couldn't remember, but for Targo to have said she couldn't be trusted with the care of a human being has to mean that part of their talk was about the hardness of her lot in having a mentally incapacitated son and what a burden he was to her.

"Bruce Mellor never did marry Eileen. They fell out and he was seen no more in Leighton Close. Targo gave up the travel agency and the boarding kennels about a year afterwards and moved away with his menagerie but not with Adele. They'd split up and were divorced after a couple of years. He went back to Birmingham and that woman he'd been off and on with for years, Tracy whatever-it-was."

"And now he's back."

"And now he's back. Living in some style. Is he still in the travel agency business? Does he still move around with a private zoo? I think he does. I saw signs of it when I went to Stringfield to have a look at his place. Perhaps it doesn't matter. I haven't a hope of proving any of this. He's got older and he may have given up this homicidal spree of his. But I've thought like that before. I thought like that when he followed me into that hotel in Coventry and when I imagined I'd seen him in London but I hadn't. Even if it's true now and he's changed, that wouldn't mean he hadn't done those things or justice shouldn't be done."

"I don't believe it, you know, Reg. I'm sorry but I don't."

"I know, and I don't care. It makes no difference."

11

THE RAHMAN FAMILY plainly disliked Hannah Gold-smith and she knew it. Not usually a sensitive woman, she did her utmost with Mohammed and Yasmin Rahman, their sons, Ahmed and Osman, and their daughter, Tamima, not to appear patronizing; the more she tried, the worse it got. Hannah's way of showing immigrants from Asia or the children of immigrants that she and they were all equally free citizens of the United Kingdom was to be excessively polite, flattering, and considerate. Of course they saw through this at once, Mohammed with amusement, Yasmin with a kind of indignant suspiciousness, and the sons with indifference.

Hannah began, not for the first time, by telling them what a "lovely home" they had. A pity the house was attached to that eyesore, Webb and Cobb, next door. She was a little abashed when Yasmin said the defunct shop and flats above it were their property. But Hannah made things worse by saying that building an extension at the rear, culminating in a conservatory, was such a marvellous improvement she couldn't understand why their neighbours hadn't done the same thing.

Mohammed smiled, said in his pleasant, slightly singsong voice, "They are far from well-off, Ms. Goldsmith. I doubt if they could afford it. We have three incomes coming in here."

Hannah had by then made up her mind that both sons probably lived on the benefit. "Oh, what do you do then?" she asked Ahmed.

"Computers," he said. "I'm an IT consultant. Work from home."

She looked enquiringly at his brother. Both were good-looking, dark, Ahmed clean-shaven, Osman with a beard like his father. All wore Western dress, while Yasmin was in the long, black gown of the traditional Moslem woman but hung with valuable-looking, heavy gold jewellery. Osman didn't answer her unspoken question, so she prompted him.

"I'm a psychiatric nurse at the Princess Diana."

Hannah nearly gushed, "How splendid!" but curbed herself just in time and said, "Really?"

In the cold voice which was the only tone Hannah had ever heard from her, Yasmin said, "If you wanted to see Tamima, Miss Goldsmith, she's not here. She's still at the shop."

"Oh, do call me Hannah. Yes, I know she is, I've been there today. She told me you and she were going home to Pakistan for a holiday."

"It is no longer home. This is home. But we are going there."

Not easily daunted, Hannah was this time temporarily silenced by Yasmin Rahman's icy, clipped tone. Every word sounded like a snub. With a faint smile, probably intended as a tribute to his mother's handling of this interfering police officer, Ahmed picked up an armful of folders and other papers and moved to a desk at the far end of the extension. Osman followed him, settling in an armchair with the evening paper. Hannah rallied, asked Mohammed what future was planned for Tamima after her return.

"Perhaps she may go to London for a while to stay with her auntie. My sister, that is. There are girl cousins to go about with and have a good time. Fair enough, don't you think, when you have worked hard for your exams? Then, she says, she would like a gap year."

"But people have gap years between school and university," said Hannah, recalling her own.

"And why not between school and sixth-form college, then? Sixteen is a difficult age, you know. Teenage is a troubling time and we should all remember that. Oh, yes, she will probably go to sixth-form college. But we don't know yet for sure. Let her enjoy herself in Islamabad first and then we shall see." With magnificent aplomb which Hannah was forced to admire, Mohammed said, "We mustn't keep you any longer, Hannah. You are a busy woman."

Hannah had hoped to have something significant to tell Wexford. She had nothing, yet she was convinced now, partly by the suave yet resolute behaviour of all the Rahmans, that the purpose of the Pakistan visit was to find a husband for Tamima. That, she thought as she walked along Glebe Lane towards her car, was exactly as such a family would behave if they intended to carry out some ancient traditional rite in defiance of laws they despised. She looked up at the windows of the flats above Webb and Cobb, and a woman looked back at her, a white-skinned woman. Hannah wondered how well this woman knew the Rahmans. A future interview with her might yield useful information.

■ ■ ■

STREET STABBINGS HAD till recently been confined to big cities. When the second happened and the victim, Nicky Dusan, died in hospital twelve hours later, Wexford feared a trend had started. People were imitative. They followed a fashion even if that fashion led to terrible consequences. DS Vine and DC Damon Coleman were the investigating officers, and three days after the knife attack Barry Vine arrested a sixteen-year-old, Tyler Pyke. Kathy Cooper and Brian Dusan, the dead boy's parents, had appeared on television with the customary emotional appeal for any witnesses, Kathy claiming that her son had been in a gang against his will. He had been forced into it, she said, by "evil" contemporaries he had been at school with who told him he had to join to defend them all against the "Pyke-Samuels gang."

"Nicky Dusan," Hannah told Wexford, "is the first cousin of that boy Rashid Hanif, who is Tamima Rahman's boyfriend and also cousin of Neil Dusan. He's Brian Dusan's sister's son."

Wexford considered the name. "You mean Brian Dusan and his sister are Moslems?"

Hannah was always happy to show off her extensive knowledge of Islam and its history. "They're Bosnians. Bosnians have been Moslem for centuries. It's a legacy the Turks left behind when they went in. Brian Dusan is presumably lapsed, though it's hard for Moslems to lapse." Wexford could see that Hannah was having problems here. A declared atheist herself and one who would have no hesitation in condemning any manifestation of Christianity out of hand, she steadily avoided criticism of Islam. "The sister is a devout Moslem," she said hastily. "She married Akbar Hanif, and Rashid is one of their seven children."

How she would have condemned so large a family if the

parents had been Roman Catholics! He smiled at her. "You've really been into this, haven't you?"

"It wasn't difficult, guv. I knew it long before this stabbing happened. It's been part of my research into the antecedents of people connected with the Rahmans."

"So you know as much about, say, Mr. and Mrs. Rahman's relatives as you do about their daughter's boyfriend's."

"More. Much more. It's a very large extended family. Mohammed Rahman has at least two sisters living in London. Yasmin Rahman has a sister in Stowerton who didn't at all object to telling me her family's history. Among the things she told me was that they've got another sister living in Pakistan whose marriage was arranged, though it sounded more like forced to me. This woman has a son who may be lined up to marry Tamima."

"'May be'? Not 'is'?"

Hannah was a good police officer. She wasn't prepared to exaggerate to serve her own ends. "Only 'may be,' guv. The sister thought this man a likely candidate, but that's all. It was really guesswork."

"Let's concentrate," said Wexford, "on Kingsmarkham's incipient gang warfare for now, shall we?"

He no more believed in the Rahman forced-marriage theory than Burden believed in his insistence on Targo as a murderer. Hannah took a few steps towards the door and turned round. She was fond of having the last word.

"Tamima and her mother go to Pakistan on Thursday. I bought a loaf from her in the Raj Emporium yesterday and she told me."

When he drove himself home, the route Wexford took was along Glebe Road into Glebe Lane, into Orchard Road, then the Avenue. He stopped when he saw a white van he thought might be Targo's parked outside Webb and Cobb. He parked his own in front of the nail bar and looked up the white van's number in the notebook he still carried. It was Targo's, but there was no sign of the van's owner. Hannah had told him one of the Rahman sons was a computer consultant, and when he had seen Targo go in there back in August, he had been carrying what was very likely a computer. Wexford's own skills in this particular technology were limited, but still he had an idea that a consultant or engineer or whatever the man was could make adjustments to what he called a machine by what he called remote control. Why then would Targo take the thing there? Or was he visiting for some other purpose?

Wexford disliked the thought of showing himself. From where he sat in his own car he could see that the driver's window in the van was open about four inches. No doubt the Tibetan spaniel was inside, no doubt waiting for an intruder to poke his face through that gap so that it could utter its single, sharp yap. I shan't give it the satisfaction, thought Wexford, laughing at his aunt's phrase and driving off.

ON THE DAY Tamima Rahman and her mother left for Islamabad, Hannah went to call on Fata Hanif. With her husband and seven children she lived in a house in Rectangle Road, Stowerton, that had once been two houses but had been converted into one by the local authority. In spite of its size and the car parked on concrete slabs in what had once been a front garden, the Hanifs were obviously doing far less well than the Rahmans. Akbar Hanif had no job, had been out of work for years, and he and his family lived on the benefit.

He was not at home and nor were five of the children, for school had just returned after the summer holidays. Fata Hanif took her time answering the doorbell, possibly due to her pausing to tie a scarf round her head in case her caller was a man. A woman can cover her hair in many ways, but perhaps the most unflattering is when the scarf is brought low down over the forehead and high up to skim the chin. A pale face that had once been pretty peered out at Hannah from inside the black cotton oval. The voice was unexpected, southeast London, which would be called cockney north of the river.

"What do you want?" It was said diffidently rather than rudely. It sounded feebly frightened.

"May I come in?" Hannah produced her warrant card, wondering if it would mean anything to this woman. "I'm a police officer but there's nothing for you to worry about. There's nothing wrong."

The door opened a few inches wider. Fortunately, Hannah was slim. She squeezed through the opening. "This is just a friendly visit. I hope to have a talk with you about Tamima Rahman."

Immediately Mrs. Hanif said, "I don't know her."

They went into a living room. A baby lay asleep on the centre cushion of a three-seater sofa. An older child, perhaps two, was strapped into a high chair with, in front of it, a plateful of some sort of cereal he was slowly and almost ritualistically transferring to the floor, scooping it up in his fingers and smiling as it flopped onto a rug. Mrs. Hanif took no notice of either child. It was the sort of room Hannah wouldn't want to stay in for more than ten minutes at the most. Though extremely clean, it showed the signs on every article of furniture of the depredations of children.

Everything was broken or battered or scuffed or chipped or
cracked or torn or split or crushed or frayed. With all those
children the Hanifs must be receiving considerable amounts
of benefit, but whatever they did with it, they didn't spend it
on improving their home.

Hannah sat down next to the baby. Every other seat in the
place was damaged in some way. A leg missing and the chair
propped up on bricks, the seat itself split or the cover ripped
off to expose splintered wood and sharp nails beneath. Mrs.
Hanif sat in the chair on the bricks, and though it wobbled,
it held her weight.

"I'd heard," Hannah said carefully, "that your son Rashid
was friendly with her."

"He's only a boy," Fata Hanif said. "He doesn't go out with
girls. His dad and me, we wouldn't have it."

Hannah could hardly say she had seen the boy and girl
together. "When he is older, will you arrange a marriage for
Rashid?"

For a moment she thought Fata Hanif would refuse to
answer. She was silent for a long time. She got up and lifted
the baby in her arms. Boy or girl, Hannah couldn't tell which
it was. The child in the high chair had emptied his bowl
and was looking with pride, Hannah thought, at the piles of
rejected porridge on the floor.

At last Mrs. Hanif spoke. "I expect we will."

"Will it be with a local girl?"

Suddenly Mrs. Hanif became talkative. "We've no relations round here except for that Nicky and his dad that's my
brother. All my husband's relations are in Pakistan. Rashid's
got girl cousins there."

Trying to treat it as if it were a laughing matter no one

would take seriously for a moment, Hannah said, "So you wouldn't consider Tamima Rahman as a possible bride for your son?"

"We don't know the Rahmans. Her and Rashid go to the same school, that's all, and my sons Hussein and Khaled go there too, and they're not any of them going to marry Tamima Rahman. You people think that because we're all Moslems we must know each other. Well, that's wrong, we don't. Is that all? Because I've got to feed the baby."

Still asleep, the baby showed no sign of wanting to be fed, but Mrs. Hanif was already unfastening the bodice of her long, lilac-print dress. Hannah let herself out.

CONCENTRATING ON THE murder of Nicky Dusan was hardly necessary now that Tyler Pyke had been charged and committed for trial. It would be months before that trial happened. Wexford sometimes thought how strange the system must be for the public, for the inveterate reader of newspapers or viewer of television news broadcasts. The killing happened and the media went mad. Photographs of the victim and the victim's family dominated front pages and screens. The "quality" papers carried statistics, giving prominence to whatever number in the list of like murders this latest one was, the sixteenth or the eighteenth in as many weeks in the south of England. The victim's "loved ones" were interviewed or appeared on television, giving appeals. Wexford dared to speculate—knowing how politically incorrect this would be—if there would ever be a death by violence after which the dead man or woman's relatives for once failed to describe them as perfect, the soul of kindness, loving, "bubbly," helpful to all, and the ideal son, daughter, or sibling. No doubt, most of the dead had in fact been much like everyone else, a mixture of good and bad with virtues and faults. A few might be as saintly as their grieving relations said they were, but others would balance that by being as satanic as—well, as Targo.

He hadn't set eyes on Targo since the day he had seen him carrying the laptop into 34 Glebe Road and seen too the Tibetan spaniel in the passenger seat of the white van. Had he ever seen the man without a dog? Perhaps not. In the travel agency he had been accompanied by a corgi, in Myringham by his own pet dogs and those in the boarding kennels, in Jewel Road, Stowerton, by what Wexford called "the original spaniel," and with that same spaniel when he walked past Wexford's window on his way to the Kingsbrook meadows. But, yes, there had been one occasion when he was without a dog. In the hotel bar in Coventry he had been on his own, and this was no doubt only because the hotel banned dogs.

It must be over a month now since he had seen Targo sitting in his van in Glebe Road. Because Targo had seen and recognised him, he had half-expected the stalking to begin again. But it hadn't, and now Wexford could see that this supposition was unrealistic. The stalking had been confined to those early days in Kingsmarkham. Later there had been the incident of the snake. But he had never again been the subject of Targo's sustained surveillance, and since the death of Billy Kenyon and the subsequent investigation, he had encountered him only once. That had been when Targo told him how he had given the puppy to Billy's mother.

Mullan had got life imprisonment for the murder of Shirley Palmer in Coventry, but Wexford still wondered. Everyone he talked to about that murder, every police officer, said that if ever there was a justified penalty, that was it. Mullan had killed Shirley just as Christopher Roberts had killed his wife, Maureen. But Wexford wondered. By this time Mullan had served decades in prison and had never admitted to the crime, though such an admission might have have resulted in his release. This was usually regarded as an argument against guilt.

Did this perhaps mean Targo had been responsible for Shirley Palmer's death? It was possible. The recent murders in the Kingsmarkham area had been knife crimes, and Targo himself had only killed by strangling and claimed involvement in murders by strangling. Serial killers gave up when they got old, Wexford thought. As he reflected on this, listing in his mind notorious killers who had in age left their life of crime behind them, he realised that there weren't so many. Most known killers had been caught before old age. Then the thought came that Targo couldn't be called a serial killer. Even Wexford, obsessed as he was, could hardly give that title to a man who was possibly responsible for only two deaths. Or perhaps three and others which Targo would have liked to be blamed for.

Now, with old age encroaching, would he have the strength to strangle someone? The method took physical strength. If his victim was a woman, he would have. Wexford conjured him up, an image of him, short, sturdy, brawny with the muscles of a mini-sumo wrestler. Did he still lift weights, do press-ups? The question really was, would he want to? Perhaps he was satisfied now with the life he had made for himself, with his wife, his house, his cars, and, of course, his dogs.

I will get him for what he's done, Wexford said to himself. Whatever it takes, I will get him. One day, no matter how far away and how long it takes. This murder of the innocent and harmless Billy Kenyon has got to me like no other death by violence I have come across for a long time. If I let myself, I could weep for Billy Kenyon, even now, after all these years, but I shan't, of course I won't. I will watch Targo and wait and one day bring him to justice for Billy Kenyon and Elsie Carroll and perhaps too for Shirley Palmer.

12

THREE WEEKS LATER they came to him with the same subject on succeeding days. Hannah first, sandwiching her information between her report on Nicky Cooper-Dusan and the health or lack of it of Tyler Pyke. Jenny avoided the police station and came to his home. But they had the same thing to tell him. Yasmin Rahman had returned from Pakistan and Tamima with her. Tamima was not married, there was no husband, and no marriage ceremony had taken place. They had come home early because Tamima was homesick.

"These children, they have their way these days, don't they?" Yasmin had told Hannah, echoing her husband.

"I hoped to have a word with her," Hannah had said.

But Tamima wasn't there. In spite of what her mother had said, she was back working for her uncle at the Raj Emporium. "She will soon be going to London to stay with her auntie in Kingsbury."

Hannah remembered that this was exactly what Mohammed Rahman had told her would happen. She asked when that would be, but Mrs. Rahman said she didn't know. She was growing indignant by this time, and Hannah finally had to acknowledge that she hadn't a leg to stand on when Tamima's mother said, "I don't know why it interests you. She is free to do what she wants. What wrong has she done? What wrong have me and her father done?"

"Nothing, Mrs. Rahman, nothing at all." Hannah was appalled that she of all people might appear to be victimizing people for no more reason than that they were immigrants. "I'm sorry. I'd no intention of upsetting you."

"Tamima is over sixteen. She can leave home if she wants. You see, I know your law."

Jenny had met with an even colder reception, in her case from Tamima's father. "Tamima is working for her uncle. She's there because she likes to earn some money, as many young people do. Would you like to speak to her uncle? Or, better, would your *husband* like to speak to him? He, I think, is the police officer, not you."

Shaken, Jenny said, "No, no, of course not." And making matters worse: "It's just that I've grown fond of Tamima and I want to see things turn out well for her."

"And aren't I fond of my own daughter? My *only* daughter? Do you think I want her to be unhappy? Perhaps you should remember, Mrs. Burden, that I am a child-care officer, specifically Myringham's teenage-care manager. Don't you think maybe I know as much about adolescents' needs as you do?"

"Of course you do, of course." Appalled, Jenny was admitting to herself that this man was too much for her. This man was a great deal cleverer, more sophisticated and astute, than she had given him credit for. "It's just that—"

He interrupted her. "I'm sorry, Mrs. Burden, but I am busy and cannot talk much longer. Tamima is planning to go to her auntie in London shortly. She will enjoy herself there, go out with her cousins. The length of time she stays is down to her and to my sister. Then she will come home and decide what her next move should be? OK? All right?"

"I had to be satisfied with that," Jenny said.

"Aren't you?" Wexford raised his eyebrows. "Dare I ask what all the fuss is about?"

"If that's your attitude, I give up."

"I'm glad to hear it." He changed the subject and spoke to Dora. "Did Andy Norton come today?"

"He always comes on Thursdays. Well, twice he's changed to a Tuesday, but he's always phoned well in advance to let me know. Three o'clock. You could set your watch by him."

On the following Thursday Wexford got home early. Andy Norton was still there, cutting back the lushly overgrown shrubs and climbers which covered the rear garden wall. Wexford saw a tall man, white-haired and gaunt. He went outside, introduced himself, and noted the mellifluous tones and fine enunciation conferred on its alumni by Eton College.

"You're doing overtime," he said with a smile.

"I want to get things shipshape before the rain starts."

Shipshape, the word Targo had used long ago. He watched Norton get into his ancient but gleaming Morris Minor and drive away, waving as he went.

Later in the evening, Dora told him. He had noticed when he got home from work how especially nice she looked in a new, dark green dress and high-heeled, dark green shoes. Her legs had always been one of her best features, with their long calves and fine ankles. Round her neck she wore a necklace of gold and green garnets he had once given her. He complimented her on her appearance.

She smiled, thanked him, said, "I've been meaning to tell you. There's been a white van parked outside here for most of the afternoon. That's the second time this week. It was here on Tuesday too. I went out to check if it had a resident's parking pass in the windscreen, but it hadn't. Still, the traffic warden didn't appear. They never do when you want them."

He felt a sharp chill, like icy water trickling down his spine, the warmth her smile and evident pleasure had brought him all gone.

"As a matter of fact, I took the number."

He looked at the slip of paper she held out to him. It was Targo's. Of course it was.

"It comes of being married to a policeman," she said.

He tried to speak casually. "Dora, don't do that again. I mean, don't check up on a vehicle's right to park. Please."

"But why, darling?"

"Suppose I said, because I say so? Would that be enough?"

"That's what you say to children. All right, then. But I would quite like to know."

THE WHITE VAN didn't come back to Wexford's street next day or the next. That meant little. Targo had at least one other car. Wexford decided not to frighten Dora by asking her if she had seen a silver Mercedes parked where the van had been. Nor was he going to ask her if there had been a dog in the van. Besides, Targo might well have a collection of motor vehicles. Or he might do his surveillance on foot, parking the van farther away and walking the Tibetan spaniel half a mile or so.

What puzzled Wexford was the question of whom Targo was keeping under observation and why. Not himself, surely. The man must know he was out of the house all day. So he was watching Dora. Wexford didn't like that at all. Only a few days ago, he had half-made up his mind that Targo had given up his need to kill, had become a law-abiding citizen. Now he thought of the two occasions he had seen that van in Glebe Road. On both Targo had been calling on the Rahmans because one of the sons was an IT consultant, a legitimate reason for a visit. But Ahmed Rahman might have knowledge of Targo which would be invaluable to him. His thoughts went back to his wife.

Two years before, along with four other people, she had been abducted and held hostage by a group of countryside campaigners. He still thought of the three nights and four days as the worst period of his life. When she came back, he had sworn to himself that he would value her more, and for the most part he had stuck to that. He had appreciated her more and had shown it. But there was no reason to suppose that what had happened then would happen again. As far as he knew, Targo had never abducted anyone. He felt that cold trickle again when he spoke aloud what Targo did: "He kills. It's a hobby with him." He had killed at least one woman and one man, possibly two women. Maybe there had been others, "unregistered in vulgar fame." He remembered what Kathleen Targo had said to him when they met all those years ago in the Kingsbrook Precinct: "He likes animals. He doesn't like people."

What was to be done? He could hardly send a PC to keep an eye on the street outside his house. In the eyes of everyone but himself, Targo had done no wrong. Perhaps he should start again on proving that the man was not the innocent he looked to be. It was Friday afternoon, a mild day in October. The leaves on the trees were a dull green and they had begun to fall. The sunshine was rather thin, the pale blue sky streaked with strings of cloud.

The walk to Glebe Road constituted half his daily exercise but he was held up—almost swept up—by the crowd of Moslem men returning home or to their work from Stowerton mosque. They seemed remarkably happy, laughing and joking with each other, though not rowdily, and he thought how different would a group of home-going church attenders have been. Be careful not to be an inverted racist, he told himself, you're just as much a racist as Hannah if you favour immigrants over indigenous people. Letting the crowd go ahead of him, he fell in behind them. Most lived in this neighbourhood, but by the time he was halfway up Glebe Lane only two young men remained and an older man. Outside Webb and Cobb, the older man paused to look between the boards which covered what had been a shop window and, apparently satisfied, passed on. They all turned into number 34. Mohammed Rahman and his sons, they must be, Tamima's father and brothers. He waited until they were inside before ringing the bell.

The door was opened by the son with the beard, the older one, Hannah had told him.

"Chief Inspector Wexford, Kingsmarkham Crime Management." Wexford produced his warrant card. He had nearly said "Kingsmarkham CID," for old habits died hard and to him the new title sounded like a mafioso managing a bunch of gangsters.

"You want my dad? He's inside with my brother. I'm off to work."

Wexford walked in and was met in the narrow passage by a man of about fifty with black hair but a gray beard. He seemed to recognise Wexford, though Wexford had no recollection of ever having seen him before.

"Mohammed Rahman." He held out his hand, then indicated the young man behind him. "This is my son Ahmed."

If the father seemed calm but wary, the son looked rather tense. He was a handsome man of perhaps twenty-five, pale-skinned with coal-black eyes and black hair. He had the face of a young mogul emperor. They were absurdly crowded together in that narrow space, three tall men so close to each other that father and son had to shrink back to avoid touching Wexford, while Wexford pressed himself against the wall.

"Come into the lounge," said Mohammed Rahman.

A ridiculous word for a living room at any time, owing its provenance, Wexford thought, to early-twentieth-century Hollywood and luxury liners. Here it was less absurd than it might have been for the room was unexpectedly spacious with ample light coming in through the conservatory. A large fireplace of stone blocks with a mantelpiece of polished granite held on its grate a bowl of dried flowers. Kilim rugs covered the floor, and the conservatory was full of plants, a pale blue plumbago, a rose-pink oleander, which, had they been outside, would by now have been killed by frost. Apart from the rugs, not a single object was what Wexford would have called oriental. He was rather ashamed to confess to himself that he had expected the décor of an Indian restaurant.

He was shown to a black leather armchair. The two Rahmans waited expectantly, the father managing a smile, the son still ill at ease. "Do you know a man called Eric Targo?" he asked them.

The tension slackened. It was interesting to watch this lightening in each of them. Had they expected him to talk about Tamima?

Ahmed spoke for the first time. "He's a client."

"Your client? You're a computer consultant, aren't you?"

The young man nodded. "I work from home. I have an office upstairs."

"You look after Mr. Targo's computer? Service it? Mend it if it goes wrong?" Wexford was aware he was using the wrong terminology.

Evidently Ahmed was also aware of it, for he smiled. "Mr. Targo has three PCs. If he has a problem, I talk him through it or I call at his house."

"He's sometimes brought a computer here, Ahmed," his father reminded him.

"That's right. So he did. His Toshiba, his laptop, that was. Look, let me explain. Some of my clients—well, they're not exactly computer-illiterate. I wouldn't say that. But they get a bit nervous. They don't quite understand that when something's wrong, I can put it right if we're—well, both of us get online. That's when I can talk him through what's bothering him." Ahmed looked searchingly into Wexford's face, in case the chief inspector failed to follow him. "Anyway, that's how it is, but a lot of clients think I have to have the PC here to look at. And that's when he brings the Toshiba in for me to deal with it."

"I see."

What Wexford really meant was that he didn't see—it amounted to mending a machine without touching it or even seeing it—but he accepted and was satisfied. He hardly knew what he had suspected, for, whatever Targo's murderous propensities, he must have constant contact in business and his personal life with people whom he knew in honesty and innocence.

The trees in Glebe Road had begun to shed their leaves. Wexford started the walk back to the police station, recalling how when he was a child, he always made a point of treading on a fallen leaf, enjoying the crunching sensation underneath his feet. He tried it now, crushing a dried, crinkled plane leaf, and was pleased to find it gave him much the same feeling. But back to the Rahmans. There was nothing sinister about the Targo-Rahman connection, he thought. Nevertheless, Targo had resumed his stalking of *him* or, rather, begun stalking his wife. It came to him then that, in accordance with the old marriage service, a married couple used to be called "one flesh," and thinking of that, he felt a pang, as if what seemed a threatened hurt were being done to himself. The first thing he did when he was back in his office was to send for DC Damon Coleman and, wondering if he might be doing something indefensible, considering that in everyone's eyes but his own Targo was an innocent man, set him to keep Wexford's own house under surveillance. The stalker stalked, he thought.

SOME YEARS BEFORE, when his daughter Sylvia had been taking a course in psychotherapeutic counselling, she had taught him about the "box" as a means of dealing with anxieties.

"If you've a problem weighing on your mind, Dad, you have to visualise a box—maybe quite small, the size of a matchbox. You open it and put your worry inside—now don't start laughing. It works. Close the box with the worry inside and put it away somewhere, inside a drawer, say."

"Why not throw it in the sea?"

"That's a bit final. You may want to take it out again one day."

"And this is going to take all problems away?"

"I don't say that, Dad, but it might help. If you find yourself thinking of the worry, you also think it's locked away in the box so you can't touch it."

He had scoffed. But still he tried it. Several times since then he had put Targo in a box, and sometimes it had worked well. He tried it again now, carefully placing Targo and the white van and a bunch of dogs and his own fear into the box and hiding it in a drawer of the desk in his office. And the white van failed to reappear. No silver Mercedes was parked in Wexford's street, and no man with cropped white hair walking a Tibetan spaniel had been seen. It had, of course, no longer been possible to tell Damon Coleman of the distinguishing mark, the naevus on the neck. That was gone.

Damon had seen Dora Wexford leave the house twice on foot and twice in her car, but he was sure she hadn't seen him. Damon was an expert in the role of the invisible watcher. A woman he recognised as Wexford's daughter Sylvia came once and stayed about an hour. Jenny Burden called with her son. Apart from these, the only caller he had seen was a man in his sixties who arrived on Thursday at three in the afternoon in an ancient Morris Minor. Damon finished his surveillance at five, by which time the visitor had not come out.

This wasn't quite what Wexford had wanted. His wife and her callers were not to be watched but, rather, whoever might be watching her. Damon's report reminded him of the kind of thing a private detective might produce for a husband who believed himself deceived. That made Wexford smile. The idea of Dora's infidelity was absurd, even the mildest disloyalty out of the question.

But his fear was in the box and the box was shut up inside the top left-hand drawer of his desk. As often when he used the box—the invisible container created by his mind—the apprehensiveness or anxiety locked inside it had faded away. Just as the box had no real existence, so it seemed that the fear had none either.

Rashid Hanif had just come out of the gates of his sixth-form college on the Kingsmarkham bypass when Hannah spoke to him. If she had simply walked up to him, he might not have been so obviously taken aback, but he had seen her car draw up and park ahead of him and this good-looking, young woman he recognised from the Raj Emporium step out of it, flourishing a warrant card. He was good-looking himself, a tall, handsome boy with pale skin, brown hair, and gray-blue eyes.

Hannah could tell he was frightened and she wondered why. After all, he might be only seventeen, but he was a man, and most men—at any rate the innocent ones—were happy to speak to her. "I'd like to ask you about Tamima," she said. "We could talk in my car. I could give you a lift home."

Making that offer was a mistake. "Oh, no. No, thanks. I don't need a lift home. I can walk."

"I know you can walk. I don't have to take you to your house, just to the corner of the street. Come on. Those books you're carrying must be heavy."

He allowed her to shepherd him into the passenger seat of the car. Hannah had no intention of driving off immediately. She sat in the driving seat and turned to face him. "I've seen you talking to Tamima in the Raj Emporium, Rashid. I've seen you quite a few times. She's your girlfriend, isn't she?"

He shook his head, said in a low voice, "I wish."

"But she's not? Why is that? Because your parents are against it or hers are?"

During a long pause, his fingers tightened on the handle of the heavy bag. "Both. Look, I mustn't talk to you about that. I'll get into trouble. My dad's told me not to see her again. But I'm not to talk about it, OK?"

Hannah started the car, said nothing for a moment or two, then, when they were in Hartwell Lane, heading for the Hart estate, said, "You can only see her in the shop, is that right?"

"I'm not to talk about it." He immediately did so. "They took her to Pakistan to keep her away from me, but she missed me and she wanted to come back. Now they'll send her to her auntie in London."

"Did she tell you this?"

"She didn't tell me, but it's what I think. I told you, I'm not supposed to talk about it. Can I get out now? I can walk from here."

"I'm sure you can. If you'll tell me her auntie's name and where she lives, I'll drive to the end of Hartwell Lane and drop you off."

The boy shifted in his seat. Now he was clutching the bag of books. "It's Kingsbury. But she's not gone yet. Maybe she won't go, I don't know."

"And the name, Rashid?" The house where his family lived was in sight. Hannah pulled over, leaving the engine running. "The auntie's name, Rashid?"

The two words came out in a choked rush, "Mrs. Qasi," and he flung open the car door and ran.

Hannah knew she must bide her time. It was true that Tamima might not go to London. If, for instance, she agreed to give Rashid up, she might remain here. But that was unlikely. The Rahman parents wouldn't trust her to keep any promise she might make, especially if she was working in that shop where anyone might come in and have access to her. Besides, their aim was not only to divide her from Rashid but to marry her to someone else.

"It would be hard to force marriage on a girl here. In a place like this where everyone knows everyone else," Hannah said to Wexford.

"Used to," said Wexford, thinking of the villagey town of his youth.

"Still is. Especially if you're an immigrant. People are always on the watch for them to do something *un-English*, something bizarre or something *they* wouldn't do. Think of the drama there'd be if Tamima ran away on the steps of the mosque or the register office or wherever. In London she couldn't do that, she wouldn't know where she was or where to go. Think about it, guv."

"Hannah, what I'm thinking about is the drama you're making out of a young girl's visit to London. To go shopping, no doubt. Maybe see a film or a show." Smiling at Hannah's mutinous expression, he said, "She hasn't gone yet. But I've met those Rahmans and they impressed me as intelligent, enlightened people, the last to force ancient traditions on a beloved daughter. I'll be very surprised if Tamima doesn't go away for a couple of weeks, have a good time, and come back to take a better sort of job somewhere."

On the way home he wondered if he had been rather rash in saying that. Was Hannah's theory so far-fetched? Perhaps what provoked his pacifying rejoinder was her vehement determination to prove that a forced marriage was intended without any evidence for it. But that was not so different from his certainty that Targo was at least twice a murderer. He had no evidence either. Yet he constantly said to himself that he knew it for a fact. Hannah too was probably even now telling herself the same, that though she had no evidence, she was still convinced that the Rahmans were planning Tamima's marriage to some old man she had never before seen. If Hannah's theory was a fantasy, wasn't his just as likely to be one too?

For once, few cars were parked along his street. No white van or silver Mercedes was among them. Of the few that were there, not one had a dog sitting on the passenger seat, the driver's window a few inches open to give it air. He let himself into his house, called out, "It's me," as if others existed who had keys.

Dora came out into the hall. He put his arms round her and kissed her with a little more than his usual fervour.

"I suppose that's because you've been imagining me lying dead somewhere," she said.

"Don't."

"And don't you set Damon Coleman to watch this house without telling me. Poor chap, he looked so bored. I nearly went out and told him my lover wouldn't be round before two."

Wexford laughed. The laughter was a bit forced.

"It was that white van," Dora said, "wasn't it?"

"It seems to have stopped. That's something to celebrate, so let's have a drink."

13

A SECOND GLASS OF red wine had been tempting but he had refused it. Not because he had some sort of premonition he would be called out, that hardly crossed his mind, but because it was early, he had only just sat down to his dinner, and if he had more claret now, he would want another before bed. So he left the silver stopper his daughter Sheila had given him in the neck of the bottle and applied himself to the fusilli alla carbonara and roquette salad he didn't much like but which Dora deemed good for him. As you got older, he thought, your taste reverted to the food of your youth. In your middle years you had quite liked deep-fried melon flowers and filo pastry and chorizo, but now you wanted what you never got, sausages and steak and kidney pudding and stewed plums and custard. On the other hand, his preferred drink used to be beer but now he hardly touched it. He was musing on this, wondering if Dora felt the same but somehow feeling sure she didn't, was on the point of asking her, when the phone rang.

She knew it would be for him. She passed it to him without answering it herself.

"I have to go." He got up, leaving half his fusilli. "Something serious." He always used the phrase to her when he was called out to an unexplained death or a lethal attack. So it had been when Billy Kenyon's body was found in the botanical gardens, so it was when Nicky Cooper-Dusan was stabbed. He was later glad he adhered to this economy of explanation. Telling her the address he was called out to this evening, though at the time it meant nothing to him, would have shocked and horrified her so that he would have baulked at leaving her alone.

She nodded, accepting. The days when she would have lamented his failing to finish his dinner were long gone. Now, his girth staying the same if not exactly increasing, she was pleased when he missed a meal or only ate half of it.

Again glad his evening's drinking had been limited to one small glass of red wine, he drove himself to Pomfret. Two police cars, a police van, and an ambulance—not to be needed—were already parked outside the row of white stucco cottages. He left his car fifty yards up Cambridge Road. A blue-and-white-striped canvas barrier with a doorway in it had already been erected to cover most of the front of number 6.

Barry Vine lifted the flap over the doorway and came out as Wexford approached. "Pathologist's just come, sir. He's with the deceased now."

"Who is it?"

"Dr. Mavrikian," Barry said.

"I don't mean the pathologist. Who cares, anyway? I mean who's what you call 'the deceased'?"

Barry knew very well Wexford's hatred of jargon and verbiage, so he said, "Sorry, sir. The dead man is called Andrew Norton. This is his home and a neighbour . . ." The look on Wexford's face stopped him. "You know him?"

146

"What did you say the name is?"

"Andrew Norton."

Wexford felt his heart pound. He could almost hear it. "He does—did—gardening for me."

"Someone put a rope round his neck and strangled him."

"I think we'll wait to hear what Dr. Mavrikian says before we make statements like that," said Wexford.

He was very taken aback. Thank God he hadn't mentioned that address to Dora. She had liked the man, they had had tea together when he took his break on Thursday afternoons. Damon Coleman had seen him come and go in his ancient Morris Minor. Wexford walked along to the living room where the body was lying on the floor between a sofa and the television set. Mavrikian got up from his knees and gave Wexford one of his impassive stares. A tall, thin, humourless man of Armenian origin, he had lined white skin and blond, nearly white hair. The only time he had been seen to be even slightly moved was when the news had been brought to him that he had a baby daughter.

In Wexford's estimation any faults the man might have were compensated for by the swift (and accurate) assessment he made of the time of a victim's death and the cause of that death.

"He's been dead since between seven and nine this morning, let's say twelve hours ago. Someone put a rope round his neck and pulled it tight. All the details to come in my report. Good evening."

As he was leaving, Hannah Goldsmith arrived. "He was my gardener, poor chap," Wexford said to her.

"My God, guv."

"He was at my house yesterday afternoon."

"Your partner may know something relevant then."

"She's my wife," said Wexford, annoyed.

Andy Norton had been a good-looking man, his regular features and still smooth skin bloated by what had been done to him. His head of white hair was as thick and glossy as a wig, but it wasn't a wig. The scene-of-crimes officer was anxious to get on with his job, so Wexford turned to Hannah and told her they would go next door to speak to the neighbour.

"She's a Mrs. Catherine Lister, sir," said Barry Vine. "She's a widow and she lives alone. Her and the dead chap, they seem to have been good friends."

"What does that mean?"

"Oh, nothing. Only what I said, sir. She's very upset."

Mrs. Lister's daughter opened the door. She was about forty, thin, her dark hair drawn back into a ponytail.

"I came over to Mum this afternoon," she said, "and I've been here ever since. I'd like to take her home with me tonight. Is that OK?"

"Once we've had a word with her it will be quite OK," said Wexford.

He had a strong sensation of déjà vu. He had been here before, yet he knew he never had. For almost his whole life, while he had lived in the Kingsmarkham neighbourhood, he could never remember having even seen this terrace of cottages, tucked away in the hinterland of Pomfret. Yet the little hallway, the stairs going straight up opposite the front door, the single living room that had once been two, the garden with its door in the wall beyond . . . He forced himself back to speak to the older woman.

She was rather like his own wife, the same type, the type that was *his*. Her figure was still shapely, her waist small and ankles fine. Her hair had once been dark and was now iron-gray, and she had large, dark eyes and the clear skin and good colour of a woman who has known little illness. If she had cried, her eyes were dry now, with no puffiness in her face.

She suddenly spoke without waiting for questions. "We were very close, Andy and I. We were more or less living together but these cottages are a bit small for that. I have a key to his house and he had one to mine." She looked down at the hands in her lap. "I spent last night with Andy as I did two or three times a week, but I came back here at about seven this morning."

Her voice was steady and cool. The daughter took one of her hands, but Catherine Lister didn't press hers in return.

"What time did you go back next door?" Hannah asked.

"Not till afternoon. I did some housework, cleaned the place, put my washing and Andy's in the machine. He didn't have a washing machine. I was going shopping for both of us later on. . . ." Her voice broke and she shook herself, steadied herself. "It was about four. I went in to him to see if there was anything special he wanted." Again her voice wavered but she kept on. "I let myself in, and I—I found him on the floor. Dead. I could see he was dead."

"Did you touch him, Mrs. Lister?" Wexford asked.

She turned her face away. "I lifted up his head. I—I kissed him."

The crying began then. Her daughter put her arms round her and Catherine Lister sobbed into her shoulder. Wexford and Hannah exchanged glances. They were silent for perhaps a minute. The only sound was the sobs and gulps from the weeping woman.

"I'm sorry, Mrs. Lister," Wexford said. "I'm very sorry but I do have to ask you a few more questions."

"Surely you can leave Mum in peace for now!"

"No, I'm afraid not. Did you hear anything from this house during the morning?"

"Nothing," she said, her voice hoarse from crying. "I heard nothing and I didn't see anyone."

"Did Mr. Norton have any enemies?" This was Hannah. "I mean people he disliked or who disliked him?"

"Everyone loved him," said Catherine Lister.

But she rubbed the tears from her eyes and, her voice made hoarse from crying, gave him all the information about Andy Norton that he wanted. He left her then. The clocks had gone back and it was dark, but light from the French window of number 6 showed him Andy Norton's garden, beautifully tended, with still a few chrysanthemums and Michaelmas daisies remaining in bloom. The grass exemplified the phrase *a manicured lawn*. Wexford walked down the path past the shed in the right-hand corner to the green-painted door in the rear wall. It had no lock or bolts. He opened it and stepped out into the cobbled lane at the back. Now he knew what this house reminded him of, what this terrace of houses reminded him of.

These cottages were the same as the row of houses in Jewel Road, Stowerton. This house had the same structure as the Carrolls' at number 16, from the narrow hallway to the shed in the garden and the door in the rear wall leading to a lane outside. Or they had once been the same when they were first built. When would that have been? Eighteen seventy? Eighteen eighty? Something like that. Probably other terraces in Kingsmarkham and Stowerton and Pomfret were of the same vintage. Much had been done to these, and no doubt by now to those in Jewel Road since he had first been in the Carrolls' house. A pair of single rooms had been turned into one double room, French windows had been put in, as had central heating and new kitchens and bathrooms. But if you had known one of these houses forty years before, if you had *lived* in one of these houses, you would know the configuration of all of them wherever they might be.

He went back into Andy Norton's garden and shut the door in the wall. The moon was rising, a red ball, streaked with bands of dark cloud. With the coming of the moon the air seemed to grow colder. He closed his eyes momentarily and was back in Jewel Road where a man opened the door to him and showed, for a few brief seconds, a birthmark like a crimson crab climbing down his cheek and his neck, before he snatched up a woman's scarf and covered himself.

There was no more for Wexford to do tonight. DS Vine and DC Coleman were busy interviewing the other neighbours. The scene-of-crimes officer had finished. Wexford walked out through the blue-and-white tent that covered most of the front of the house and opened the gate. A man was walking his dog in the direction of the cross street. He was an elderly man, well above medium height, not wearing a scarf, and the dog he had on a lead was a boxer. But it was the déjà vu all over again.

He half-expected cold blue eyes to stare into his. The man looked curiously at the tent and the police tape and passed on.

Wexford went home to tell Dora before anyone else did or she saw it on the news, and when he turned into his garage drive and switched off the engine, he saw an image of Targo opening that door in the wall in the dark and seeking a hiding place in the shed until the time was ripe. He was a man of such self-confidence that he would see no need to bring the instrument of death with him. The world was full of strips of cloth, rope cutoffs, pieces of cord, scarves, ties, straps, and belts. Such a thing would be waiting in Andy Norton's house or garden for him to lay his hand on.

ANDY NORTON WAS a widower. He had three children from his marriage, only one of which, a daughter, was living in England. Of his sons, one was in the United States, the other living in Italy. Prior to his retirement he had been an official—with one of those permanent or private secretary titles—in the Department of Social Security. His wife had died fifteen years before. He and she had lived in a South London suburb, but he had sold the house when he retired and bought this Pomfret cottage. Mrs. Lister, a widow, was already living next door.

Mary Norton, a teacher whose home was in Leicester, arrived the next morning. Talking to her in his office, Wexford found himself with a not uncommon dilemma, how to avoid asking her when she had last seen her father. He slightly changed it.

"When did you last see your dad, Ms. Norton?"

She had a hard, crisp voice, was a thin fair-haired woman. No one could be less like Mrs. Lister. "He came up to stay with me the weekend before last. That often happened. Or I came down to stay with him." Her tone remained the same, steady, clear, and calm, when she said, "We were very close, father and daughter, the way a father and daughter should be.

"I don't know how much you know about him. He had been a civil servant—that is, an official in a government department. Dad retired eight years ago and came to live here. He had an excellent pension but he liked to keep himself busy and he went out gardening. He was a good gardener and he loved it. He enjoyed the chats he had with elderly housewives over a cup of tea."

Though he knew it was unreasonable, Wexford resented her patronising words. When she had finished he kept silent for a while, moved a pen on his desk, straightened the blotter. "And Mrs. Lister," he said quietly, "how did you feel about her?"

Mary Norton plainly resented the question. She had calculated, Wexford thought, that she would have everything her own way in this interview. She would fix the time of it, organise the structure of it, pass on the information she thought the police should have, deliver her planned speech, then terminate it. Though she wasn't in the least like him, the way she stared, her blue gaze steady and unblinking, reminded him of Eric Targo.

"What's that got to do with Dad's death?"

"I ask the questions, Ms. Norton." The words were harsh but the tone was gentle. "Would you answer the one I asked you?"

"If you must know, she's a pleasant enough woman. It was good for him to have companionship."

It was more than that, Wexford thought, much more. He asked her if her father had made a will and, if so, what was in it.

Incredibly, she answered him in lawyer's jargon. "His testamentary dispositions divided everything he left between my brothers and myself. There was this cottage and his savings, not a great deal." She hesitated, then softened a little. "My father gave away most of what he had to his children. He sold his house and got a good price, which enabled him to leave quite large sums to each of us under the seven-year rule. You know what that is? The beneficiaries get a tax concession if the donor lives for seven years. He did, in fact. Just."

"Very well, Ms. Norton. That will be all for now."

Even though he hadn't yet received Mavrikian's report, he knew Andy Norton had been strangled. What he had at first thought to be a length of rope, but which turned out to be a window-sash cord, had been used.

"All the sash cords were in place, sir," DS Vine said to him. "This one wasn't new. It had been in a window somewhere, it was a bit worn and frayed at one end, and my guess is it was lying in a kitchen drawer or cupboard."

"Your guess?"

"I realise we're going to have to find precisely where it came from, sir. They're doing a house-to-house in Cambridge Road now."

"Yes, well, don't let me hear of any more guesswork, right?"

Wexford went back to Pomfret. The house-to-house, which he could see going on, reminded him of Jewel Road all those years ago. How many house-to-house enquiries had he instigated since then? Yet this procedure again brought Targo to mind. Andy Norton had been strangled and Targo was the arch-strangler. It was absurd. Why should Targo kill the harmless and innocent Andy Norton? Come to that, why had he killed Elsie Carroll and Billy Kenyon? They also had been harmless and innocent.

Damon Coleman and Lynn Fancourt were doing the house-to-house at this end of Cambridge Road. He went up to meet them when Damon came away from the doorstep of number 18 and Lynn from number 20.

"Any luck?"

"A woman opposite, sir, at number five, seems to have kept

the house under surveillance, especially in the early mornings and late evenings." Lynn Fancourt smiled. "She disap-
proves of Andy Norton's relationship with Mrs. Lister. She
watched their comings and goings."

"She'll have to look elsewhere for her kicks now," said
Wexford.

"Yes, sir. She swears no one went into the house this
morning. She was watching from the moment it got light,
and that's at about seven. She saw Mrs. Lister come out and
go into her own house next door at seven fifteen."

Wexford went back to number 6 and made his way in
through the blue-and-white-striped awning. Barry Vine was
inside with a PC from the uniformed branch.

"Suppose," he said to Vine, "the perpetrator came into the
back garden here while it was still dark. Say at five. Come
with me."

They went out by way of the back door into Andy Norton's garden. Something was particularly dreadful about
looking at this trim and lovely place, the small lawn weed-
less and neatly mown, the borders rich with autumn flowers,
the four sculpted stone tubs still holding their cargoes of red
and apricot and pink begonias. From the moment the culti-
vator of this garden had died, it too had begun to die, gradually withering, abandoned to its untended state. Tomorrow
it would be a little drier, the grass a little longer, or a little
wetter, nearer to drowning, the dying petals starting to fall.

"He could have come through the gate from the lane. And
suppose he came in before it got light. That means before
seven. Let's say he waited out here, with his sash cord. He
could have hidden in the shed. He would have seen a light go
on in the house and taken that as a signal. Did he know about
Mrs. Lister? It doesn't really matter. If she had been there,

would he have killed her too? But she wasn't. She had gone."

"You sound as if you know the perpetrator, sir?"

"Do I, Barry?" Wexford shook his head. "What happened next? He went up to the back door and knocked. There's a knocker but no bell. When he heard someone knock at his back door, Andy Norton went to answer it and admitted him. Why? We don't know. Perhaps because it's natural for older people, brought up in a safer age, to open their doors to whoever knocks. Maybe it wasn't like that and the back door had been left unlocked overnight. Maybe it always was. We shall know more than that when I get the pathologist's report."

It was Targo's murder of Elsie Carroll all over again. So many small properties in these towns had lanes running at the backs of houses. So many gardens were impossible of entry except over or through those walls if the doors were locked or bolted. All the houses had back doors. Many householders still left theirs unlocked. Wexford thought of 32 Jewel Road, where Targo had once lived, of 8 Glebe Road, where he had lived later on in his stalking days. He would know the layout, he would know which moves were feasible.

Wexford rang Mrs. Lister's doorbell. Her daughter let him in, explaining that instead of taking her mother away, she had stayed the night.

"Mum's lying down."

"I'd like you to go up to your mother and ask her two questions, whether Mr. Norton's back door was left unlocked overnight, and whether there was a piece of sash cord in Mr. Norton's house. You know what sash cord is?"

"A kind of rope that opens and shuts windows."

"That's right. Now your mother will probably guess what this cord was used for if she didn't actually see it when she found the body. I hope she didn't see it and won't guess, but if she does, that can't be helped. Is all this clear?"

"Yes, of course. I suppose it was used to strangle the poor man."

"What I want to know is, did this sash cord belong in the house or was it—well, brought there."

She went upstairs. Wexford sat there, thinking about Targo. This was more than obsession, this was paranoia. It was impossible Targo was responsible for this; wild imaginings, fixation, a kind of madness. The daughter came back into the room.

"Mum did see it when she—found him. She recognised it. It was a piece of sash cord that had been rolled up and put in the garden shed along with balls of string and a length of rope. She says she's glad to help. She wants whoever did this caught."

"And the back door? Was it left unlocked?"

"She doesn't know. She says it often was and she told Andy she thought that wasn't a good idea, but he said this was the country and there wasn't much crime in the country."

Wexford sighed.

THE BOX HAD burst open and Targo come out of it, strutting, staring, defying him. His dilemma was the same one, the old one. How to interview—interrogate—a man lacking even a tenuous connection with the murder victim whose death he was investigating.

"This woman," said Burden, "the one who lives at number five, she saw no one but Catherine Lister when she left just after seven?"

"She wouldn't have seen Targo if he came into the garden from the lane. If he came the same way as he came when he killed Elsie Carroll all those years ago."

"A *man* who came into the garden, Reg. A man or a woman, but not Eric Targo. He's old now. If he did in fact kill Elsie Carroll—and I have my doubts about that and about Billy Kenyon—would he have the strength to strangle a man a head taller than him? Would he have the strength to strangle anyone?"

"*He* would," said Wexford. "What excuse can I have for going to talk to him?"

"A white van parked outside Andy Norton's house on two occasions—how about that? Or a silver Mercedes?"

"They weren't, though. Not so far as we know. And, no, Mike, we're not going in for fictitious scenarios because the fact is we don't need them. We don't need an excuse. What's to stop us questioning anyone we choose about any crime committed on our patch?"

THE DAY AFTER Andy Norton's death, Donaldson, who was Wexford's driver, took him and DS Lynn Fancourt to Stringfield. Passing through Stoke Stringfield village, Wexford thought briefly of Helen Rushford, his girlfriend of a few months when he lived in Brighton, she who had told him she loved him and that he was everything she wanted. She lived here somewhere, a grandmother no doubt, and he would long have ceased to be what she wanted. In that house by the green or down that lane? In one of those pretty cottages? If she came out of one of those houses, would he recognise her? Probably not.

They drew up outside Wymondham Lodge. No cars were

on the driveway, but the big garage had space for two vehicles, so they might have been hidden from view.

"Look, sir," Lynn said, "those animals. Aren't they lovely? Are they llamas or alpacas?"

"No idea," Wexford said, smiling at the benign-looking creatures who came up to the fence in quest perhaps of treats. "Targo's got some big felines too, I think. Only they're behind bars."

When he rang the doorbell, a dog started to bark. It sounded, as Lynn remarked, like two dogs, and so it was, the Tibetan spaniel and a Staffordshire bull-terrier puppy, the latter on a lead held by a woman in late middle age with the brightest red hair Wexford had ever seen. He had seen geraniums that colour but, not previously, hair. It was woven into a helmet shape that fitted over a large head and a face not resembling the terrier's or the spaniel's, but with its squashed features and a turned-up nose, perhaps a Pekingese's. Thickset and stocky, she was expensively dressed in a beaded brocade jacket and black trousers. She looked impassively at their warrant cards. Her eyes, prominent and very blue like Targo's, met Wexford's.

"Oh, yes," she said, "I've heard him mention you."

This was unexpected. "Mrs. Targo?"

"I'm Mavis Targo, yes." Her manner was charmless, her voice gruff.

"We'd like to speak to your husband."

She unfastened the lead on the bull terrier and it immediately jumped up at Wexford. She gave it an indulgent smile, which she switched off when she spoke. "He's not in."

He gave the dog a push. It was unexpectedly strong. "When do you expect him home?"

"I don't. He comes when he's ready. He pleases himself."

"May we come in, please."

Wexford put his foot over the threshold and she had no choice but to let him in. Lynn followed quickly to avoid the door's being slammed in her face. The old house had a graciousness its furnishings did their best to diminish. They found themselves in a big hall out of which an elegant curved staircase climbed, but it was furnished with gilded tables and chairs of the imitation eighteenth-century French variety, set about on a pink-and-white Chinese carpet. A large chandelier, a glittering waterfall of prisms, was suspended from the ceiling. The puppy jumped on one of the tables and stood there, wagging its tail.

"Get down, sweetheart," said Mrs. Targo in a halfhearted way.

"I don't know what you want to come in for," she said to Wexford. "I said he's not here and I don't know when he will be. I haven't seen him since yesterday morning."

"Sixty percent of the population of this country has a mobile phone," said Wexford. "I think that's the correct figure. I'm sure your husband is one of them. Would you like to call him and let me speak to him?"

"What, now?"

"Now."

"You'd better come through."

Coming through meant entering a large living room, furnished in much the same style as the hall but with a blue carpet. A blue, white, and pink silk rug, spread across quite a big area of this carpet, had extensively been chewed and most of its fringe was missing. The puppy homed at once on the rug and began gnawing with gusto on the edge where the fringe had been.

"Leave it, sweetheart," said Mrs. Targo, unperturbed when

the dog took no notice. She picked up a pink-and-silver mobile phone from one of the tables and dialled a number in a lethargic, vaguely depressed way. Her fingernails were the same colour as her hair.

When there appeared to be no reply, she dialled a second number, beginning to shake her head. Targo stared at Wexford from a silver-framed photograph standing on a piano. It had been taken not long ago and after the treatment to remove the birthmark. Targo was smiling—*smiling*—proud, no doubt, of his new unblemished appearance. In anyone but this monster it would have been pathetic, even touching. For the one of him, there were four of his wife, taken when she was younger and slimmer, in one of the photographs wearing a wedding dress embroidered in sequins.

"He's not answering," she said. "D'you want me to leave a message?"

"I'll do that," said Wexford. "Give me the phone."

He asked Targo to contact him and gave him a number to call. If it was Targo, if the numbers she had called had been his.

"Where was he going when he left here yesterday morning?"

"He had a call to make in Kingsmarkham. I do know that. He did say that much, but not when he'd be back or nothing."

"What does your husband do for a living?"

"He's mostly retired but he still does a bit of property."

"You mean he's a property developer?"

"All those right-to-buy flats, that sort of thing."

"So where is he, Mrs. Targo?"

"I don't know, do I? I've tried to get him for you and he's not answering. What more can I do?"

"Your dog is eating the flowers in that vase," said Lynn.

Wexford suppressed a smile. "It's now ten past three. I shall phone you at six, but whether he is back or not, we shall come back at seven. If your husband phones you, please tell him I shall see him here at seven."

At this point, as they were returning to the hall, a disconcerting thing happened. From somewhere in the grounds behind the house came a deep-throated roar.

Lynn said, "That sounded like a lion."

"It *is* a lion." Mavis Targo sighed. "That's King. My husband's crazy about him but I don't know. . . . Well, I'll have to feed him before Eric gets back or he'll go on like that for hours."

"Is he allowed to keep a lion like that?" Lynn asked when they were outside.

"God knows. I'm not going to worry about that now." Another roar and another sounded more loudly. "Good thing he hasn't any near neighbours." Put the lion in a box and shut it up in a drawer . . .

At seven, when he and Lynn went back, the lion was silent, and in the darkness no other animals could be seen. The sky appeared starless, the land an undulating, gray expanse dotted with black trees which the imaginative might have compared to the plains of Africa. Targo was still out. He had phoned, his wife said, or someone had phoned, and left her a message on the landline.

"You mean you were out when this person phoned?"

"I had to feed King, didn't I? And that scares me to death. And then I had to take the dogs out."

"Who was it left you a message?"

"I don't know. I thought it was someone in his office, but he's told me he's got no one working for him just now."

"Are you saying it was Mr. Targo himself disguising his voice?"

"It could have been. I couldn't tell, I was in a state worrying about King."

Perhaps you need a box of your own, Wexford thought. "What did the message say?"

"Just that he was OK and he'd call me."

"What, this mysterious voice simply said it was speaking on behalf of your husband and he'd call you tomorrow?"

"That's right."

"I'd like to listen to it, please."

"Oh, it's not there now. I erased it. I always do that with messages to avoid getting in a muddle."

"All right. I want the address of his office, the numbers of all the phones he has. The number of his car. DS Fancourt will take those numbers from you. Come along now, Mrs. Targo."

When Lynn had taken them down, having some difficulty in extracting the number of the Mercedes from her, she asked about the white van and was told it was in the garage. Mavis Targo was at last beginning to show signs of agitation. It had taken a long time to shake her out of her apathy but she was shaken now.

"I keep telling you I don't know where he is. I don't keep tabs on him. I wouldn't be here long," she added with a flash of bitterness, "if I did."

"His son and daughter live here or near here. I'd like their addresses and phone numbers."

"I haven't got them! I've hardly ever seen them. He doesn't have them here, he goes to them. I don't know where they live."

"Then I suggest you get busy with the phone book. I suppose you know his daughter's married name?"

She did. Eventually, Lynn found the phone book and looked up the names while Mrs. Targo smoked a cigarette and, fetching herself a gin and tonic, asked Wexford if he and "the young lady" would like a drink. This was refused. The Tibetan spaniel began to whine, its note growing shriller until the puppy followed suit, first yapping, then emitting a full-throated bark.

"They're asking for their dinner," said Mavis Targo.

Lynn patted the puppy on its head. "Missing his master too, I expect."

The office address was in Sewingbury, three or four miles away, in a small, two-story building on the edge of the industrial estate. Streetlamps were on but most buildings were in darkness, including Targo's office. Like the place he had had in Myringham when he was a travel agent, it appeared to consist of one room. The door was of glass and the window a sheet of plate glass, through which, as at Myringham, a desk and two chairs could be seen by the light of Lynn's torch. On the floor were two empty bowls, one for water, the other for dog food. All that was missing were the posters of exotic locations and the proprietor. Neither Targo nor anyone else was about, and the door was locked. No cars were on the parking spaces adjacent to the building. The whole place seemed infinitely desolate.

Back in his own office, Wexford phoned all the numbers he had been given. On Targo's he was put onto message. Alan Targo answered his own phone, was polite and pleasant, but had no idea where his father was. He hadn't seen him for three weeks.

"I'm a solicitor," he said. "My firm's in Queen Street."

Wexford thought of telling him they had last met when Alan was a child of four, but he thought better of it.

"My sister's here, as a matter of fact, if you want to talk to her. But I know she hasn't seen Dad for weeks."

She hadn't. He recalled that other evening, long ago, when Alan had been sitting at his father's feet stroking the dog and this woman he was talking to had still been in her mother's womb. Nothing odd about that, though. Half the people he talked to had yet been unborn when he was young. . . .

He was wasting his time, Burden said when they met for a drink. When they met for a drink and dinner, Wexford corrected him, for they couldn't go home yet. He had phoned Mrs. Targo five minutes before to be told her husband was still out.

"I shall go back to the zoo. You can come with me if you feel like it. He has to get home sometime."

They had deserted the Indus for the restaurant whose gimmick was that it served only old-fashioned British food. Not "English" because haggis was sometimes on the menu and so were Cornish pasties.

"Cornwall's in England," said Burden.

"Not according to the Cornish. They say England starts when you cross the Tamar." Wexford had less than happy memories of the county (or country), the awful Medora in Port Ezra, but happy memories too in that his first meeting with his wife was in Newquay. Strange, though, to remember that he had already come across Targo in those days, that Targo had been with him for the greater part of his life.

"*Why* does he do it, Mike? Elsie Carroll, Billy Kenyon, and now Andy Norton. He didn't know any of these people. All he had in common with them was that they happened to live in the same neighbourhood. But why those? Would anyone have done for him? Oh, I know I've yet to convince you that he killed them."

If a reply was needed, Burden failed to give it. "I'm going to have the fish pie. I fancy all that sauce and mashed potatoes. My mum would have called it nourishing, though I don't know if nutritionists would agree with her these days. Too much fat, probably. Not that I have to worry about that."

"Please don't preen yourself. I've enough to bear without that."

Burden laughed. "A glass of sauvignon, I think. Shall I have potatoes as well or just the sprouts and the carrots?"

"Potatoes would be adding insult to injury." Wexford looked up from the menu, said to the waitress, "Fish pie over there, please, and roast beef without the Yorkshire pudding, sadly, for me. Oh, and a glass of *tap* water. I shall be driving us back there. But I'm not wasting money on bottled fizz, the biggest ramp of all in these extravagant days."

Burden studied the décor. A mural of morris dancers covered half a wall, jousting knights the other half. "On the wall behind you that you can't see they're changing the guard at Buckingham Palace."

" 'Christopher Robin went down with Alice,' " said Wexford. " 'Alice is marrying one of the guard. "A soldier's life is terrible hard," said Alice.' That's the first poem I ever remember reading."

Burden sighed a little. "Are we really going back there tonight? What *for*?"

"Well, in part to ask Targo where he was between seven fifteen and nine thirty yesterday morning." Their drinks came, Burden's sauvignon filling a large glass. "Have you ever thought how much less depressing water would be if it had a colour? I mean, if it was light blue or pink like rose? A natural colour, of course, not some sort of dye they put in."

"No, I haven't. If we weren't going back there on a wild-

goose chase, you could have a big glass like mine full of burgundy."

"I have often wondered," said Wexford, "why it should be
so difficult, if not impossible, to catch a wild goose. A tame
goose is quite easy to catch, and it's hard to understand why
catching a wild one should be so different." The waitress
brought their food and another came with vegetables. "I
wish I'd had the Yorkshire pudding, but it's too late now." He
applied his knife to a slice of beef. "I asked you why he does
it. Why does he kill people he doesn't know? It was a rhetori-
cal question really because I know how he chooses the people
if not what impels him to kill them."

"Go on then, tell me. This fish pie is very good."

"He picks a person," said Wexford, "that someone wants
to be rid of."

"He *what*?"

"You heard me, Mike. He doesn't have to know the person,
but he has to know something about them. First there was
Elsie Carroll. It was quite well-known in the neighbourhood,
if not to poor Mrs. Carroll, that her husband wanted shot of
her in order to have a free run with Tina Malcolm. Billy Kenyon was expendable because it was only if he was out of the
way that Bruce Mellor would marry Eileen Kenyon. Possibly
there were others in Birmingham and Coventry similarly in
need of someone to rid them of an encumbrance, but if there
were, we don't know about them. And so to Andy Norton . . ."

"His girlfriend said everyone who knew him loved him.
No one wanted to get rid of him, that's for sure."

"*I* did, Mike," said Wexford, "or Targo thinks I did."

• • •

167

"You? Why you?" said Burden. "What on earth do you mean?"

"I'll tell you. Targo, though quite sane, is a psychopath. He is a monster, entirely callous, indifferent to others' pain. But for some reason—and I don't know what that reason is—he needs to give people in need of it some help in dealing with their trouble. Perhaps he has a conscience of a kind. Perhaps he does it so that he can say to himself, 'I'm not so bad. I did him a service.' Or maybe it gives him a reason for what he does. He needs a death and he needs a hook to hang a death on to."

"It sounds mad to me. What sort of service are you saying he did you?"

"Think about it," said Wexford, then drank an inch down the glass of his tap water. "He was parked outside my house day after day, watching. He must have seen Andy Norton go in—not by the front door, mind, but what he would think of as sneaking round the back. He would have seen him park his car, go in the back way, and stay for three hours. He'd never see Dora, but he would have known she was in. Do you see now?"

"I don't believe it!"

"That means you do. It always means that. Look, I hate thinking like this because I know what would be impossible to my wife, but to Targo it would be all in the day's work. I was the deceived husband and Andy Norton my wife's lover."

Burden shook his head, but in wonder rather than disbelief. "Do you mean he likes you? He cares about you?"

"Liking and caring don't come into it with him. It's dogs he likes and cares for. And llamas and lions. He was performing a service or restoring order where before there was chaos. Or maybe doing this makes him see himself as a just judge, a justified executioner. I rather prefer that line." Wexford laid down his knife and fork. "I don't want a pudding. All this speculating about Targo takes away my appetite. He's my new slimming regime. My thin guru. If we don't get him for killing Andy Norton, what do we do? Keep searching the town, maybe the country, for people other people want out of the way? Such is the sorry state of the world that there'll be thousands."

"But he doesn't ask people if they want rid of someone, so how can he be sure?"

"He didn't ask me but maybe he sometimes asks. Perhaps he's asked others. When, for instance, he's sure the husband or parent or whoever it is will be thankful and keep quiet about his part in it."

Burden sat in silence. After a couple of minutes—a long time for two people sitting at a table not to speak—he signalled to the waiter and, when the man came over, asked for a crème brûlée. Wexford was looking at his watch.

"It's ten past nine."

"All right. I won't be long. It's not as if we've an appointment set in stone with the man."

"I've a feeling he'll be there. I wonder if he still exercises. Works out, as they say these days."

"What if he does?"

Wexford was good on feelings. His intuition usually served him well. But not this time. Last night's moon, a little thinner but just as red, loomed half-risen when Burden rang the Wymondham Lodge doorbell. There was no sound from the menagerie. More lights came on inside the house, and the dogs set up an optimistic barking. The puppy rushed out when Mavis Targo opened the door.

"Disappointed, are you, poor chap?" Burden said to the

puppy, and it plainly was, sadly slinking away when scent and sight told it someone not Targo was on the threshold.

"He's not here."

Once again Wexford had to force his way into the house.

"Where is he, Mrs. Targo?"

"I haven't heard from him. I don't know where he is."

"Has he got a passport?"

"Of course he has."

"Then would you like to see if you can find it?"

She had not far to look, lifted the lid of a bureau and produced Targo's passport, the small, red booklet sheathed in a leather-and-gilt case. "He wouldn't go abroad if that's what you're thinking. He hates abroad. He took me to Spain on our honeymoon, and he hated it so much we came back early and he said he'd never go again."

Wexford was unconvinced by this, but the passport bore out what she said. It was almost unused, in pristine condition. "Has he ever been absent from home this long before without letting you know?"

"Oh, God, yes. He's a law unto himself, he is. He'll have business dealings somewhere. Birmingham, Manchester, Cardiff, you name it. He could be away for days, maybe a week. And when he comes back it won't be to see me. It'll be to see if King and his dogs are OK."

Wexford pondered for a moment. "These right-to-buy flats you mentioned. Where are they?"

"Some are round here and there's some in Birmingham, I reckon. I don't really know. I never had anything to do with them. Why would he go there, anyway? He's not a rent collector."

Nothing more was to be done at Wymondham Lodge.

"What's this about right-to-buy flats?" Burden asked when they were in the car. "Some property dealing of Targo's?"

"I don't know, but I can guess. It works like this. There was a housing bill which made it possible for council tenants to buy their homes. As sitting tenants, you got your flat at the market value minus three percent, and a couple of million people bought their homes. There was some sort of time limit on when you sell your house or flat on, but when you did, you could make an enormous profit."

"OK, where does Targo come in?"

"Well, suppose you knew of some particular block or better still terrace of houses and you know there are ten original tenants in them. Each can exercise his or her right to buy. So you give each one a big cash enticement to buy on your behalf. That way, even allowing for the bribe, you get a property for half what you'd pay on the open market. Then you lease them back to the council, who put people from their housing list in. You can make a packet. From what Mavis Targo says, I think that's what he's been doing."

"So that's the business he's got in Cardiff or Birmingham or whatever, and allowing for that you've said, there's no reason to suppose it isn't legitimate. As far as staying away, his wife isn't worried about him. She's used to this behaviour."

"I've phoned both those mobile numbers repeatedly and they're always on message. Since we went there, I've phoned his office landline and it doesn't even have an answer phone, it just rings and rings. Why would a man live like that if his business was legitimate?"

"I don't know, Reg, but nor do you. People are peculiar. How many times have I heard you say that there's nowt so queer as folk?"

"I'm going to trace that Mercedes of his and put out a call for him. Oh, all right, I know I've no grounds, no evidence, as you keep telling me, but I'll see Freeborn first. I'll get to see him first thing tomorrow." Freeborn was the assistant chief constable. "I think I've got a case."

"I don't," said Burden. "Listen to me. You'll tell him that God knows over how many decades Targo murdered three people in Kingsmarkham and environs. How do you know? You intuited it. 'Where's the evidence?' he'll say, and you'll give him all that stuff about Targo killing people other people want out of the way and how once upon a time he stalked you. So now you'd like to track his car and put a watch on all UK exits in case he tries to go abroad on a fake passport. 'You what?' he'll say, and then he'll say, 'Go away and stop wasting my time.'"

And this was what happened—with small variations. Freeborn didn't tell Wexford to stop wasting his time or to go away, but he did tell him there could be no question of putting a watch on ports and airports. Targo was not even a missing person. Old he might be, but if what Wexford said about his physical health and strength was accurate, to believe that his disappearance was in any way age-related was nonsense.

"Has his wife reported him as missing, Reg?"

Wexford shook his head. "She says that going off like this and switching off mobiles isn't unusual with him."

"Well, then."

There was no more to be said.

Damon Coleman and Lynn Fancourt had questioned everyone in the Pomfret neighbourhood of Cambridge Road without any positive result. Wexford went back to Cambridge Cottages and carried out, purely for his own satisfaction, a reconstruction of what he thought had happened on the morning Andy Norton was murdered. He played Targo's part himself. Being Targo, he let himself into the shed and found the box of rope coils and balls of string from which the killer had taken the window-sash cord. Straightening up, he banged his head on the roof. Targo was about seven inches shorter than he, so he wouldn't have done that. Holding a short length of rope—a length just short enough and long enough to strangle someone—he sat down on a stool and asked himself what sort of time he was trying to re-create. Five thirty? No, too early. Six, then. And how had Targo got here? In one of his vehicles, parked it anywhere in Pomfret, and walked to Cambridge Cottages. It wasn't a very big place.

The back door was unlocked, but when had it been unlocked? Wexford got off his seat and, carrying the length of rope, walked down the path past the chrysanthemums and the Michaelmas daisies to the small area of yard between the back door, the wall, and the kitchen window. Targo would have wanted to be invisible while he was doing that under the cover of darkness, but once at the house there was no hiding place for him. It seemed likely that the back door was unlocked. Did he go in without knocking? Or knock and fetch Norton down? How did he know Catherine Lister had left? Because he saw a light come on in the house next door. Wexford looked over the dividing wall and saw that this would have been quite possible. Wexford did what Targo may have done and rapped on the glass with his fist. Lynn came to open it and Wexford stepped inside.

Surely the first thing Andy Norton would have said was to ask him what he was doing there and how had he got in. Well, no doubt he had asked. That wouldn't have deterred Targo once he was inside. It hardly mattered what he said, for the grim truth was that Norton would never see him again.

The most likely thing was that he said he had been attacked and had come into Norton's garden to escape his pursuer. Could he come in, please, and be let out into the street by the front door? What did it matter if Norton was mystified and suspicious? The two men would never meet again.

Wexford walked into the living room as Targo must have done, following Norton, and there got the sash cord round his neck from behind, the way the thugs of India had once done with their garrotes. He felt his anger rise as he thought of this gentle and innocent man becoming another of Targo's victims.

All I want, he thought, sitting in the car later, is a small breakthrough. Just something to make one other person believe me or approach believing me. One person to give me the benefit of the doubt. I don't know what to do now, short of trying to call all those numbers all over again, short of going back to Wymondham Lodge and talking to that woman and being assaulted by a pack of crazy dogs. I don't know what to do unless I get a breakthrough.

Lynn Fancourt had seen him sitting there and was coming up to the car. He opened the driver's window.

"I've been talking to a woman in Oxford Road, sir," she said. "That's the street that runs parallel to this one. The lane's between the gardens. But maybe you know that."

"I know that, Lynn. What have you got to tell me that I don't know?" Make it good, he didn't say aloud.

"She's called Wentworth, Pauline Wentworth. On the morning Andy Norton was murdered, she came downstairs to answer her phone just before six. She hasn't got an extension upstairs. She answered the phone because her daughter's due to have a baby, and she thought that was what it was about. It wasn't, it was a wrong number. But she didn't go back to bed because she knew she wouldn't get to sleep again. It was dark, of course, but there was a big moon, if you remember. She went into the kitchen and put the kettle on for tea. It was then she looked down the garden and noticed that the door in her rear wall was flapping open. No mystery about that, she'd left it open the night before. She went down the garden to close it, and as she did so, she saw someone go through the door in the wall into Andy Norton's garden."

"Why didn't she call us?"

Lynn cast up her eyes. "She says because she thought she recognised him. This person, she meant. She *thought* she recognised him as a man she'd seen a couple of years ago out walking his dogs. One of his dogs had gone after her cat, and she'd told him to put it on a lead. She said he was a small man, no taller than her, and not young, but—listen to this, sir—and when she'd seen him before, he had a big birthmark on his neck but this man didn't."

Wexford kept his excitement under control and spoke calmly. "What did she think he was doing?"

"She didn't know, of course. But she thought it was all right because he was what she called 'a respectable person' and an animal lover. Maybe, she said, one of his dogs had got into his garden and he wanted to get it back without disturbing the householder. In my opinion, sir, these animal people are a bit nuts."

He laughed. "Thank you, Lynn. Well done."

I know him, Wexford said to himself. I know the way he works, and the way his mind works but this new scenario I am imagining—it can't be that way. And, letting himself into his house, Wexford went to find his wife.

175

14

I FELT I KNEW him really well," she said slowly. "He was a friend. As you know, I don't usually feel like that about someone I've only known a few weeks." She suddenly thought of something. He guessed what it was from her face and knew it was the very thing he wanted her not to feel. "He wasn't killed because of anything to do with this house and— well, me, was he?"

"I don't know why he was killed," Wexford said truthfully, and then he lied. "But it couldn't have had anything to do with you. That's out of the question."

"Only I'd hate to think that. I'd never get over that. Oh, Reg . . ."

He held her close. She put up her face for a kiss. It was just the way she had done this the second time they had gone for one of those evening walks at Newquay. The most trusting act he had ever known . . .

LATER HE WAS back in Pomfret.

"Can you describe him?"

"Not very tall," said Mrs. Wentworth. "I mean, nowhere

176

near your height." The look she gave Wexford, wondering, unflattering, slightly disapproving, made him feel like a giant in a freak show. "I used to live in Stringfield and I'd seen him about once or twice, always with a dog, but not for years. I mean I hadn't seen him since I came here. I told the young lady I thought it was him, but then I wasn't sure because he used to have a birthmark and this man didn't. You can't get rid of something like that, can you?"

"Wonderful things are done with plastic surgery these days, Mrs. Wentworth," said Wexford.

"When I saw him in Stringfield, he used to wear a scarf. Even in the summer in quite hot weather he wore a scarf. And then someone told me he wore it to cover up that mark, and one day he took the scarf off when I was looking at him and I saw it. So you say he had it taken off?"

"It's possible."

"Well, then, it was him. I did think it was him, but when I saw he didn't have that awful birthmark, I said to myself, 'Well, it can't be him, can it?' But it must have been. He wasn't with a dog that morning, though. I thought that's why he was going into Mr. Norton's garden. I thought, maybe his dog's got in there and he's looking for it."

WOULD THAT BE enough to persuade Freeborn and the chief constable of the need for a call to locate Targo's car? Enough to put out a watch for him at Heathrow, at Gatwick, and other possible airports? That he had left his passport behind meant nothing. He was the sort to have several passports. And a lot of time had been lost. It was now two days since Andy Norton's body had been found. But Wexford had got his breakthrough. For the first time in all his years of watching Targo and being stalked by Targo, of suspecting him and of being certain of his repeated guilt, he had concrete evidence that Targo was a murderer.

"Are you convinced now?" he said to Burden.

"Well, yes, I'm coming close to it. And I'm sorry, Reg, for doubting you all this time. I'm convinced because you've given me so much background, but I don't know that anyone else will be. The Wentworth woman's evidence is a bit shaky, isn't it? Imagine it in court, an even moderately clever counsel telling her it would still have been dark at six in the morning at the end of October, and asking her how she could have seen a birthmark or the lack of one. She couldn't see, could she? She's seventy-two years old and lawyers are all ageists."

"We've got enough," said Wexford, "for me to start a countrywide search. Don't look so worried. I'll go back to Freeborn and ask him first. But he'll say yes when he knows the facts."

He said yes. A reluctant yes but a considered one, put into a word after several minutes' thought. The first thing was to find that missing Mercedes. But who had made that phone call to Mavis and left a message? Was it possible that a man could disguise his voice so that even his wife wouldn't recognise it?

TARGO HAD LEFT home, Wexford thought, on the same day he had killed Andy Norton, within hours probably. He marvelled at a man so removed from all human feeling, from shock, from simple self-questioning, that he could go about his normal business after committing a crime of such magnitude. It wasn't quite normal business, though. He had gone without a dog and he had gone in the Mercedes. What was the significance of that? Perhaps only that he had intended to stay away a long time. Days, anyway. Where had he gone first? His children lived here, but Targo hadn't been to see his children.

Had he been to see his first wife? When Wexford had last seen her, that day in the Kingsbrook Precinct, she had said of their divorce that it was "good riddance to bad rubbish," but people change, people become reconciled to those they would once have passed in the street without speaking.

It was a long time since he had seen her too. In her late sixties now, she appeared to be a strong, healthy woman, pleased to see him.

"You haven't changed a bit," Kathleen Targo said.

Gallantly, he told her she looked younger than when he had seen her all those years ago in the Kingsbrook Precinct. "I know you're called Mrs. Varney now, but I had a bit of a job finding you with only Sewingbury to go on."

"That's because I married again. Jack died a few years back and I married his best friend. He'd been a widower for about the same time."

She took him into a living room and offered him coffee. "I won't, thanks. Things are a bit rushed at present." He remembered the child in the pushchair. "How's Philippa?"

"Just qualified as a doctor. Working all hours, but you have to, don't you, your first year or two?"

"You must be proud of her."

"No doubt of that. I'm a very lucky woman, Mr. Wexford. All my children have done well for themselves. I've got my health and strength and I've had two good husbands after starting off with a rotter. I can't complain and I don't."

She invited him to sit down. Photographs of her children were on the mantelpiece, tables, the top of an upright piano, and alone on what looked like an old-fashioned music console, one of her as a bride for the second time. He wondered how he would have felt if Dora had been married before and kept a photograph of her earlier wedding in the living room. He would have hated it, but then he and Dora had been young and in love, not like this couple marrying for companionship in impending old age.

"You're no longer Mrs. Varney," he said, "so what do I call you."

"I'm Mrs. Jones now, but you call me Kathleen."

"I don't suppose you know where your first husband is? He's missing."

That made her laugh. "A good miss, I should think. If he's disappeared, you can bet your life it's on purpose."

"I'm sure it is."

"You don't suppose right. I don't know where he is. He'd go to any one of his women before he'd come to me. Left Mavis, has he? They weren't getting on, I know that. Joanne tells me. Alan won't have a word said against his dad, God knows why not, but you've got to hand it to him."

Strange and interesting, Wexford thought, how grown-up children can be devoted to a bad parent—more devoted often than to a good one. Because they still hoped to please them, even so late in the day, and thus at last win their love? "He's left his wife only in the sense that he's gone away somewhere. Do you have a name and address for the woman he was living with in Birmingham?"

"Tracy something. Wait a minute. Tracy Cole. He left me for her. Well, the fact is I threw him out and he was with his mum in Glebe Road for a bit, and then he went to her. It took a bit of nerve on my part to get him out, but I had good neighbours and they came in and helped me. Between us we manhandled him out of the house and then I changed the locks. He never tried to come back, though. He'd found this Tracy, you see. I've got the address she was living at then. Well, it's somewhere. I'm one of those people who never throw anything away, so I reckon I can find it."

"I think I will have that coffee," said Wexford, "if it's not too much trouble."

"No trouble at all."

Did this propensity of hers extend to never forgetting anything? Perhaps. People who hoard, people who save every useless scrap and fragment, the anal ones, as psychologists call them, usually have good memories, he had noticed. He would ask her. Those hard times—hard in more ways than one—in Jewel Road, Stowerton, might not be lost in the mists of time. In his mind's eye, as in a dream, he saw Targo sitting by the appliance everyone in those days called "an electric fire," the little boy, Alan, who was loyal to him still, going up to him, kissing him good-night, then stroking the spaniel's silky head. Kathleen had been thin as a famine-stricken woman but for the swollen belly which carried Joanne. . . .

She came back with coffee and two cups on a tray. Also on the tray was a yellowing sheet of paper on which, long ago, someone had printed an address. "He wouldn't write me a proper letter. Wouldn't even buy a stamp, and stamps weren't the price then they are now. He put this bit of paper through my front door without even an envelope, to show me where he was living. He knew I'd see the address was in the best part of Birmingham. That Tracy Cole was loaded. Her dad had died and left her the house and wads of money. Him and her, Eric, I mean, it was one of those cases of a couple who never really get away from each other, one or the other of them will always go back."

If she still lived there, Wexford thought, if she did after so long, could Targo have taken refuge with her?

"Kathleen," he said, feeling a little awkward as everyone does when using a given name for the first time, "do you remember the evening I came to talk to Mr. Targo when you were living in Jewel Road? It was in connection with the murder of Mrs. Elsie Carroll. Do you remember that?"

"Of course I do. I remembered you, didn't I? And that was the only time we met till we ran into each other in the Precinct, apart from me being rude to you on the doorstep."

He laughed. "You weren't rude, just a bit sharp. This is very good coffee. Do you also remember that I asked your husband where he was on the night Mrs. Carroll was killed and he said he was babysitting Alan?"

"I'd been giving Alan his bath," she said, and incredibly to Wexford, so excellent was her memory, "and I wasn't there when you asked that. I came in and heard him say that bit about me being at my dressmaking class. I didn't say anything when he said he'd been here all the time doing pressups and all that rubbish. I didn't because I was scared of him. You could tell that, couldn't you?"

"I was very young, Kathleen. I didn't know about domestic violence. Well, no one did much then. It was talked about as a private thing in a marriage, not to be interfered with by outsiders."

"That suited men all right, didn't it? Eric didn't knock me

about much in those days, but I didn't want him hitting me at all when I was so near my time. I mean, I didn't want to fall over. What I'm trying to say is that night you were asking about, I came back early from my class because the teacher was taken ill. Oh, I remember all this even though it was so long ago. When I came back, Eric wasn't there, he'd left Alan alone. Only for ten minutes maybe, but he had left him and it was that made me think I'm not putting up with this, him leaving his kid alone at night, him hitting me if I step out of line, and making more fuss about that dog than he ever would about the baby I was expecting."

His belief needed no confirmation, but she had made assurance doubly sure.

"Joanne was born two weeks later. You stayed in hospital a lot longer then than they do now, but he came to see me just the once. Once in ten days when I'd just had his child. He wasn't at home looking after Alan. He was at home looking after the dog while Alan stopped with my mum. I did put up with it for nearly two years more. Alan was six and Joanne was getting on for two. He hit me then, a punch in the breast. They thought punching a woman's breast brought on cancer—it doesn't, they know that now, but I believed it then and I said to him, 'That's it, what you've done is going to kill me anyway, but this is the end.' Next day me and the neighbours threw him out and he went to his mum and to Tracy, who was another mum to him."

Wexford's next call was to an old people's home. It might still have been called that but political correctness and a general mealymouthed PC-ness had renamed it the Seniors' Sanctuary. He had been directed there by the woman who had lived next door to Eileen Kenyon on the Muriel Campden estate.

"Alzheimer's is what it is," she said to Wexford on her doorstep. "She's only in her sixties but that's what it is. You won't get any sense out of her. I know, I've tried, and you'll just be wasting your time."

It wasn't the first time he had visited such a place, and this one depressed him anew. The décor, the smell, the half-circle of chairs in front of the television set in which sat the elderly inmates, all dressed in a jumble of ill-fitting, bizarrely coloured clothes, none of which looked as if it had originally been bought for its wearer. But perhaps the worst thing was the programme showing on the screen, a display of acrobatic dancing by beautiful teenagers in tight-fitting sequinned costumes, their lustrous hair flowing, their skin like a new-picked peach.

Like half the spectators, Eileen Kenyon was in a wheel-chair, sitting in that characteristic pose of the sick elderly, her shoulders slumped, her back rounded almost to a hump, and her head lolling to one side. Like most of them, she seemed to be staring at something, but not the screen. The sequinned young people cavorted and performed impossible leaps and gyrations while the old sat, twisted and sunken, not watching them. Golden lads and girls all must, thought Wexford, as chimney sweepers come to dust. A carer whispered to him that he would get nothing out of Eileen Kenyon. She no longer knew who she was or where she was. When the carer moved her wheelchair away from the semicircle of viewers over to the window where he was, he realised she was right. Eileen Kenyon was now only dimly recognisable as the woman she had been. It was as if a hand, dipped in some viscous, grayish matter, had passed over her head, whitening and thinning her hair, dimming her eyes, and slurring her features.

"Do you remember me, Mrs. Kenyon?"

No response at all. The eyes, which had gazed at the wall some ten feet away from the television, now stared at the floor.

Inspiration led him to ask, "Do you remember your dog, the dog you got from Mr. Targo?"

One of her eyelids flickered. He tried to remember the dog's name. It was maddening that he remembered the names of Targo's own dogs, Buster, Princess, Braveheart, but not the one Eileen Kenyon had when Billy was killed. But then it was true that he had almost total recall of the things Targo had said to him.

"Dusty's puppy," he said. "Do you remember Dusty's puppy? Dusty was Mr. Targo's."

She lifted her head a little. The eyes opened. "Snake," she said quite clearly, then mumbling, "Snake he had. Scary snake, don't like snake." Then: "He asked . . ."

"What did he ask?"

But there was to be no more. He had been given nothing to make him think Eileen Kenyon would have finished her sentence with the words *if she wanted Billy killed.* Asking her if she knew where Targo might be now seemed ludicrous. He thanked the carer and made his way out along a gloomy corridor to the stained-glass double doors which were the entrance to this place. There must be more places in Kingsmarkham he might have gone to. Something Kathleen Jones had said had briefly alerted him. But what was it?

Of course she had told him not what he came for, but what was almost more important, that Targo hadn't stayed in babysitting that evening so long ago. What else was it? Philippa becoming a doctor? No. Tracy Cole? Yes, definitely, but that could wait. Glebe Road, he thought, she had mentioned Glebe Road. That was where the Rahmans lived. Nothing had happened to make him think it possible except the knowledge that Targo had visited Ahmed several times in the past. So suppose he had called at the Rahmans after he had killed Andy Norton?

15

HE TOOK HANNAH with him. They knew her, and if she was to be believed, they hadn't resented her suspiciousness. Hannah was honest and quite openly confessed that Mohammed Rahman had firmly but amiably put her down. He was, she told Wexford, a master of the smiling snub. Wexford expected Mohammed to be at work, but Yasmin told him that her husband was ill in bed with flu. He had come down with a virus a couple of days before.

Ahmed was upstairs, taking his father a hot drink, but he came down after a few minutes. On the previous occasion that Wexford had seen him, when he and his brother had just come back from the mosque, he had been struck by Ahmed's good looks and air of health, perhaps too of contentment. All that had changed. Both sons had pale skin while Tamima's was a dark gold, but today Ahmed was white with a sickly pallor. Dark shadows were under his eyes, and a day's growth of beard was on his chin. This was of course becoming a fashionable way for a young man to look, but Ahmed's seemed the result of indifference to his appearance, as if something more important than trends and style brought about that careworn look. He had probably picked up the virus that had laid his father low.

"Yes, Mr. Targo came here in the afternoon," he said in answer to Wexford's enquiry.

"You were expecting him?"

"No, we weren't. When the doorbell rang, I thought it was the doctor for Dad." Ahmed hesitated. "I was surprised to see Mr. Targo. He wanted to order some software."

Aware that this left Wexford in the dark, Hannah said, "He didn't do that himself? He asked you to do it for him?"

"Oh, yes."

Ahmed looked at his mother. She was sitting stiffly in a straight-backed chair, no jewellery but for her rings to be seen this morning, her head covered in Wexford's presence. Her expression was rather stern, her hands clasped together, but she got up at Ahmed's glance and said she would make coffee.

"What kind of software?" Hannah asked

"Some floppy disks and a home manager CD."

"What exactly is that?"

"A home manager CD?" Ahmed suddenly seemed on surer ground. "Put simply, you plug it into your PC and you can control your lights and electrical appliances by sending a signal from your PC to the switch modules. It goes via the electrical circuit of your home. It turns on the radio if that's what you want. It even sticks the kettle on."

"And that's what Mr. Targo wanted?"

"So he said. He'd read about it somewhere."

"You could get it for him?" Wexford asked.

"Oh, yes," Ahmed said confidently. "The point is, I know where to get it and how to order it, that sort of thing. You can buy the floppies anywhere, but he always likes me to do that stuff."

Yasmin came back with the coffee. When she had handed the cups to them, Wexford noticed her eyes go to the polished granite mantelpiece. She looked at it as if she detected something not quite right about it, then looked sharply away. As she sat down again, picked up the sugar basin to pass to them, her hands were shaking. Not strongly, but the merest tremor, which she conquered by stiffening the fingers and holding them out straight.

"Do you know where Mr. Targo went when he left here?"

"Home, I suppose. I didn't ask him."

"Were you surprised," Wexford asked, "that he didn't have a dog with him?"

"I wouldn't allow a dog in my house," Yasmin said.

How would Targo have reacted to that? Her remark caused a silence. Hannah broke it. "Is Tamima still working at the Raj Emporium?"

The sternness of Yasmin's expression concentrated itself on two deeply cut parallel lines between her dark eyes. "My daughter has gone away to stay with her auntie. We have told you she was going many times before. Now she has gone. My son Osman had the day off work and drove her there."

They drank their coffee, Ahmed filling up the silence by giving a gratuitous lecture on innovative autonomous robotic kits with forward, back-up, and turn actions. To Wexford it might as well have been delivered in Swahili, and he got up to leave before his cup was empty. But before going to the door, he crossed purposefully to the fireplace, put one hand on the shiny granite, and looked closely at the right-angled corner of the mantelpiece. He touched it with one finger, and at a soft indrawing of breath from Ahmed, turned away with a polite smile. Mrs. Rahman's expression was unchanged. Ahmed got up to show them out.

"What was all that with the fireplace, guv?" Hannah asked outside.

Wexford was contemplating the Harley-Davidson which had joined the other vehicles on Burden's former front garden. "Something happened there not long ago. I don't know what it was, but Yasmin and her son know. They're scared it may have left some sort of mark."

"Has it?"

"Not so far as I could see."

"Tamima's aunt is called Mrs. Qasi and she lives in Reservoir Road, Kingsbury, London, northwest nine. Do you think Tamima really has gone there?"

"I don't know, Hannah, and I don't care. At present the missing Targo occupies all my thoughts."

WEXFORD HAD DECIDED that unsatisfactory though she was, Mavis Targo must be the best source of information available on her husband. She opened the door of Wymondham Lodge, said, "He's pining away. He won't eat."

These were the first words she addressed to him. There had been no greeting, not even an enquiry to know what he wanted. For a moment he had thought she was speaking of her husband, that he had come home, that he was ill and somewhere in the house. He should have known better, he told himself. Of course it was a dog she was talking about, probably the cream-and-white, fluffy one, which sat disconsolately in its basket in a corner of the ornate living room. He wondered if it was a shared passion for canines which had brought this ill-assorted pair together. But perhaps it was not so incongruous a match; for now, looking at her, he saw that she and Targo were rather alike, they might have been brother and sister, the same sort of height, the same stocky build, coarse features, staring blue eyes. If this were horror fiction, he thought, she would turn out to be Targo himself in disguise and she a corpse in the cellar. But how then had he achieved that formidable cleavage which showed at her neckline? He almost laughed.

She was still talking about the Tibetan spaniel missing Targo when the puppy appeared at the French windows, yapping and flinging itself against the glass. She rushed to let it in, opened the windows, and as she did so, from somewhere in the grounds came a shrill, chattering sound and a low, resounding roar. The puppy scampered about, jumping up at Wexford and covering the pale carpet with muddy footprints.

"He doesn't miss his master," she said. "He's too young, aren't you, sweetheart? I can't say I'm sorry. I couldn't be doing with two of them breaking their hearts."

"I don't suppose you've heard from your husband?"

"Nothing. Not a word. It's a long time now, even for him."

"I am sorry to have to ask you this, Mrs. Targo, but I'm afraid it's necessary. Does the name Tracy Cole mean anything to you?"

"Oh, God, yes. You needn't be sorry. She wasn't the last one before me, she was the last but one. She's not called Tracy Cole now, she's been married twice since him and her split up."

"Would you have a phone number for her? An address?"

"You're barking up the wrong tree if you think he'd go to her."

The hackneyed metaphor, used in this house, made him smile.

"Just the same, do you have a number?"

Her answer came reluctantly. "He's got her number on his mobile. I know he has, though he denies it. It's not written down anywhere, I wouldn't have that. I've got her married name somewhere. She wasn't married when he was with her, in case you didn't know." Wexford said nothing. He waited. "I don't know if you do know, but she was very young. Her dad had just died and left her that big house and what they call a portfolio of shares. She was only eighteen and she had to wait till she was twenty-one to inherit the rest."

Mavis Targo was no Kathleen. She boasted that she never kept anything, often threw things away and regretted it afterwards. Tracy Cole's second married name couldn't be found, but Mrs. Targo said she had remembered it. She remembered it because it was the same surname as Targo's own second wife: Thompson. She was Tracy Thompson and the second wife had been Adele Thompson.

"He was married to her when he was living in Myringham?" Wexford thought how odd this conversation would have sounded to him in the days when he first met Targo. Not merely odd but bizarre, incredible, having no possible connection with an English middle class as it then was, in which the great majority married and remained married until one of them died. Today's serial polygamy would then have been associated only with Hollywood. "When he had the boarding kennels?"

"What, Adele? I suppose he was. I hadn't met him then. It didn't last long, that marriage. She didn't like dogs. She kept it from him when they met but after a time it showed. Well, it would, wouldn't it?"

Wexford said nothing, only looked encouraging. He welcomed Mrs. Targo's new loquaciousness. "The other Thompson," she said, "Tracy, I mean, she lived in Edgbaston, still does for all I know. That's the poshest part of Birmingham. He brags about that. Lovely house she had, he says, more a palace than a house. It's nothing for him to be proud of, is it?"

"You said he wouldn't go to her, but are you sure of that? He wouldn't hide out with her?"

At last some kind of realisation dawned. "What d'you want him for? You've never said. What d'you think he's done?"

"We need him to help us with our enquiries into the death of Mr. Andrew Norton."

"Who is he? I've never heard of him and I'll bet Eric hasn't."

Wexford got up. His rising to his feet was a signal for the bull terrier puppy to rush over and jump up at him. Addressing the dog as "sweetheart"—perhaps it had no other name—Mavis Targo told it in the gentlest possible tone, quite unlike her rough manner with Wexford, to get down.

"Tell me something," he said as he was leaving, "when did your husband have the naevus removed?"

She laughed. "When we were first married. I asked him to. He did what I asked him in those days."

Wexford made no comment. "You'll let us know if you hear from your husband, won't you, Mrs. Targo?"

IF SHE WAS to be found, if she was still alive. He suddenly had one of his hunches that Tracy Cole, the rich woman, the woman who lived in the best part of Birmingham, she to whom Targo had fled when his wife turned him out, was the refuge to whom he had gone now. Alan Targo had been six, his mother said, and now he was what? Forty? Would Targo still want the woman he had wanted thirty-three years ago? He might. People do, and Wexford thought of his own wife, to whom he had been married for so long. The former Kathleen Targo had said that, no matter who else intervened, Eric Targo and Tracy Cole always went back to each other. . . .

With the information he had, Tracy wasn't hard to find. Over the phone she said she hadn't seen Eric Targo for more than a year but had several times spoken to him. Wexford wondered if Mavis Targo knew that and doubted it. Tracy, who called herself Miss Thompson, said that she had quite a lot she could tell Wexford about her former lover, but she would prefer to do it face-to-face. Would he come and see her?

First he cleared it with West Midlands Police. The officer he spoke to on the phone was a Detective Superintendent Roger Phillips. It had to be the same one. After all this time, the occasional phone call, one or two letters, then years of silence.

"I was best man at your wedding," Wexford said.

"So you were. And a very good one, as I remember. I'm still married to Pauline and will be till death do us part. How about you?"

"The same. Still married to the same woman, thank God." Wexford told him about Tracy Thompson and the hunt for Targo. "I'd like to talk to her if it's OK with you."

"Sure. You want me to send a DC with you?"

"Thanks, but I'll have my sergeant."

"Bring him in afterwards for a cup of tea."

Wexford said he would, tried to remember, when the call was ended, what Roger had looked like, failed, but recalled perfectly the pretty face of his wife. It was her parents who had been friends of the people who brought Medora Holland to the Phillips wedding. . . .

HE TOOK BARRY Vine with him and they went up by train, a long journey if you start from Sussex. Wexford seldom went anywhere by rail, but he read his newspapers and watched television and knew how liable trains were to delays and cancellations and he feared the worst. But the train from Euston to Birmingham, if not on time, was only five minutes late, and they made it to the place that was "more a palace than a house" at the appointed time.

This added up to four women with strong connections to Targo he had talked to, and of them Tracy Thompson was the youngest and the smallest. A tiny woman, no bigger than a child of ten, she could have been taken for a teenager until seen close to. Then the lines which crisscrossed her face showed, the white threads in her limp brown hair. She was dressed like a teenager in jeans and a Disney T-shirt printed with dalmatians, and her background of this house showed her up as an even more incongruous figure than if she had been living in a social housing flat.

Palatial it was, grand and somewhat awe-inspiring, but as Barry Vine remarked to Wexford afterwards, also "weird." The furniture in the large, high-ceilinged rooms looked as if it had been there, standing precisely where it was now, through several generations, untouched, never renovated, the wood surfaces never polished, curtains, though intact, faded to a gray pallor by decades of sunlight, carpets bleached or irredeemably stained. If the place was not quite Miss Havisham's abode, it was Satis House after a halfhearted cleaning.

There was no suggestion, Wexford thought, of Tracy

Thompson having been left at the altar and abandoned to the life of a recluse. Rather, she had inherited this place with everything in it but was simply indifferent to her surroundings so long as she might be warm and comfortable when she chose.

She saw him looking, said, "It's a bit shabby, isn't it? Shame really. I keep meaning to do something about it, but I don't suppose I ever shall. You see, I don't like having people in unless they're my friends, I can't stand cleaners, builders, whatever." She flicked back her long little-girl's hair. "What did you want to ask me?"

"It's more a matter of what you want to tell us, Miss Thompson."

"Well, the first thing is, what d'you want Eric *for*?"

And then she said something which nearly made Wexford shoot out of the shabby floral armchair he was sitting in. "He hasn't gone and killed someone, has he?"

BARRY VINE WAS nearly as astonished as Wexford. He had gone a little pale. "What exactly do you mean by that?" he asked her. "Were you serious?"

"I think I was." She seemed not in the least alarmed. "I don't know if he was when he asked me."

"What did he ask you?"

"Perhaps I'd better start by telling you about us, Eric and me, that is. I suppose I ought to offer you something, but I don't drink tea or coffee. I expect there's some Coke."

"Please don't bother," Wexford said. "You were going to talk about your relationship with Mr. Targo."

"Yes, well, we've known each other since forever. He'd just come to Birmingham and my dad had just died. I was feeling pretty low. I was only just eighteen, you see, and I'd no one. My mother was dead, I'd no relatives. Everyone kept telling me how lucky I was to have so much money and this house. I was sitting on a bench in the park, thinking about things, what loneliness was and not being able to see any future, when this dog came up to me. It was a spaniel, quite old but so *sweet* and gentle. It licked my hand, and when I stroked it, it climbed up onto the bench and snuggled up beside me. It put its head in my lap. And then the owner—it was Eric—came up and he said his dog was like that with people he liked. We talked and I told him about myself and he said I ought to get a dog, he'd get me a dog. And, well, he did."

It didn't sound much like Targo and yet it did. It wasn't quite true that he liked dogs and disliked people, but rather that he only liked people who liked dogs. "Go on," Wexford said.

"We started seeing each other. I suppose you could say we fell in love. He wasn't my type and I wasn't his, but we sort of clicked. His wife had left him, he wanted sometimes to see his kids, but he didn't want a share of their house. I had enough for both of us, you see, but if you think he took up with me because I was rich, you'd be wrong. He was crazy about me. And I was the one who got tired of it first. I gave Eric the price of a house and enough to start a business—a driving school it was—paid him off, you could say, and I married someone else. But I could never get Eric out of my head. His divorce had come through and then I got divorced. Eric didn't move back with me, he had his own house, and when I found out he'd a woman living with him there, I was so mad I got married to someone else on the rebound.

"Well, after that it was sort of on and off with us, though you could say he was really the only one for me as I was for him. I've been single for years now and there's never been anyone else. Eric married this Adele he'd been living with and moved to Myringham in Sussex. She came from there. And he came from a place called Stowerton. He'd already got property he let out, and he started a dogs' boarding kennels. Just up his street that was with him being so mad about dogs. I helped him with the money to set it up. I thought we might get back together because Adele only lasted a few months more, but he'd met that Mavis and married her and that was like the end for me. I'd invested in this property development of his, getting hold of right-to-buy properties it was, and it was doing well, but he still married Mavis and bought a big house somewhere with her money. And that's it really. Up to a year ago we were still meeting sometimes and still talking on the phone, but when he asked me if there was anyone I wanted rid of—well, that was the end, the really final end."

Wexford had listened to all this in silence. Now he said, speaking quite slowly, "What exactly did he ask you, Miss Thompson?"

"You want the details?"

"Please."

"He phoned and said he had to come up here on business and he'd like to see me. Time was when he'd have come up to see me and found a bit of business to do while he was here. But never mind, that's all water under the bridge. He came and I asked him if he'd be staying. No, he said, and he wanted to tell me that we wouldn't see each other again. He was with Mavis now and they'd settled down. He was getting on and having a bit on the side was no longer on. I said to him, 'Is that what I was, a bit on the side?' and all he said was 'You know what I mean.' He was always saying that, that I knew what he meant—especially when it was hurtful, what he said. Then he said he'd like to do something for me as a kind of thanks for all the years. Was there anyone I wanted rid of? I didn't understand him—well, no one would. He said he'd put it more plainly. Was there anyone I wanted out of the way, disposed of, and no questions asked? I thought he'd gone mad, I really did."

"He meant, did you want someone killed, is that what he was saying?"

"That's what he was saying. As a kind of *compensation* for leaving me and maybe for us not getting married in the past."

"What did you say to him?" Vine asked.

"What do you think? I said I was glad he'd said he wouldn't see me again because I felt exactly the same about him, and if there was anyone I wanted rid of, it was him."

"You didn't think of contacting us?"

"Well, I did. But what had I got to go on? It would be my word against his. I thought they'd say it was a case of a woman scorned. I mean, look at it this way. He was married, doing well, living with his wife. I was a single woman with two failed marriages behind me, a woman who'd given him God knows how much money over the years, and now he'd rejected me. How would that look to the police? Like revenge, don't you think?"

"You've told us now," said Wexford.

"Because you asked about him. And I thought you wouldn't if you hadn't good reason. Right? And you do believe me, don't you? You don't see me as a woman scorned?"

"I believe you."

TEA WITH ROGER PHILLIPS terminated in a bottle of port being brought out. Wexford had resolved some years before

never to drink port again, but he had one glass with Roger
while he told him about the interview with Tracy Thompson and the "compensation" Targo had offered her, told him
too about Elsie Carroll and Billy Kenyon and Andy Norton.
Roger echoed the words Wexford himself had used to Tracy.

"I believe you."

"She says she hasn't seen him since. He's tried to phone
her, left messages, but she hasn't answered them. That offer
he made her shocked her to the core."

"Well, it would, Reg. We're used to violent death and
death threats so we often fail to appreciate how shocking
ordinary members of the public find that sort of thing. Society hasn't really become depraved, whatever the media says.
Most people lead pretty sheltered and certainly law-abiding
lives. Are you thinking that he may have made that sort of
offer in the past to the people who would benefit from what
he was about to do?"

"He didn't make it to me," said Wexford, "and he expected
me to benefit from the death of Norton. I'm sure he didn't
make it to George Carroll. If he had, what would have
stopped Carroll telling us about it when he was charged with
murder? But it may well be that Eileen Kenyon knew. He
could have suggested it to Eileen Kenyon after he'd given
her a puppy and seen how she was with Billy. If she knew he'd
killed Billy, it was in her interest to keep quiet about it."

"And now he's disappeared?"

"I don't think he's with a woman. There's only this Adele
left and we'll contact her, but it appears she was with him for
a shorter time than any other woman in his life. He could be
anywhere."

"He must be getting money. Have you looked at his bank
account?"

"I've had no grounds to do that till now. It's my next step."

With undertakings (neither would adhere to) to keep in touch, meet for a meal when the Phillipses were in Sussex visiting Pauline's aged mother, they parted. Wexford took the *Birmingham Post* he had bought that morning out of his raincoat pocket and read it on the train, while Vine, afficionado of Donizetti, listened to *L'elisir d'amore* on his CD Walkman.

When he was reading a newspaper belonging to a distant city or even specifically to London, Wexford always looked at the births, marriages, and deaths. Time was when people he knew were getting married, then having babies, now, some of them, dying. The last name in the deaths column was Trelawney. He knew no one called that, yet . . . "Trelawney, Medora Anne, beloved wife of James Trelawney, on October 31 at Sutton Coldfield, sadly missed. Funeral at All Saints' Church, November 3 at 10 a.m., no flowers, please. Donations to the British Heart Foundation."

It was almost certainly the same one. The boyfriend who had tried to blackmail him she had called Jim, and Trelawney was a Cornish name. No age was given for her, he noticed. It looked as if she had died of heart disease. What had she been doing in Sutton Coldfield? Living there with Jim, no doubt, and maybe children who sadly missed her. He folded up the newspaper and went back to thinking about Targo. There was little doubt now that Targo had disappeared.

16

HANNAH GOLDSMITH PICKED Jenny Burden up at the school gates at four thirty in the afternoon. It was pouring rain, which meant that all had covered their heads or put up umbrellas and were scurrying through the downpour. This suited Hannah well. She didn't much want to be seen having secret or at any rate private meetings with Mike Burden's wife. The café they went to in a side turning off Queen Street would have been called when Wexford was young a "pull-up for carmen." If they had heard the phrase, they would have supposed it had something to do with the opera.

The shabby little place was ill-ventilated, with condensation running down the windows. The tea was the mahogany-coloured kind they used to say you could stand a spoon up in but now was called builder's.

"I wanted to share with you what I'm doing," Hannah began, "because I know you're concerned about Tamima Rahman the way I am. I went along to see the family with the guv yesterday—it was about something quite different—but Yasmin Rahman happened to say that Tamima had gone to

London to stay with her auntie. Her brother Osman—he's the nurse—drove her up there the day before."

Jenny nodded. "So she's there, is she? Where exactly is she?"

"Auntie's called Mrs. Qasi and she lives in Kingsbury. That's a London suburb in the northwest, sort of west of Hendon if you know where that is. But as to whether she's there, I don't know. They say she is and maybe it's all right. But I found Mrs. Qasi's phone number and called her and asked to speak to Tamima. That was this morning. She said Tamima was out with her cousin. Apparently she's got a lot of cousins, all of them in that sort of area. They'd gone to Oxford Street shopping, she said. I asked when she'd be back, but Mrs. Qasi didn't know. I phoned again at three and this time there was no answer. I left a message."

"What is it you suspect?" Jenny asked.

"I don't know. All these weeks since Tamima left school in July I've thought there was a possibility the Rahmans would arrange a marriage for her."

"Not force a marriage?"

"I think they are anxious to keep her and Rashid Hanif apart, but sending her to London shows they haven't succeeded. Now this is perhaps the point where the idea of an arranged marriage becomes a forced marriage."

"You mean send her to London and introduce her to some relative, of whom there are dozens up there, and if she's OK about the idea so well and good, but if not . . ."

"If not, it would be much easier to compel her to marry in London than down here where everyone would know what's going on."

"And if," said Jenny, "she won't, she refuses, what then?"

"I don't want to go there. Not yet. First of all I want to find out if Tamima's with Mrs. Qasi and, more to the point, if she's happy to be there."

But Tamima didn't call her back as Hannah had asked her. Nor did she call Jenny, though she had her number. Teenagers don't write letters, but they send e-mails. Jenny got an e-mail from her, though there was nothing to prove Tamima was the source of it.

Hi Mrs. Burden. I am having a great time in London with my auntie Mrs. Qasi at 46 Farmstead Way, Kingsbury, and my cousins. I didn't really know them till now and it's so cool. I may decide to stay for a while and get a job.

Tamima.

"Anyone might have sent that," Hannah said.

"Yes, I don't know *why* she would send it. After all, I haven't made any enquiries about her since before she went to Pakistan. Why not contact you?"

Hannah said thoughtfully, "Let's give it a few days. If we haven't heard any more, would you feel like going to London on Friday or Saturday and pay this Mrs. Qasi a visit?"

"Saturday would be best for me. No school."

But on Friday, when Hannah went with Wexford to check with the Rahmans that Ahmed had heard nothing from the missing Eric Targo, Osman had the day off and was at home.

Looking very much like his father and half-smiling in the same supercilious way, he told Hannah that he knew she "took a great interest in Tamima's activities. You may care to know that she's going to share a flat with her cousin and a friend for a while and get a job. Quite enterprising, don't you think?"

. . .

It was one of those areas of not-quite-outer London that still retained vestiges of countryside, spoilt countryside where chain-link fencing, concrete, and abandoned factory buildings scar the fields, but where the fields still exist. You could see how Farmstead Way got its name. The road Hannah drove along to reach it skirted the Brent reservoir, and there was even a small herd of black-and-white cows chewing the cud under a stand of chestnut trees. The rain had cleared away, but only temporarily, and the blue sky would be short-lived. It was Saturday, when Hannah should have had a day off.

Faduma Qasi's home was a bungalow, semidetached, as were all the houses in the street, though their designs had been varied and green-tiled roofs were among the red. Hannah had phoned to warn Mrs. Qasi of their coming, and she let them in promptly. Both Hannah and Jenny had expected a black-robed woman who would have covered her head before answering the door, but Tamima's aunt was dressed much as her non-Moslem neighbours might be in a black-and-white dogtooth-check skirt, black sandals, and a red polo-neck sweater.

When the introductions had been made, she said she would make tea. Jenny and Hannah sat down in a living room in which not a piece of furniture or ornament had its provenance in an Asian subcontinental culture. Hannah was reminded that Mrs. Qasi was Mohammed Rahman's sister. His home had taken on a similarly indigenous British end-of-the-twentieth-century atmosphere. A bookcase was full of English books and, even more to Hannah's astonishment, a bottle of sherry stood on a tray next to two glasses.

The tea came, much like the tea in the Queen Street café, strong, aromatic, dark chestnut colour when a drop of milk was added to it.

"Now," said Faduma Qasi, sitting down to pour, "I'd like to begin by setting you right on a few matters. I know what you're thinking. I can see it in your faces. It's written all over them, if you don't mind me putting it that way." She passed Jenny's cup, indicated the bowl of loaf sugar. "You expected to see a downtrodden old woman in a burka, didn't you? You think all Moslem women are like that and your mission in life is to set them free and emancipate them. But I don't quite fit the picture, do I? I'm a teacher"—she looked at Jenny—"like you. But I'm not married. I was and my marriage was arranged, but we were each shown pictures of possible people to marry and we chose each other. We met and liked each other and went out together. Arranged marriages are a tradition in our family. My brother's marriage with Yasmin was arranged and you couldn't find a happier one. I'm divorced now. My husband didn't say, 'I divorce you,' three times and throw me out, like the newspapers say. We were divorced properly in the court. I've a man friend—I refuse to call a man of fifty a boyfriend—and eventually we shall get married." Hannah received her teacup and the sugar pushed towards her. "My brother was born in Pakistan but I was born here, and English is my native tongue. I was born a British citizen of enlightened, intelligent parents. I don't cover up my head because there's nothing in the holy Quran about a woman having to cover her head. I try to be a good Moslem and I don't drink alcohol. Yes, I've seen you looking at the sherry bottle—that's for guests. Would you like a glass? No? A bit early in the morning, I expect."

"Mrs. Qasi," Hannah began, "we don't mean to—"

"No, I know you don't mean to. I know you think you're quite without prejudice, but you're racists like English people are. Benevolent racists, is what I call you. OK? Now we'll talk about what you came for."

Jenny said, "I think you've taken the wind out of our sails a bit. Out of mine, at any rate. What we came for was really to ask if your niece Tamima is all right, if she's staying here, you've seen her since she came back to London, and if—well, if you're happy about her sharing a flat with your daughter and a friend. I mean, they're very young, aren't they? Tamima's only sixteen and I don't suppose your daughter's much older."

"My daughter is also sixteen," Mrs. Qasi said, "but when Tamima speaks of her cousin, she doesn't mean Mia. She means her cousin who is my sister's daughter—we are a large and united family, Mrs. Burden—and who is twenty-seven. The friend is my niece's friend Clare, and they have been sharing a flat for five years."

Hannah asked, "Would you give us the address of that flat and your other niece's name, Mrs. Qasi?"

"My niece who owns the flat is called Jacqueline. Her father is an Englishman, you see. But I don't think I shall give you the address. I would if you had an order or a warrant or whatever you call it, but you haven't. Tamima has done nothing wrong and nor have Jacqueline or Clare. As you must know, Tamima is in London with the full approval of her father and mother. She intends to return home at the end of the year. At Christmas, I believe. You see I celebrate that like any other British citizen while not believing in the faith behind it—again like most British citizens. Incidentally, Tamima was here until yesterday. She left with Jacqueline and Clare just about the time you phoned to make this appointment. If you want her address I suggest you ask my brother for it.

"By the way," she added, speaking to Jenny. "The e-mail Tamima sent you was written on my suggestion. It seemed a sensible and polite thing to do."

The interview had turned out very differently from the way Hannah had expected. Much as she hated being called a "benevolent racist," she was obliged to admit, if only to herself, that Faduma Qasi had been precisely correct when she described—in cringe-making detail—the kind of woman she and Jenny had expected to find. Some of the expressions she had used, especially with regard to dress and marriage, were the very things they had discussed while driving along the road from West Hendon. Hannah, who had prided herself on her utter lack of race prejudice, her persuading of herself that all people, regardless of race and skin colour and origin, were equal, must now thoroughly examine her attitudes and revise them. She felt humiliated, an unusual sensation for her. But she was anxious not to show it.

"Tamima lived here with you for how long?" she said.

"About a week. It was like a holiday for her. Jacqueline works from home so she could take days off, and she took Tamima about in London. To a theatre matinee, you know, and the cinema and to museums. We are not entirely uncultured, our family. Then she and Clare suggested Tamima get a job at the Asian supermarket Spicefield and move in with them. She asked her parents if that would be all right and they agreed."

"I believe," said Jenny, "that it's a fact that Mr. and Mrs.

Rahman were anxious to separate Tamima from a boy she was friendly with, Rashid Hanif."

"I know nothing about that. Tamima never mentioned him."

Hannah spent the rest of the weekend preparing a report for Wexford. It outlined her suspicions but also contained incontrovertible facts. There was no proof that Tamima Rahman had ever been in London, only the word of her parents and her aunt Faduma Qasi. Mrs. Qasi had refused to give the details of her niece Jacqueline's flat, so Hannah had no idea where it was, who the friend was apart from her being called Clare, or which branch of Spicefield was supposed to be employing Tamima.

Preoccupied with Targo, Wexford nevertheless took the time to read it.

"I've asked you this before, Hannah, but I'll ask you again. What is it you suspect?"

"That they're forcing her to marry someone."

"But what makes you think so?"

"It's in the report, guv."

"I've read the report. Now I'd like you to answer a few questions I'm going to put to you. Has Tamima or anyone in the family ever spoken to you of forced marriage, as something they favour or, conversely, are opposed to? Have any of them ever told you they disapprove of Rashid Hanif? Or named someone they prefer over him to be a boyfriend or fiancé or husband for Tamima? You say—though not in the report—that the Rahmans are an enlightened westernised family, yet you suspect them of inflicting on their daughter a cruel and ancient custom. Why? Above all, why have you, whom I always take to be particularly pro-Moslem and anti-racist, suddenly begun showing what seems to me like unreasoning prejudice?"

This last was too much for Hannah. She burst out with a passionate rejoinder. "Oh, guv, I haven't. It's not like that. I'm trying to be open-minded. I'm afraid that if I—well, veer too much to being pro-Moslem, I'll lose my judgment."

"No fear of that," Wexford said briskly. "Now there's a lot to do here. We've got someone missing who's almost certainly committed at least one murder. And I've just heard that the Mercedes has been found, parked by the roadside in a village in Essex. Apart from Targo, wherever he is, crime goes on. Petty crime if you like, but you wouldn't call it petty if it was your house that had been broken into and pillaged and wrecked. So you can have one more go at finding where Tamima Rahman lives and works, and if that fails, you have to give up. Are you happy with that?"

"I have to be if you say so, guv." But Hannah made a mental note that on her own, without backup, without even Jenny's support, she would pursue her enquiries into Tamima's whereabouts. She would start with the supermarket and find which, if any, of their branches employed her.

17

T HIS TIME THEY met in the Olive and Dove's "snug." Ashtrays on the tables were piled with ash and cigarette ends, the ceiling yellow and polished with tar deposits.

"If the day ever comes when they bring in a smoking ban," Wexford said, "this place will get a cleanup. They might even get new curtains."

"More likely to close down. People won't come. Smokers like to smoke while they drink."

"Or we shall have the place to ourselves."

Wexford went to get their drinks. The saloon bar was quieter than usual as if in anticipation of restrictions to come. Two girls sat chatting and smoking at a corner table. In his youth, Wexford thought, they would have been in a tea shop, but they would have offered each other cigarettes then as now. The elderly man who sat alone with his yellow Labrador—did people now refer to *him* as an elderly man?—had a pipe in his mouth. Pipes would disappear. Even now his grandsons talked of seeing someone smoke a pipe as he when a boy might have spoken of seeing an eccentric in galoshes or using a monocle. The man with the dog brought Targo to mind—not that he was ever far away.

"What we need to know," he said to Burden, "is what he was up to in Kingsmarkham between the time he left the Rahmans at around three—say, three-thirty—and came back to fetch the Mercedes *sometime after eight fifteen.* We know it was still there after eight fifteen because the girl from the nail bar saw it. So even if he drove it away at half past eight, it had been there for nearly six hours.

"He didn't go home. Mavis Targo says he didn't and why should she lie? He didn't call on his children. He didn't go to his Sewingbury office. Bescause if he had, he would have gone in his car. It's too far even for him to walk."

Burden took a sip of his wine. He wrinkled his nose but made no comment on the quality or taste of what he was drinking. "Why didn't he have a dog with him? Oh, I know Mrs. Rahman wouldn't have a dog in the house, but when he'd been there on at least one previous occasion, he brought the dog but left it in the car. Why didn't he have a dog this time? Because of what he intended to do *after* he'd been to the Rahmans? He left the car where it was because there are no parking restrictions in Glebe Road and he went off to do whatever he did."

"Yes, but what was that? His not bringing a dog suggests to me that he knew he wouldn't be going back home. He was running away. He'd committed another murder, and this time he knew he'd been seen going into his victim's garden."

"But did he know that, Reg? Surely he didn't. If he had, he wouldn't have wasted time ordering fancy computer equipment. Wouldn't he have been off as soon as he could pack a bag?"

"You're right," said Wexford. "He couldn't have known. He wasn't in a hurry. It looks as if he expected to return home. His wife says he took no clothes with him. So did something happen while he was at the Rahmans' or soon after he left the Rahmans to make him realise he might have been seen? Perhaps. Maybe we should go and ask what used to be called gentlemen's outfitters, but no doubt are no longer, if they sold a whole new wardrobe to a single customer that afternoon."

"What, and carry the stuff all the way back up Glebe Road to the car?"

"I know it's not a brilliant theory, Mike. How about he went to get a false passport from some mate?"

"I know this place has degenerated along with the rest of the countryside, but surely you'd have to do that kind of thing in London or maybe his other favourite haunt, Birmingham?"

"Mike, I just don't know. The whole thing doesn't add up. But I got busy with a map of Essex before we came down here. Melstead, where the Mercedes was found, is about seven miles from Stansted Airport. That's why I thought about the clothes and the passport. He could have got out of the country before anyone started looking for him. Of course that doesn't answer why he left the car where he did. It was bound to be found, so why not leave it in the long-stay car park at Stansted?"

"Come to that," said Burden, "why go to Stansted at all when Gatwick is on our doorstep?"

"I know. I thought of that. I phoned Mavis Targo and told her about finding the Mercedes. She just said, 'Abroad?' in the sort of tone a woman might use if I'd suggested her husband had gone to Mars. Then she repeated that stuff about him hating abroad. He's only once been out of this country and that was to Spain on their honeymoon.

"I said he'd renewed his passport just the same. That was

because they were going to New York, she said. Her daughter was getting married in New York and she wanted to go to the wedding. I didn't know she had a daughter. She's not Targo's of course. Targo was apparently going too, but when it came to the crunch, he couldn't face flying and he's seasick on boats. When I said it was still possible he'd left the country, all she said was *she* was left to feed the bloody animals. Every time she goes in the cage to feed the lion, she's so frightened her hands shake and she can hardly hold his steak dinner."

Burden laughed. "I don't hold with keeping wild animals—dangerous animals—as pets. Why does he do it?"

"I suppose he has an affinity with them. He's a dangerous animal himself. He's a monster."

"What d'you think made him leave the country—if he has?"

"While the car was parked outside the Rahmans' and while he was walking about Kingsmarkham, shopping or seeing someone or, for all I know, revisiting the scenes of his past crimes, he spoke to someone or saw or read something and realised he was in danger. I don't know what that something was, but it's the only thing that accounts for his not going home as he planned. Instead he had to get away fast."

"Yes, but, Reg, he didn't get out fast even then. This discovery of his—I mean that he would be a suspect—was probably made during the afternoon, at latest by about six when it's dark and the only people about are in the pubs. But we know he didn't leave Glebe Road until after eight fifteen. When he did leave, he drove, not to the nearest airport, but up to north Essex, a long way, taking in the Dartford Crossing and endless miles of motorway. That's not getting out fast."

"No, you're right. And what we haven't considered is how did he get from where he parked the car to Stansted if he did. Walked? In the middle of the night? If it's anything like most of these country places—think of the villages round here— he'd be walking along narrow, totally unlit lanes, sometimes no houses for miles, and if there were any, they'd be in darkness at that hour. Did he know the way? Had he ever been there before? I asked Mavis that and she said not that she knew of. She did know he'd never been anywhere from Stansted Airport."

"The prints on the Mercedes—I take it they're his?"

"His and Mavis's. Whatever she says, Mike, he's at the other end of the earth now and he's not planning on coming back. There's only one thing that really worries me about that theory. Would he leave all those animals? Would he leave his *dogs*? Oh, he could rely on her to look after them, but surely only for a while. The dogs permanently maybe, but the llamas? The lion? That's the part I don't understand. I have to see this place where the car was parked. I'm going up to Melstead tomorrow."

THE ROUTE FROM the Dartford Crossing along the M25 and the M11 was almost uniformly ugly and spoilt. But beyond the hoardings and the proliferation of road signs, behind the flower stalls, the prefab cafés, and the golf courses, meadows and untouched woodland could distantly be seen, with here and there a church spire or an ancient half-timbered house. The scenery improved once Donaldson took the turning for Braintree, and Wexford, who had heard, along with most Sussex people, that Essex was generally a flat eyesore, was surprised. He had only previously been to Colchester and hadn't expected gently hilly country, willow-bordered streams, and pretty villages boasting more thatched cottages than in his own county.

Melstead was such a village. It was approached—and apparently exclusively approached—along a network of narrow lanes without pavements. At one point Donaldson was forced onto the verge and halfway into the hedge when a woman sped past them without any relaxation of speed. Wexford considered doing something about it, then told himself he wasn't a traffic cop and had better things to occupy his time with.

The street where Targo's Mercedes had been found ran from the heart of the village where there was a green with a war memorial, the church, and the vicarage, up to a pub called the Prince of Wales Feathers and a small council estate. Donaldson parked the car and Wexford and Lynn Fancourt walked up to the middle point of the street. Here were the only two shops remaining in the village, a butcher, which had about it that indefinable atmosphere of pride and conceit that proclaims its reputation as "the best butcher in Essex," and a general store and post office.

Recently converted to vegetarianism, Lynn shuddered theatrically at Mr. Parkinson's display of locally shot pheasants and turned her face away to follow Wexford into the general store. Another surprise was in store for him. Out here, in this rustic and intensely English spot, the proprietor and postmaster was Asian. A particularly dark-skinned, hooknosed Asian at that. Wexford wondered if it was politically incorrect even to think these things. He showed Anil Mansoor his warrant card and introduced Lynn.

"Sussex, eh? I have cousins in Sussex. Maybe you know them?"

This reminded Wexford of the sort of people who, when you tell them you're going to Sydney, say that maybe you'll see their brother who immigrated to Perth ten years before. He ignored the remark and asked about the car.

Mr. Mansoor said he hadn't noticed it until a customer told him it had been there four days and asked him what he thought should be done about it. Minding one's own business seemed to be a watchword of the postmaster's.

"I said it was nothing to do with us. There are no parking restrictions in this street. Anyone could leave a car here if he wished, plenty of room for us remains."

"Do you live over the shop, Mr. Mansoor?" Wexford asked.

A note of pride came into Mansoor's voice. "No. I have a home in Thaxted. I drive here each day, it isn't far."

"You didn't see the man who parked the Mercedes here?"

"As I say, I go home to Thaxted each evening sharp at five. Indeed, you might call that afternoon rather than evening, but that is when I drive to my home."

"If someone wanted to get to Stansted airport from here and had no car, what would he or she do?"

"He could walk." This was such an alien notion to Mr. Mansoor that he burst out laughing as if he had been exceptionally witty. "If he was mad or stricken by poverty, yes, he could walk. It is seven miles. Better get a taxi. You will find the taximan's home opposite the pub. It says Tip-Top Taxis on the gate, which is rather a silly name, in my opinion."

Today Mr. Mansoor's side of the street had parked cars almost nose to tail, there being just two gaps large enough for someone to squeeze a vehicle in. If even a single car or van had been on the other side, the space left between would have been wide enough for no more than a bicycle. As it was, a car driving through had to negotiate a passage perhaps eight feet wide.

"What happens when something comes the other way, Lynn?"

"That happens, sir," she said, pointing.

A van which had just about passed the halfway mark in the street moved relentlessly on while the Fiat coming towards it was forced to reverse, a manoeuvre which was a challenge to the old man at the wheel, who was several times in danger of scraping the bodywork of a Rolls-Royce, a VW, and a Transit van. They watched with interest but desisted from applause when the older driver succeeded in escaping with no damage to his own car or the others. They walked up the path to Tip-Top Taxis.

Wexford was almost certain the taxi driver was going to tell him he had received a phone call from someone requesting to be driven to Stansted Airport or even to a station on the London-to-Cambridge mainline at midnight on the relevant date. But the owner of Tip-Top disappointed him. Mr. Davis kept his books efficiently. No such call and no such appointment were recorded.

"I'd have remembered anyway."

"Why is that, Mr. Davis?"

"Because I'm sixty-five years old and I reckon I'm past driving some lazy sod to Stansted at that hour when there's no flights before six in the morning."

"It could have been in the morning," said Lynn, thinking of Targo sleeping in his car. "Have you any bookings to the airport or a train the next morning?"

"Not a sausage, miss. I do a regular run Wednesday mornings without fail. Take a lady to see her mum in an old folks' place in Newmarket, wait for her, and bring her back. That satisfy you?"

So Targo had parked his car and vanished. He was strong and fit and resourceful. He could have walked. "Along those lanes, sir?" Lynn asked as they walked back to the car. "In the dark? You noticed how fast the locals drive. He'd have been lucky not to be killed. Do you remember that woman that passed us on the way here?"

"I do. A pedestrian would get short shrift from someone like her."

HANNAH WAS PUT on to someone called a personnel coordinator at the Spicefield supermarket headquarters. This was far from London and even farther from Kingsmarkham on an industrial estate outside Peterborough.

"Kingsmarkham Crime Management. This is Detective Sergeant Goldsmith. Can you tell me if you're employing a Tamima Rahman at any of your branches? R-A-H-MA-N."

"I'll check."

In the days when such information was kept in files, she would have had to call Hannah back. As it was, she didn't even have to ask her to hold the line. She knew within thirty seconds. "No, we don't employ anyone of that name."

Hannah was always thorough. "Would you check again, please?"

The second check afforded no different data. Hannah's next call was to Mrs. Qasi. Her tone was waspish. "Don't ask me. I haven't seen Tamima since she left here. I've told you. She's living with Jacqueline and Clare in Wandsworth."

As soon as the words were out, Faduma Qasi realised she had inadvertently let Tamima's place of residence out. Using a wheedling tone usually foreign to her, Hannah asked if Mrs. Qasi could, *please*, be more specific.

Tamima's aunt hesitated—or had she put the receiver down?

"Are you there, Mrs. Qasi?"

"Oh, well, I suppose it won't do any harm. Mancunia Road, Wandsworth, SW eighteen. It's number forty-six."

"Thank you very much."

While she had been checking on supermarkets, Damon Coleman had also been round the shops. When Wexford was young, engaged to Alison, Kingsmarkham's men had only one shop in which to buy their clothes, an old-fashioned (even then) outfitters in the centre of the high street. This was Prior's, where women also bought skirts and suits and their children's school uniforms. Now there were six, one of them in the run-down Kingsbrook Centre, one (very trendy) in York Street, the rest in the high street, where Prior's still held a preeminent place but under its new name, minus the apostrophe, of Priors Prime of Life. Damon went there first and met with no success. The smart place in York Street was no help, and nor was Young Adult three shops along from Priors. The last shop he visited was called Heyday, its window full of jeans, sweaters, baseball caps, heavy, metal-studded belts, and Wild West ten-gallon hats.

No, Mr. Targo hadn't bought anything there on the afternoon in question, but they knew him. He wasn't what you'd call a regular customer, but he had bought a couple of pairs of jeans there, one pair two or three weeks before.

"You're a snappy dresser, Damon," Wexford said. "Is that expression still used?"

"Not so far as I know, sir."

"You'd know. Let's say, you care how you look. Would you leave the country with only the clothes you stood up in?"

"No, I wouldn't. But then I wouldn't be fleeing from justice, would I?"

Fleeing was hardly the word. *Shilly-shallying, loitering, hanging about,* would be more appropriate. Targo hadn't even been shopping. Surely if you embarked on a flight without a suitcase full of clothes, Wexford thought, you would only do so because you'd find clothes at your destination. Not necessarily in the shops of some foreign city, but because you kept them there in a friend's home. He phoned Mavis Targo.

"My daughter? Lois? He wouldn't go to her. The only time they met they didn't get on. It was here and she's allergic to dogs. She only stayed one night, but I had to lock the dogs up, and you can imagine the sort of fuss Eric made."

"Just the same I'd like her phone number, please."

"What time is it? Two p.m.? Well, it's only seven where she lives. I'll give you the number, but you'll have to wait till a more civilised hour."

Wexford didn't bother with civilised hours but called Mrs. Lois Lidgett in Colorado Springs five minutes later. Her "I wouldn't have him in the house" had a familiar ring. He remembered that Adele Thompson had said she wouldn't be in the same room with Targo, and Mrs. Rahman wouldn't allow his dog to cross the threshold.

People had been telling Wexford over the years that a good way to think clearly was to go for a walk. If you sat down in a chair and tried to think, the chances were you'd go to sleep. First put the monster in the box, he thought. Throw the box away—but he couldn't do that, it was the monster he had to think about. He had always considered walking as therapeutic in that if you did enough of it it would use up some of the calories you put in by means of red wine, cashew nuts, Chinese food, fruit pies, and snacks. Might it also be beneficial in a psychological way? That is, affect the mind so that it was concentrated on the problem in hand?

Beautiful the botanical gardens were no longer. Or perhaps it was only the time of year, the untidiest time when lawns are brown with scattered leaves and a few dying roses linger on straggly bushes. The tropical house had become a coffee bar, the pinetum had been vandalised by those such as the Molloy gang, and the rare-trees enclosure had been turned into a (seldom used) children's playground with swings and seesaws. The grass was too wet to walk on, so he kept first to the main drive, then turned off along a path between lawns shaded by great cedars and beeches shedding copper-coloured leaves.

A woman was coming towards him, and because he was always aware of women's fear when encountering a lone man in a lonely place, he took a few steps off the path onto the wet turf. He smelt her scent, then heard her say, "Keep off the grass, Reg. Do you remember saying that to me before these gardens were here?"

He had no idea who she was, a tall, thin woman, very upright, white hair piled on her head in a chignon. Unrecognisable—yet she had recognised him.

"Why did I say that?"

"Most of those words weren't needed, you said. Cut out *keep* first and you get 'off the grass,' then *the*, which isn't necessary, finally *grass*, because what else? You've just got 'off' left and that says it all. I've never forgotten it. You don't know who I am, do you?"

He did now. "Yes, Alison, of course I do. How are you?

Tell me you don't live here and I couldn't have seen you all these years."

She laughed. "I live in France. I lost my first husband and married a Frenchman. I'm here because my mother died. She was immensely old, but it's still awful, it's still a shock."

"Let's walk."

They went back the way he had come. So much for thinking and concentrating on his problem. He was telling her about his life, his children, his grandchildren, when she took his arm and, looking down at her right hand resting on his sleeve, he saw the ring she wore on her third finger. It was the engagement ring he had given her when he was twenty-one and she had kept when he offered it. He looked at it and she saw him look, but neither of them said anything.

At the gates she said, "I'm staying at the Olive. Where else? Back to France tomorrow on the Eurostar."

"Good-bye, my dear," he said, and took her in his arms and kissed her. She walked away, waving once.

BACK TO THE police station and back to earth. DS Goldsmith, he was told, had gone to London in pursuit of Tamima Rahman but was expected back shortly. He felt vaguely annoyed. He had told her to have one more go at finding Tamima's whereabouts. Perhaps it was that word *shortly* which irritated him. What was wrong with *soon*? He was trying to do the thinking which the fortuitous meeting with Alison had put an end to when Burden walked in frowning, the corners of his mouth turned down. He seldom swore but he did now.

"That bloody lion's escaped."

"What?"

"King or whatever it's called, it's escaped. Mavis Targo's been on. She went to feed it and it got out."

"For God's sake, Mike. When did this happen?"

"Early this morning. She was scared to tell us, thought it might come back of its own accord. She phoned the RSPCA first and then something called the Feline Foundation, then us. We were a poor third. The media haven't got it yet, but they will without help from us. I've been on to Myringham Zoo and they've got someone coming over, their big-cats expert apparently."

"How did it get out?"

"Well, normally, she says, she wouldn't go into its enclosure. Targo does and apparently he strokes the thing. She throws half a side of lamb or whatever over the wire—he hangs it on that hook thing—only she missed and it caught on the top. She unlocked the gate, went in, and tried to reach it, but failed. The lion was in its cave. She fetched a pair of steps to climb up, forgetting that the gate was unlocked. When she came back, the gate was open and she saw the lion out in the meadow where the muntjac deer are. She was so frightened she ran back to the house, locked herself in, and drank some brandy. I don't know what she hoped for, some miracle, some waking up from a nightmare maybe, but it wasn't till half an hour ago that she phoned us."

Wexford's phone was ringing. He picked it up.

"*Kingsmarkham Courier* here. Lionel Smith speaking. What can you tell us about this escaped lion?"

18

THE WIDESPREAD PUBLICITY was welcomed by Wexford. If anything could bring Targo back, this might. The news that his wife was missing or one of his children would likely leave him indifferent, but the loss of one of his precious pets would be a major disaster in his life.

Of course the story figured mostly in the British media, but Damon Coleman found, via the World Wide Web, references to it in French, German, and Spanish newspapers. Bulls might stampede through the streets, wandering bears terrorise the unwary, or animals resembling a lynx be spotted on the moors, but this was a lion, a man-eater, truly the king of the beasts. British newspapers loved it. The *Sun's* front page was all lion, a magnificent full-page photograph under the single-word headline "Escaped!" Whether this was a picture of King hardly mattered. One lion is very much like another, and this one had the recognised leonine attributes, a noble head, a flowing mane, and a powerful, muscular torso. The *Guardian* scooped with a photograph of Targo inside his lion's cage, the animal standing six feet away from him. Mavis must have saved something after all, Wexford thought. He liked the *Daily Mail's* version best, its headline "A Double Flit" with a picture of Targo jogging in shorts, T-shirt, and scarf and another of some unnamed lion crouching and poised to spring.

Kingsmarkham filled with reporters and photographers, all hoping, Wexford said, for King to emerge from his hiding place to attack and devour some unsuspecting citizen, preferably in public, preferably a woman, and preferably a blonde.

Burden laughed. "I don't know about 'unsuspecting.' The whole place is galvanised with terror. Down the high street half the shops aren't opening. Their staff haven't come in to work. There's no one about on foot, but the traffic's heavier than usual. Everyone who's got a car is out in it."

"He'll come back, won't he, Mike? He won't be afraid of the wretched beast not being found. He'll be afraid of its being seen and shot."

"What good would his coming back do? He'll no more know where his lion is than we do."

"Maybe not. But you say that because you can't imagine being as attached to any animal the way Targo is to that lion. And to his dogs, come to that. If you were abroad and one of your children was missing, you'd come home, wouldn't you?"

"Well, of course," said Burden. "But that's different. They're my children and they're human beings."

"It's not different for Targo. He's got children too, but his animals are more important to him. Always have been. Once, long ago, I saw him smile fondly at his son, Alan. Not because he felt tenderly towards the boy, but because the boy was being specially nice to his spaniel. I think he'll come back."

"The big-cats bloke's told me he'll shoot it with an anaesthetic dart if he gets the chance. The trouble is, he knows how it's done but he's had no experience of actually doing it.

The chap from the Feline Foundation's got a twelve bore and a licence for it. That was the first thing I asked. He doesn't want to have to use it, but he will if it's a matter of saving human lives. I hope they don't have to kill the poor thing."

"So do I," said Wexford.

At the last minute Hannah had decided to take Jenny Burden with her to Wandsworth if Jenny would come. She would and the two women set off for London in Hannah's car, threading their way through late-afternoon traffic but finding Mancunia Road, which abutted the Wandsworth Common, without difficulty.

The flat was the top one in a Victorian terraced house. The nameplate under the bell said Clare Cooper and Jacquie Clarke.

"I expected to take longer getting here," Hannah said. "We may be in for a long wait."

She had parked rather nervously on a space where a ticket from a machine on the pavement was required. Or that was how it seemed. Things were very different from what prevailed in Kingsmarkham. The horrors of possibly having her car clamped had occurred to Hannah even before she got here. But she put her coins into the machine and a ticket emerged, entitling her to park for two hours. She and Jenny went up the steps to the front door of number 46 and rang Clare Cooper and Jacquie Clarke's bell. Rather to their surprise a voice answered, said it was Clare Cooper and would open the door. Hannah felt sure their luck wouldn't hold and she was right.

A tall, fair-haired young woman admitted them to the light and airy flat. She looked for rather a long time and with

227

great interest at Hannah's warrant card. "Tamima's not here," she said. "She left—oh, a week ago at least."

"What, just left?" Hannah said. "On her own? Where did she go?"

"Home to her parents, I suppose. I didn't ask. She's Jacquie's cousin. I never met her before she came here. She tried to get a job in a supermarket, I do know that, but she didn't get it. That was when she started going out every evening with some boy. I think Jacquie saw him but I don't really know. Anyway, she said she was leaving and she packed her cases and went."

"When will Jacquie be home?" Jenny asked.

"Not till Monday. She's gone away for the weekend."

They hadn't come near to using up the allotted two hours' car parking. They sat inside the car, at a loss for what to do next.

"She's definitely not at home with her parents," Hannah said. "I spoke to Mohammed Rahman this morning. He was a bit cold with me, but there's no doubt she wasn't there. He said she'd be home for Eid al-Adha, whenever that is." She caught herself up and blushed. She had done the unforgivable thing, the counter-PC thing, and spoken in a disparaging tone, if not in disparaging words, of a time-honoured Islamic tradition. "I mean, she'll be home for a holy festival."

"Then where is she now?"

"I don't know. Do you think we should go over to Kingsbury and see if Mrs. Qasi can tell us anything?"

"It's miles," said Jenny rather dismally. "It's not so much the distance as going right through central London in the rush hour. But it's not for me to say. You're the one that's driving."

Hannah never let a little difficulty such as driving through

London at five in the afternoon on a Friday put her off. "That's OK. Let's go."

It took a long time. Hannah would no more have talked on her mobile while at the wheel than she would have parked on a double yellow line. She gave the phone to Jenny and told her Mrs. Qasi's number. By this time they were crossing Wandsworth Bridge so were almost committed to going northwards. And Faduma Qasi was at home. Her tone sounded amused when she told Jenny that of course they could come. She would be delighted to see them and would get tea ready.

"I thought she was going to start laughing," Jenny said. "It was really very odd. I could almost think there was a conspiracy going on between all these people to keep Tamima hidden somewhere."

"Not 'almost.' I expect there is. What did that Clare woman mean by 'out with some boy'? Tell me if what I'm saying is too far-fetched, but it's not a forced marriage I'm thinking of now. It's an honour killing."

Jenny was silent for a moment, then said, "There was a story in the paper yesterday about some Indian widow who'd committed sati and thrown herself on her husband's funeral pyre with all the relatives standing round."

"It's *become* sati, not *commit*," Hannah corrected her, "and it's Hindus who do that, not Moslems. It's been against the law for about two hundred years."

"Come to that, honour killings are against the law but they happen."

"I know."

∎ ∎ ∎

NEXT DAY HANNAH managed to see Faduma Qasi again, and this time she went alone. As had happened the day before, Mrs. Qasi refused to discuss Tamima, and Hannah's questions met with silence. Not, of course, absolute silence, for Mrs. Qasi, once more offering tea or coffee or, with a half-amused glance, oloroso sherry, was happy to talk about the weather, a small earthquake in Pakistan, and the long hours of fasting she and her family observed at Ramadan. But when Hannah took the conversation to the subject of Tamima, Mrs. Qasi said she really couldn't discuss family matters.

"You seemed quite willing to talk about her the first time I came."

"Yes. Perhaps that was a mistake on my part. I've reason to believe my brother objects very strongly to his private affairs being discussed."

"If it's a matter of breaking the law, Mrs. Qasi, these aren't his private affairs. I've reason to believe Tamima has antagonised her family by meeting a young man her father and mother can't accept and that they may take steps to stop it."

"I really can't say."

"Perhaps you can say where she is now. Clare Cooper, your other niece's flatmate, told me she was no longer living with them. She hasn't succeeded in getting a job. She isn't at home in Kingsmarkham. Clare mentioned some involvement with a boy. Tamima is only sixteen years old."

"I know nothing about this." Faduma Qasi got up. "I think you should go."

Hannah had no choice about it and she went. But every word on the subject that Mrs. Qasi had uttered increased her anxieties. The picture that formed before her eyes was as yet only of Tamima imprisoned, Tamima in the home of some relative unknown to Hannah, not restrained to the point of being tied up like an animal, but possibly locked in a bedroom belonging to this gaoler until she "came to her senses." The boy she was involved with must surely be Rashid Hanif, and it was to the Hanifs' house that Hannah went as soon as she was back in the Kingsmarkham neighbourhood.

At first, parking her car in the only vacant space she could find in Rectangle Road, Stowerton, Hannah wondered why so few people were about. Cars, yes; pedestrians, no. She was halfway to the Hanifs' house when a car pulled up alongside her and a woman put her head out of the driver's window.

"You don't want to be outside," she said. "The lion's been seen in Oval Road. I'd get inside somewhere if I were you."

Hannah thanked her, resisted saying she wasn't her, and walked up to the Hanifs' front door. It was opened by Fata Hanif, her head bare. "I saw you coming," she said. "I thought, 'Maybe she's seen the lion.' Come in quick. My husband just came home. He says it's been seen in the high street."

"I've come to talk to you, Mrs. Hanif. It's nothing to do with the lion."

Akbar Hanif was sitting in the living room, the baby on his lap, an older child on either side of him. He was a heavily bearded, rather fat man, wearing a loose white shirt over black trousers. He nodded to Hannah, looked at her warrant card with an amiable smile, and asked her what the police were doing about the lion, an enquiry Hannah ignored.

"I hoped your son Rashid might be at home," she said. "Or isn't he back from college yet?"

"They are on half-term."

This fact was already known to Hannah. "But he's not at home?"

Fata, a small girl now in her arms, said, "No, he is not at home because he has gone away camping with his cousin.

He works hard. He's entitled to a break sometimes. Now his great-auntie has died and left him some money. A little bit of money, so he is spending it on a tent and other equipment for camping. Is there something you don't like about that?"

"Fata," said her husband, the intervention evidently intended as a reproof but uttered in a mild, gentle tone.

"Where is he camping?"

"In somewhere called the Peak District, if it's any business of yours."

This time the reproach came in a sad shaking of Akbar's head.

"When do you expect him back?" Hannah asked him.

"Wednesday or Thursday." Fata spoke for her husband. "I don't want him back here while that lion's about. I don't want any of my children out on the streets."

Hannah was heartily sick of the lion. "And this camping is just with his cousin?" What numbers of relatives these people had, Hannah found herself thinking, a reflection she caught up short, horrified at yet another example of racism in her uncontrolled thoughts. "Just he and the cousin on their own?"

"Oh, no," said Mrs. Hanif. "There are three or four of them, another cousin and two friends from college." She gave Hannah a penetrating glance. "But if you're trying to make out a *girl* is with them, you are wrong. And now I think you should go," she said, thus becoming the second woman to have addressed those words to Hannah in four hours.

The street was empty. It was late afternoon and already growing dark. She drove back to Kingsmarkham, where she encountered Lynn Fancourt in the police-station car park.

"I'm really scared of this lion," Lynn said, "especially after dark. Cats are nocturnal, aren't they? I expect it only really starts prowling around, looking for something to eat, in the nighttime."

"It won't come into urban areas. It's probably more frightened of people than they are of it."

"I hope you're right."

Hannah went up to Wexford's office.

He was looking at his computer screen with Damon there to guide him through the Web. The glance he gave Hannah was less than pleasant.

"Well?"

Damon was going and Wexford said nothing to encourage him to stay.

"I've been in London, guv," Hannah said, "and since I got back, I've had a talk with Rashid Hanif's parents. I think Tamima Rahman's gone off with Rashid, they're hiding out somewhere. I don't believe for a moment her parents' story that Rashid's gone camping with a bunch of friends and relations."

"So she's somewhere, as you put it, with her boyfriend. She's over sixteen. I've yet to learn that fornication's against the law in this country."

"It's against sharia law. Asian people have killed a daughter for less. They may have killed her or be planning to do that. May I tell you what I've found out?"

"You'd better sit down," said Wexford rather sourly.

Hannah told him about Clare Cooper, her two visits to Mrs. Qasi, and the reaction of the Hanifs to her questioning. "You can see why I'm anxious, guv. No one's seen the girl for days, weeks maybe. Everyone's got excuses for her not being where she's supposed to be. But Clare Cooper did mention her being involved with a boy, and as Rashid Hanif's gone off somewhere too, surely it's obvious they're together. Or they've been together until—"

"All right, I see all that. But none of it leads me to your conclusion, that she's a victim of an honour killing. You've absolutely no evidence for thinking that way. It's pure assumption."

"Would you OK it if I went to see the Rahmans tomorrow and put it to them? Asked them, I mean, if Tamima's away because she's with Rashid?"

Wexford was silent for a moment, then said, "Let me tell you what I should really like, Hannah. Firstly, never again to hear the name Tamima Rahman coupled with the term *forced marriage* or *honour killing*. Then, if you go to talk to the Rahmans, I'd like you to find Tamima there, alive and well and in the bosom of her family. But preferably not to tell me about it."

"All right, guv. I get the message." In the doorway, Hannah turned. "D'you know, guv, you're the only person I've talked to since I've been back here who hasn't mentioned that lion."

PERHAPS HE HADN'T mentioned it because he had heard little else all day. When Hannah came in, he had been looking at lion pictures on the Internet, a video that claimed— surely erroneously—to be of King ranging the open space outside its cave in the days of its captivity. He phoned Mavis Targo. No, she had heard nothing from her husband. She would have told him if she had. At present she was afraid to go outside and did so only to reach the white van in which she went shopping. This meant a walk of maybe three yards. She described to Wexford the agonies she went through each time she made that short journey, waiting for King to spring at her from out of the bushes.

"And one of the muntjacs has gone."

Wexford had to think what a muntjac was. A sort of small deer? "You mean one of yours?"

"Excuse *me*. One of Eric's. He had three and now there's only two. I watched them through binoculars. I was scared to go out there."

Wexford would be with her next morning, he told her. It was now nearly two weeks since her husband had departed.

19

THE LION WAS still at liberty. In this countryside, Wexford thought, there was little reason why it shouldn't retain its freedom for weeks, months even, provided it found enough small animals to feed on. The area abounded in wildlife, badgers, foxes, hares and rabbits, pheasant and partridge. On his way to Stringfield, he found himself noticing all the roadkill, squashed bloody pelts and bundles of black and brown feathers. Would a lion eat carrion? Probably, if it was hungry.

While Donaldson stopped at a red light at the Local Traffic exit, Wexford made a phone call to the Rahmans. Yasmin answered, and once again her magisterial tone and economy of speech impressed him.

"Hallo? Who is speaking?"

Wexford said he wanted to talk to her and her husband, her son Ahmed too if that was possible.

"My husband will be here," she said. "My son Ahmed also." The faintest hint of humour came into her voice. "And my son Osman too if you want the whole family."

"That must include Tamima, of course."

She was annoyed. "How many times do we have to tell you? Tamima is in London with her cousin."

"No, she isn't, Mrs. Rahman. But we can talk about that later."

It was a fine sunny day; the grounds of Wymondham Lodge and the downs beyond looking at their autumn best. English woods have few trees in them which turn red in November. That display is confined to North America where forests have a preponderance of maples. Here, in Sussex, the fields were green and the woods dark green and yellow and brown, the gold coming from the birches and the tawny colour from beech and oak. A little breeze ruffled the treetops, making the different shades mingle and shiver. On some distant slopes sheep grazed, with black-and-white cattle in the meadows by the Brim. But nearer home was more exotic fauna, the llamas enjoying the sunshine, the two remaining muntjacs running for the cover of the hedge at the sound of Wexford's car. No lion, of course, to greet him with a roar.

The front door wasn't immediately opened. Mavis Targo called out, "Who is it?" Wexford couldn't help smiling as he answered. Did she imagine the lion would reply with "It's me, King!"

She was very much dressed up for his visit. Or dressed up for her own satisfaction. A tight black suit and green blouse set off her heavy gold jewellery, several necklaces, earrings as large as coat buttons. Her thick fingers were stiff with gold and diamond rings. Wexford imagined her, forced by her fear to stay at home, diverting herself by trying on various outfits and hanging jewellery on some designer creation, experimenting with colours and shapes in front of the mirror, like a little girl playing with mother's clothes.

"I haven't heard from him," she began, and she didn't mean the lion. "Not a word since he went off that morning. I don't believe he's abroad. He wouldn't go abroad. And now Ming's ill. He's pining for Eric, that's what it is. I had to take him to the vet yesterday and she says it's a virus. It's no virus, it's missing Eric."

The Tibetan spaniel lay curled up on a pile of silk cushions in the corner. "Poor lamb, he won't go in his basket. All he wants are those cushions, and Sweetheart keeps annoying him. Well, he's only a puppy, he wants to play."

"May I sit down, Mrs. Targo? I want you to tell me all over again but in greater detail this time what happened on the day your husband went missing. Starting with first thing in the morning, please."

They went into the ornate drawing room.

"Eric was up very early," she began. "But he often was. He went out somewhere—in the van, I think it was."

To take himself to Pomfret and what he meant to do in Cambridge Cottages, Wexford thought. "Did he take a dog with him?"

"I don't know. It was five in the morning. I woke up when he left and then I went to sleep again. When I got up, he was back and both the dogs were there. Oh, yes, I remember he said he'd taken them out for a walk. I went shopping later on, and when I got back, he was out in the grounds with the animals." She gave Wexford an exasperated look. "You don't know how many times I've been over this in my mind. I've nearly done my head in, trying to think what he said and if he said where he was going. But he never did say, I'm certain of that."

"When did he go out again?"

"It would have been two or three in the afternoon. He

phoned someone on his mobile first, but I don't know who that was. Then he went off in the Merc."

"Not taking a dog with him?"

"I didn't know that till he'd been gone half an hour. I hadn't seen Ming for a bit, I'd seen Sweetheart, so I thought, 'He'll have taken Ming.' But he hadn't because Ming came in from the garden soon after that."

"He said nothing to you about where he was going?"

"No, but he often didn't. If I thought about it, I'd have said he went over to the Sewingbury office or maybe to see a tenant. And when he didn't come back, I thought, 'No, he's gone to Birmingham and he's stopping overnight.'"

"I know this is very personal, Mrs. Targo, but I have to ask it. Yours wasn't a very happy marriage, was it?"

Cagily, she said, "What makes you say that?"

"What, when a man goes off without a word to his wife as to where he's going, no phone call to her from wherever that is or from his car on the way there? He stays away for days on end and doesn't contact her?"

"It's just his way. He's always been like that. Maybe you'll say most women wouldn't put up with it, but I don't care that much, I'm OK. I've got this place and the dogs and most of what I want. I don't complain."

It was useless pursuing this line. "The phone call you received, the message from someone whose voice you didn't recognise, are you sure of that? Are you sure you didn't know the voice?"

"It wasn't Eric's and it wasn't Alan's, I do know that. But I do think I'd heard it before. It sounds a funny thing to say, but I think it was the voice of someone who's been here to do some work, a builder or a gardener or maybe someone to do with the animals."

"Can you be more specific?"

"I don't think so. I just know it was a voice I'd heard before."

"Someone employed by your husband at the Sewingbury office?"

"I never met them—well, there was only one and he left before Eric went missing. I never heard his voice."

Wexford sighed internally. "The forensic tests on your car—that is, the Mercedes—have been completed. It will be brought back tomorrow."

She nodded indifferently. "I never drive it." Sweetheart came padding in, its tail wagging when it saw Wexford. Mavis picked it up and held it in her arms. "Poor lamb hasn't been out walkies for three days. But what can I do? I can't risk my life to take a dog out."

Targo would, Wexford thought irrelevantly. With nothing more in view than to provide her with some reassurance, nothing but to look at the quiet, empty, sunlit land, Wexford got up and approached the French windows. He put his hand to the doorknob. "May I?"

"You can if you want, but be careful."

"Mrs. Targo, your lion isn't going to be waiting outside, enjoying the sunshine."

But it was.

Wexford stepped back, closed the door again. King was fast asleep. It lay curled up on the terrace like the big cat it was, at the foot of its marble facsimile and its woman attendant, a yard or so from him the pathetic remains of what had once been a small deer. Only the deer's almost fleshless long legs had been rejected. The rest had been King's breakfast or perhaps the previous night's supper.

• • •

"I PHONED THE big-cats man from the zoo," Wexford told
Burden several hours later. "I'm probably being unfair, but I
thought the Feline Foundation chap might be a bit trigger-
happy. Then I sat down with Mavis in that awful pseudo-
Versailles room and she kept saying over and over, 'What am
I going to do?' I kept telling her to do nothing, just wait for
the man with the anaesthetic to come. 'You could make us a
cup of tea,' I said, but she's no Yasmin Rahman. It took her a
good fifteen minutes, and when the tea came, it was pale gray
and tepid. Made me wonder if she'd ever made tea before.
While I was drinking it or pretending to, Ming the spaniel
was sick."

"But the zoo man did come?"

"Oh, yes, he came. By that time I was wondering how long
that lion would stay asleep and what if he woke up before Big
Cats arrived. However, King stayed asleep, the man came—
accompanied by two other chaps, God knows who they were,
maybe what we used to call zookeepers—a shot was fired into
King's flank, he rolled over quietly and sort of collapsed into
unconsciousness. Mavis started screaming that he was dead
and what would Eric say when he came back. I felt like saying, 'He won't come back here, he'll be in custody,' but of
course I didn't."

"What's happened to the lion?"

"Big Cats and his mates lifted him up onto a sort of
stretcher and put him into the back of their van. A black
van, incidentally, with Myringham Zoo's logo on the side, a
giraffe gobbling up the top of a tree. One of the mates came
back and cleared up the remains of the unfortunate muntjac.

He told me that if no one claimed him, they'd keep King. Apparently, they're looking for a stud male for their three lionesses."

"So a happy ending for King and his harem."

"Yes. At least there's been something good coming out of Targo's disappearance. Have we time for lunch before I go to the Rahmans?"

"I've ordered Indian takeaway," said Burden.

Wexford sat behind his rosewood desk, which was his own private possession, and Burden—his attempts to perch himself on one corner of it meeting with a frown—took the only other comfortable chair in the office.

"I'm going to see the Rahmans, all of them except Tamima, of course, to try and lay to rest this obsession of Hannah's with Tamima's forced marriage or honour killing. But if I get nothing out of them except denials, we're still left with the dilemma of where the girl is. Now what I think is that she's simply gone off with Rashid Hanif. His mother told Hannah he'd inherited 'a little bit' of money. That might be ten thousand pounds or fifty, depending on whether you yourself are rich or poor. Whatever it is, I don't think he's camping as his mother says he is. I think he's having a teenage honeymoon with Tamima somewhere."

"You mean her parents know this?"

"I doubt it. But they must know she's not in any of the places she's supposed to be, that is, with her aunt, Mrs. Qasi, her uncles and aunts, or with the two girls who share a flat in Wandsworth. In any event, I expect them to be worried and therefore glad to see me. I'm also going to ask Ahmed and his mother—she was in the house at the time while Osman was out and their father was ill—exactly what happened when

Targo called at their house in Glebe Road some eight or nine hours after he'd killed Andy Norton."

The takeaway that arrived came from the Dal Lake, chicken korma, *aloo gobi*, rice, and mango chutney, plus a plateful of chapatis, all brought up by Lynn Fancourt, who also provided on the tray a jug of iced water and a packet of paper napkins, rather incongruously printed with a design of holly and mistletoe berries.

"Left over from someone's Christmas party, I suppose."

"You're out-of-date," said Burden. "Shops in the high street have been selling Christmas stuff since September." He spooned out some rice and korma for himself. "Surely," he said, returning to the subject of Targo, "we know why he went there. He wanted that computerised thing that switches lights and heating on."

"Yes, maybe. But doesn't it strike you as very odd that a man who apparently hasn't basic computer skills—like me—a man who needs help with using the equipment in his office, wants to buy a device that presumably demands those skills for its functioning? His wife is at home all day to see to switching things on and making the heating work. Also there's the matter of why he stayed so long. He came in the afternoon—half past two or three, nobody seems sure—but it's sure when he left. Not till at least eight fifteen because the nail-bar lady and Mrs. Scott saw his car still there 'after eight fifteen.'"

"It looks as if he didn't want to leave until after dark."

"Yes, but it would have been dark at five, so that doesn't really answer the question."

"We've thought he might have been buying clothes and maybe a suitcase and just left the car there."

"But we know he wasn't buying clothes, Mike. No one sold him clothes in Kingsmarkham that afternoon, and if he went to Stowerton or Myringham to buy them, why would he, for instance, take a taxi or a bus when he could have used his own car? I'm starting to wonder something quite different. Suppose he was with Ahmed and his mother for only an hour or two, and when he left, he left on foot? Took himself off somewhere by train or took a taxi to Gatwick?"

"He can't have done that." Burden took some more spinach on the grounds that his wife, though she wasn't there to see, would approve of healthy eating. "He can't have gone on foot because his car was found up in north Essex."

"He isn't the only person in the Kingsmarkham area who can drive a car, Mike. Suppose he went off walking and someone else—later on in the dark to avoid being seen—drove the Mercedes up to within easy distance of Stansted to make it look as if he had gone there."

"Some pal, d'you mean? Some accomplice? How about his wife?"

"Mavis says she never drives the Mercedes. But that means nothing. She could have driven it. Her prints were all over the interior, as they would be whether she drove it that day or not, and no one else's were. She could have taken the van down to Glebe Road at nine, say, or ten, left it somewhere not in Glebe Road, and driven the Mercedes up the M11 to north Essex."

"Wait a minute, Reg. We always come back to the problem of whoever drove the car up to that village having to get to Stansted or, harder, get back to London. Say she drove the car away from Glebe Road at nine, she'd have had a three-hour journey ahead of her, through the Dartford Crossing, up the M25, onto the M11, *past* Stansted Airport, out along the A120 to Thaxted or Braintree, and then to that village. So she gets there at midnight more or less. How does she get back?"

Wexford looked out at the gathering clouds, uniformly gray overhead but on the distant horizon black and thick. A storm was coming. He turned back to Burden. "There are trains early in the morning from Stansted into London. But she wouldn't be in Stansted. And the Tip-Top man I saw drove no one out of Melstead that night and no one the following morning. Besides, we saw her in Stringfield at ten the following morning. No, you're right, it can't be done. Besides, I don't believe her capable of doing it. The answer has to be that whoever drove that car up there had an accomplice driving another car in which to fetch him or her back. Who these people are we don't know and are no nearer knowing than we were a week ago."

A sudden gust of wind blew the half-open window wide. Wexford went to close it as thunder rattled.

"Is it true that when I was young, storms only happened in the summer, or am I imagining it?"

"Well," said Burden, "as I often tell you, you've got too much imagination."

20

No ROOFS WERE torn off, no building collapsed. Perhaps a dozen trees were blown over, one of which blocked the Kingsmarkham-to-Brimhurst road, another wrecking Burden's rock garden. Heavy rain swelled the Kingsbrook and it burst its banks at the point where Wexford's old garden used to reach, flooding a small area where nothing much grew and nothing grazed.

"It's like that joke about the dullest headline you can think of," Wexford said to Burden. "'Small Earthquake in Chile, None Injured.'"

Burden smiled politely, the way he did when Wexford's humour failed to amuse him. "I know it's going to cost me a fortune to have that tree moved."

Wexford reflected on his own garden, which was fast returning to its normal condition of untidiness and neglect, then he thought of Andy Norton, who, however you looked at it, had died because of him.

LIKE SOME CHARACTER in nineteenth-century fiction, searching the metropolis for a fallen woman, for some girl who had

gone astray, Hannah Goldsmith was scouring London for
Tamima Rahman. She actually told herself this as she drove
from Mrs. Qasi in Kingsbury to Mrs. Clarke in Acton, reflecting that these days it was only among Moslems (or perhaps
Orthodox Jewry) that a young girl's chastity would be so valued or its loss so productive of danger and even death. She
had started with an optimistic view. Wexford didn't believe
Tamima was in danger either of a forced marriage or, much
worse, being injured or even killed for the honour of the family. He was usually right while she was often wrong. What she
wanted now was simply to find Tamima—in almost any circumstances—find her alive and well and with Rashid Hanif.
Sympathetic to a Moslem culture she might be, but still she
found it impossible to believe that anything was wrong in a
girl who was over the age of consent spending a week or two
alone with her boyfriend. In her view, the only fault would lie
in their missing out on their education.

Rashid Hanif had money. Not much probably, but enough
to take Tamima to some cheap hotel for a couple of weeks.
That the pair could be staying with relations was not to
be considered. No good Moslem would give sanctuary to
Rashid and Tamima in defiance of their parents. But a relative might have some clue as to where they would likely go.
That was why Hannah was seeking out a small colony of
Rahman relatives living in Acton, as well as Akbar Hanif's
sister in Ealing. For all that, a small voice echoing somewhere inside her head kept telling her, "You won't find
Tamima. You know you won't. She's dead. Rashid may be
dead too. They're a modern-day Romeo and Juliet."

Mrs. Clarke, née Rahman, lived in a small semidetached
house and appeared to be the only one at home. In her fifties,
she was a handsome woman if rather too thin, her eyes mid-

night brown, her hair unnaturally black, and the rainbow-shaded trousers and silk top she wore she could just carry off with that colouring. No, she hadn't seen her niece Tamima for four or five years. Of course she knew the girl was staying with her daughter, she and her daughter were close, but she couldn't recall that the subject of Tamima had ever been discussed between them. From what her daughter Jacquie had told her, she understood Tamima had stayed for a while in the flat Jacquie shared with a friend she had known since university. *Uni* was what she called it, a term that grated on Hannah's ears. I'm getting as precious and fussy as the guv, she told herself. It must be catching.

Next door lived Amran Ibrahim, Yasmin Rahman's brother, with his wife, Asha. Both insisted to Hannah that they hardly knew Tamima and hadn't seen her since she was a little girl. Hannah drove to Ealing. Akbar Hanif's sister Amina lived in a handsome detached house of 1920s vintage, a far cry from his home in Rectangle Road, Stowerton. She was a big, expensively dressed woman in her late forties and had no objection to talking about family matters. Childless herself, she was very attached to her brother's children.

"I'd be very surprised if Rashid did what you're suggesting," she said over the coffee she made for herself and Hannah. "He's not only a good boy who works hard at school—gets very good exam results—but, well, he's been brought up to respect his parents. It wouldn't be too much to say, *fear* his parents, especially his mum. They'll arrange a marriage for him one day, and he's told me he's happy with that. It won't be till he's finished university anyway. What makes you think he's not camping in Derbyshire the way Fata says he is?"

Hannah had been in contact with Derbyshire police, suggested they should find Rashid Hanif (while certain they wouldn't be able to), and been told, politely, that they had no time to waste on such things.

"I think he's somewhere else with Tamima Rahman. Or he has been."

"It seems very unlikely to me. He's simply not that sort of boy."

It was Rashid's uncle, Fata's brother in Hounslow, a disabled man who came to the door in his wheelchair, who gave Hannah the first clue. While he was still mobile, he and his wife had twice been to Brighton, where they had stayed in a B and B. "Very lovely," he said. "Very good. Nice people run it. You know they are not allowed by the law to turn people away because they are Asian—well, Moslem, we are not Asian—but my wife is from south India. They are not allowed, but some people when they see a brown face—well, they make it clear one isn't wanted. But Mr. and Mrs. Peddar at the Channel View showed us nothing like that. They welcomed us."

"And you told your sister and her husband?"

"Yes, we did. But they never went there. How can you have holidays when you have seven children?" He laughed. "You can do nothing when you have seven children."

Would Rashid take Tamima there? Hannah thought it possible. She took the precise address from Rashid's uncle and, in high hopes that they had at least been there, phoned the Channel View private hotel. Mrs. Peddar at once came over the line as an indiscreet woman.

"We have many Asian visitors. I really like them, they're so well-behaved. In fact we've thought of specially advertising for Asians, but we can't, it's against the law."

"The people I have in mind," said Hannah, "are very

young, a man and a young woman." It went against the grain
with her to refer to any female person as a *girl*.

"That sounds like Mr. and Mrs. Khan. To tell you the truth,
I don't think they're Mr. and Mrs. at all, I'm sure they're not
married, but nobody cares any more about that sort of thing,
do they? I think it's rather nice, calling themselves Mr. and
Mrs., it sort of shows—well, *respect.*"

Hannah thought she'd come across some daft opinions in
the course of her work, but few dafter than that. "I'd like to
come down and see them, Mrs. Peddar."

"They haven't done anything wrong, have they? I'd find
that hard to believe."

"No, nothing wrong."

"I've been going over what we talked about yesterday,"
Wexford said when Damon brought in tea for himself and
Burden, "and I've been thinking some very politically incor-
rect thoughts."

"I think them all the time," said Burden rather gloomily.
"What are yours?"

"I told you that when I went up to Melstead, I talked to the
Asian man called Anil Mansoor who runs the general shop
and post office. It's in the street where Targo's Mercedes was
found. Nothing he said was much help, and certainly nothing
was suspicious. But one thing he did say I ignored at the time,
but it's come back to me now. He said, 'Sussex? I have cousins
in Sussex. Maybe you know them?'"

Burden had begun taking sugar in his tea. This had been
going on for perhaps a couple of months. He fancied a
change he said when asked, which Wexford thought an inad-

equate explanation. He watched Burden wistfully, hoping to see him put on weight, but if anything he seemed thinner than before. Now, as if in defiance, he loaded three spoonfuls into his teacup.

"So?" he said.

"This is where the political incorrectness comes in. If he'd been—well, white, I'd not have stored that remark of his in my mind. So he had cousins in Sussex? So what? But because he's Asian, I'm thinking of other Asians, I'm thinking of the Rahmans."

"But there are hundreds if not thousands of Asians in Sussex."

"I told you it was politically incorrect."

Burden drank some of his syrupy tea with evident enjoyment. "OK, but what are you getting at?"

"We'd considered that Targo might not have driven the Mercedes himself. Suppose one of the Rahmans drove it? Drove it to Melstead because he knew the place, knew how to get there down all those narrow lanes, because he had been there before to visit his cousin the postmaster?"

"That's pure speculation."

"A lot of what we do is."

"Are you saying that the Rahmans and this postmaster—what's his name? Mansoor?—were in cahoots with Targo and this was done to help him with his getaway? Make us think he'd left from Stansted when in fact he left from some other airport or exit or never left at all but is still in this country?"

Burden poured himself another cup of tea and, with a glance at Wexford which the latter interpreted as challenging, ladled in the sugar. "There's no sign they're in need of money, is there?"

"Well, you could say that everyone is in need of money. Often for reasons one knows nothing about."

"If you're right," Burden said thoughtfully, "and more than one member of the Rahman family is involved, it solves the problem of how Targo got from Melstead to Stansted Airport in the middle of the night. Targo, accompanied, say, by Osman, drove the Mercedes to Stansted from Sussex. Osman, on his own, drove it to Melstead, left it there, and was taken back to Sussex by Ahmed or their father in their own car."

"I'm going to talk to them. Come with me, why don't you."

The fallen trees had been cleared away, but the back streets of Kingsmarkham, thickly treed, were littered with broken branches and twigs, the last of the fallen leaves, and here and there a dislodged roof tile. Wexford and Burden encountered Hannah standing outside Webb and Cobb, facing the window, part of which was exposed by a board which had come adrift in the previous night's storm. She seemed fascinated by the interior, which was already familiar to Wexford, the crates, the boxes, the stepladder, and the tray on the table filled with shards of crockery.

"I was just about to go into the Rahmans', guv," she said.

As she spoke, the front door of number 34 opened and Ahmed came out, holding a hammer and a bag of nails. In a rather hoarse—perhaps nervous?—voice, he said he wouldn't be more than five minutes. He had come out to nail the board back in place.

"We're in no hurry," said Burden in a cold tone.

Mohammed was sitting in the armchair the family seemed to regard as exclusively for his use, while Osman was in the conservatory watering plant pots. He set down the can, came in as his father said, "I'm glad you've come. We're worried about my daughter. She's disappeared."

"At least you acknowledge it," Wexford said. "I confess I was afraid you would stick to this story of yours that she is happily spending time in London with this relative and that."

Wexford looked from one to the other of them, Yasmin sitting statue-still, her hands, heavily beringed, lying in her lap, her head wrapped more strictly than usual in scarves, one black, one Prussian blue; Osman, as handsome as his brother but bearded, still in his nurse's attire of dark blue trousers and mandarin jacket; Ahmed and his father both dressed like businessmen in white shirts and dark suits. Wexford glanced at Hannah, said, "Detective Sergeant Goldsmith believes Tamima is in Brighton with Rashid Hanif but I don't. What do you think?"

The elder Rahmans were silent. Like one putting off the evil day as long as he could, Osman said, "I've seen Rashid today. He's been camping but he came back last night and his mum brought him into A and E with a suspected broken ankle. He hasn't seen Tamima for weeks."

"I believe that," Yasmin said reluctantly, as if the words were being forced out of her.

Wexford turned to Ahmed. "Tamima will have to be reported as a missing person. But I warn you that if she is not missing and you in fact know where she is, you will be arrested and charged with wasting police time. Is that clear?"

Ahmed nodded. Silent, he seemed in a trancelike state or hypnotised. By fear? By knowledge? Yasmin wore one of her habitual expressions, scorn this time. She looked down at the hands in her lap as if admiring the load of rings which adorned them.

"I'd like you to tell me the truth about what happened

when Mr. Targo came here that afternoon, ostensibly to talk about you ordering some remote-control device for him. What was the real reason, Mr. Rahman?"

Ahmed tried to clear his throat. He appeared to be one of those people whose voices apprehension paralyses. The throat-clearing served its purpose, but only up to a point, and when he did speak, his voice was hoarse. "He did want that—that software."

"And what was the other purpose of his visit?"

Yasmin's voice was quite clear, unimpeded by nervousness. "You had better tell him, Ahmed." She paused, stared Wexford in the eyes, said, "It wasn't my son's fault."

"What your mother says is sound," Burden said. "You had better tell us. Just you without your family, if that's what you want, here or at the police station. Which is it to be?"

Wexford hadn't expected what followed. It seemed unlike Targo, it went against all his preconceived notions of Targo. He looked at Ahmed, said, "Come along. What happened?"

"I'll tell you." Ahmed took a deep breath, exhaled, and spoke in a steadier voice. "I haven't told my father this. My brother doesn't know either. My mother was here. She knows. Targo—I don't want to call him mister anymore—he came here and asked about the software. Then he said he knew my sister was going about with a boy our family didn't like. He'd seen her, he said. That was Rashid Hanif, of course. He said a white boy, but Rashid's not really white, he's just pale-skinned because his mother's Bosnian."

"What else did he say, Ahmed?"

Ahmed looked from one to the other of them as if he expected the help that was not forthcoming. He lowered his head and shook it. "All right, I'll tell you. He said he knew we wanted my sister killed to save the family honour, and if that was what we wanted, he'd do it. He'd kill her, he said. We didn't have to pay him. He'd do an honour killing and no one would suspect him or us if we kept quiet. There, I've told you."

"Not everything, Ahmed," said Wexford. "Not by a long chalk. You can't leave it there. You have to go on."

Ahmed put his head in his hands. Through his fingers he whispered, "I can't, I can't."

"I can," said Yasmin.

Seeing the shock and distress in his father's face, Osman had gone to sit beside him. Wexford asked himself if he had ever before seen a grown-up son take his father's hand as Osman took Mohammed's now, holding it tightly in his own. This family had a solidarity he had seldom seen before the immigrants came. He turned his eyes to Yasmin.

"Well, Mrs. Rahman?"

"I was there. What Ahmed says is true." Her tone changed and the note of her speech altered subtly. Wexford wondered if it was a fact that lying raised the blood pressure. She looked suddenly as if her systolic had gone up to two hundred. "He was disgusted by what the man had said to him. So was I." She repeated it, "So was I. We are not the kind of ignorant, cruel people who would want a daughter killed for the sake of some outdated honour." The last word she came danger-ously near to spitting out. "Honour!"

Incongruously, a line from Anne Finch, Countess of Win-chilsea, came into Wexford's head from that little book he had given to the now dead Medora: "The pale, the fall'n, th' untimely sacrifice / To your mistaken shrine, to your false idol, honour!" All he said was "Well?"

255

"Ahmed told him to go. He said we would have nothing to do with what he said. Go, he told him, and he left."

"How did he go, Mrs. Rahman?"

"In his car, of course. He came in his car and he went in it."

Ahmed spoke again. "He went in his car, he drove off in it. I saw him. But he must have come back later."

Mohammed spoke. His voice sounded small and subdued. "I wasn't well, I was in my bedroom. I looked out of the window at six thirty, I know it was six thirty, I looked at the clock. That car was there. It was still there."

"Very well," said Wexford. "I want this house searched and, if necessary, the building next door searched. You can either give me permission to do that now or I can get a warrant. A warrant will delay things, but it's your choice."

"We are law-abiding people," Mohammed said. "All we want is to do what is right. You may search."

"You're looking for my sister's body?" Osman had perhaps misunderstood or had failed to follow what had gone before. He suddenly looked years older than he was. "You think he killed her just the same?"

DAMON COLEMAN AND Lynn Fancourt carried out the search with a uniformed officer. Lynn said afterwards she had never searched such a clean house, all the furniture polished to a high gloss, baths and sinks gleaming, linen sweet-smelling and carefully ironed. Tamima's room distressed her when she contemplated what she was sure had become of the girl. Posters of pop singers were on the walls. Tamima had a tiny pink radio, a pink straw basket lined with pink-and-white fabric and laden with a teenager's cosmetics. The room Ahmed shared with his brother—the largest in the house—was a temple of technology, full of cables and computer attachments as well as a desktop and a laptop, while Osman had apparently left no mark of his personality on the place. Perhaps he did no more than sleep there, bed down for seven or eight hours each night in the small single bed which seemed removed by design as far as possible from Ahmed's way of life and means of livelihood. Wexford, looking in there, while the search progressed, thought that if what he believed was true and Ahmed and his mother had been lying, if Ahmed himself had assisted at Tamima's murder, the Rahman sons would soon each have a room to himself. Or only one son would remain to take his pick of the rooms.

It had been dusk growing dark when they arrived, and now it was the deep dark of a winter's evening. The search of 34 Glebe Road had been completed and nothing had been found. All the time it was going on, the Rahman family had sat in their living room, Wexford, Burden, and Hannah Goldsmith with them, and for once Yasmin had made no offers of tea or coffee. The lights were on, mainly from table lamps, and after a while Ahmed had picked up the evening paper. He sat looking at it. Reading it? Wexford wasn't sure. Perhaps he merely stared at the print with unseeing eyes. Yasmin got up and drew the curtains on the dark, wet night.

For his part, Wexford was turning over in his mind the extraordinary phenomenon of Eric Targo. The man had killed three people or possibly more, but the ones Wexford was concerned about were Elsie Carroll, Billy Kenyon, and Andy Norton. In all those cases he had killed someone another person apparently wanted out of the way. Another person or people might well want Tamima Rahman out of the way if the propensities of some immigrant families for killing a daughter who had dishonoured them were taken into consideration. But if he had killed her—if, come to that, she was dead—why had he broken away from his usual procedure of carrying out the act without asking for leave, without seeking permission? It seemed a total break from custom, a departure from the way he usually acted that had kept him safe. Except that it wasn't total. Wexford remembered what Tracy Thompson had told him, that it was Targo's asking her if he could kill someone for her which had put an end to their relationship.

Wexford got up and, saying nothing to the silent people in the room, went outside into the front garden and the street. A thin drizzle was falling. Strangely, someone had parked a Mercedes at the kerb directly outside the Rahmans' house, but this one was black. He thought, Ahmed's story isn't right, but it's right in parts. That's why Targo didn't bring a dog; he was going to drive off, find Tamima, and kill her. Because Ahmed and his mother were lying in one respect? They had wanted Tamima killed to save the family honour, and if it had been done, they would never have spoken out, never have betrayed Targo. But Targo might have had another reason for asking permission, in other words for telling them what he meant to do. They would be blamed for her death and not he. No one would believe that he, a mere client of Ahmed's, had been involved. . . .

Wexford went back indoors as Lynn, Damon, and the uniformed officer came downstairs.

"Nothing, sir," Lynn said.

"All right. We start next door in the shop called Webb and Cobb." He went into the living room and asked Mohammed for the key.

Tamima's father handed it to him in silence. Wexford gave

the key to Damon, and they all went to the brown-painted door, which Damon unlocked.

"*Cobb* means a 'spider,' doesn't it?" Damon asked.

"When it's only got one *b*," said Wexford.

They went in, Burden with them. There was a strong smell of musty airlessness, paint, and a hint of mildew, nothing else. The mushroomy scent would have been from rising damp, which had made a kind of tide of black fungus climbing up the wall. Burden switched on lights, which hung from leads in the middle of the ceiling. No spiders and no cobwebs were to be seen. This ground floor, the area which had been the shop, comprised three rooms, the large front one, a small but still fairly big one beyond, and behind the stairs a kind of dilapidated kitchen. It was all clean in here too, and Wexford concluded that Yasmin kept this place almost as spotless as her house. Almost, for she hadn't attempted to clean off the fungus or had attempted and failed, nor had she had much success with removing dark gray stains from the kitchen tiles.

The largest of the rooms was of course the one which could be seen from the street between the window boards. Two built-in cupboards were empty but for a cracked jug and a spoutless teapot standing on shelves. Stacked up on the floor were perhaps twenty large wooden crates and as many cardboard boxes. Nothing was on the table except a trayful of broken pottery, with nothing at all in the table drawer. They opened crate after crate and box after box, found nothing.

The kitchen was bare, but in the back room were several crates of the same type as those in the shop room. Only one cupboard here, and the crates. Again the crates were opened, this time by Lynn. She lifted out pieces of china, a flowered tea set, about twenty tiny coffee cups, each one wrapped in tissue paper. Underneath or in the next crate she expected to find Tamima's body. She had been sure she must find it here ever since she had driven away from Brighton, leaving behind an indignant couple in their thirties who had insisted in angry tones that their name really was Khan and offered to show her their marriage certificate.

The crates were empty now and there was nothing for it but to put everything back. Wexford had opened the only cupboard in this room, which, because it was without shelves and was no more than a foot wide and less than that deep, seemed to serve no useful purpose. He had such a shallow, narrow cupboard in his own house, but it housed the electricity meter and fuse box. No such equipment occupied this space. On the left-hand side the wall was not of brick but of hardboard, as was the wall between it and the window. He now noticed that the whole room had recently been painted. That accounted for one of the ingredients of the smell. The paint was a creamy ivory shade famous among builders' merchants as "magnolia."

"How has that board been—well, fixed there?" he asked Damon.

"With screws, I should think, sir. Under the paint you'd probably find screws hidden under some sort of filler."

"Then find them, will you? I want that wall taken down. Just the bit between the cupboard and the window."

The uniformed officer, Moyle, took over. As Damon had said, Moyle soon exposed the screws, eight of them. He went back to the van he had come in and returned with a screwdriver. Hannah, watching, was shivering. PC Moyle began methodically removing the screws, and the hardboard panel loosened until he was able to take hold of it with both hands, free it, and set it against the opposite wall. An empty space was revealed with another such panel screwed in at the back, as this had once been a large walk-in cupboard, including the one next to it.

Moyle said, "D'you want me to take the screws out here, sir?"

"Yes, please."

Hannah smelt it first. Not a strong smell, not yet, but enough to conflict with paint and mildew scents. Charnel house, Wexford thought because he had long ago read the expression somewhere. The smell strengthened when Moyle lifted away the rear panel, became a reek, a stench. Hannah covered her nose and mouth with her hands, and Burden screwed up his face in distaste. Inside the compartment at the back a parcel tightly wrapped in green plastic sheeting and brown sacking, perhaps five feet six or seven long and tied with rope and electricity cable, had been leaning against the wall.

While Moyle cut the ropes and he and Damon started to remove the mummylike wrappings, Wexford examined the inside of the cupboard. But it was totally empty. The thing inside its shroud of man-made materials had left nothing of itself behind. The foul smell of corruption assailed him as he stepped back into the room and the corpse was exposed.

He found himself looking into the contorted face and the staring eyes no one had bothered to close, of Eric Targo.

21

I T WAS ALMOST the middle of the night. The police station car park was empty but for Wexford's car and Hannah Goldsmith's. Ahmed Rahman would not be going home that night.

Walking down the stairs to Interview Room 2, Wexford thought how he had been thwarted of the great coup he had for most of his life hoped to bring about. No longer a creator of victims, Targo had become a victim himself. Three times a killer, a motiveless, cold-blooded murderer, he would soon be remembered as a respected citizen, and no doubt whatever obituary he earned would dwell on his successes as a self-made man, his "beautiful home," his menagerie, his dogs, and his love of animals.

Ahmed sat on one side of the table with a cup of tea in front of him. Standing behind him beside the recording equipment was PC Moyle, keeping an eye. Wexford thought of the days when everyone questioned in this room or the one next to it—where, currently, Yasmin Rahman would soon be questioned by Burden and Damon—smoked like furnaces, chain-smoked, and had to be supplied with Rothmans King Size or Players Capstan as well as tea and, sooner or later, sandwiches. As a nonsmoker himself, he had suffered, had coughed and grown hoarse. But nothing was to be done about it until now, when they had a smoking ban throughout the police station.

Hannah came in, sat down opposite Ahmed, then rather slowly and deliberately, Wexford joined them. It had been a shock for Hannah, finding dead Targo encased and swathed like a mummy. She had been sure the unwrapping would reveal the slender, pathetic body of Tamima, and now her hunt had to begin again. Wexford hoped what she said was true, that she was enormously relieved, but knowing her need always to be right, her often unjustified certainties, he wondered.

Having told Ahmed that the interview would be recorded, that they were Detective Chief Inspector Wexford and Detective Sergeant Goldsmith, and that the time was 11:37 p.m., Wexford began by asking Ahmed to tell him what had really happened at 34 Glebe Road that afternoon when Targo called.

"You can forget that stuff about the home-management device and forget too about Targo driving off but coming back before six thirty. Inspector Burden is questioning your mother next door, and I don't think your mother will lie, will she?"

"No, she won't lie," said Ahmed.

"So tell me."

"I shall have to, I suppose. Will I go to prison?"

"Probably. That depends on what you did."

"I killed him, but I didn't mean to. It was an accident."

Hannah said, "Begin with what he said when he made the offer to kill Tamima."

Ahmed nodded. He pushed away his half-empty teacup.

"My mother was there. She was sewing something. I think Targo wanted me to send her away, but I couldn't do that in her own home. Then he sort of shrugged as if he was saying, 'OK then, if that's what you want. Let her stay.' After that he asked about this office-manager thing, and I showed him some pictures in a brochure I had. 'Get one for me, will you?' he said, and I said I'd send for it and it'd be about ten days. Well, what I said was, five to ten working days. Then he said, quite pleasantly, in the same sort of voice, 'Your sister's going about with a white man, isn't she?'

"I was so surprised I just stared. My mother laid down her sewing, but she didn't say anything, not then. Targo said, 'You people don't like that kind of thing, do you? It's bad for your family honour or whatever.' Those were his words, 'honour or whatever.' My mother spoke then. She said, 'We can't discuss that with you.' He took no notice. He said, 'You'll want her out of the way, won't you? Dead and gone and no questions asked. I'll see to that and it won't cost you a penny.'"

"What did you say to that?" Wexford asked.

"I said I thought he should go. My mother got up. She was wearing the hijab, of course, and a shawl round her shoulders. But when she looked at him, she pulled the shawl over her head as well and held it in front of her face. I think she wanted to hide herself from him, he was such a monster."

Yes, thought Wexford, that is what he was, a monster. A chimera, an abomination. "Go on."

"He didn't go. He laughed. He said, 'I know that's what you want. I've seen them kissing—that's not the way a good little Moslem girl behaves, is it? You won't want her in your home again, and you need not. Just leave things to me. I'll find her wherever she is.'

"I hit him then. He was an old man and shorter than me

and I know I shouldn't have done that, but I was so angry. I saw red, I really did, red in front of my eyes. I hit him on the jaw and he fell backwards." Ahmed was speaking now at great speed. "He fell backwards and crashed against the fireplace and hit the back of his head on that granite shelf, the what d'you call it?"

"The mantelpiece," said Wexford.

In Interview Room 1, Yasmin Rahman had reached much the same point in her account. She was heavily veiled, much as she had been when Ahmed described her, the shawl on top of the hijab pulled down to form a peak over her forehead. Her strong, handsome face—the long, straight nose, the dark, liquid eyes—was almost hidden but for the mouth.

"My son Ahmed hit him. He asked for it—isn't that what you say in this country? He asked for it. That man—Targo—he fell down and there was blood coming from his head. I thought he was dead—how would I know? I went to the kitchen to get water and something to wipe away the blood, and when I came back, Ahmed was feeling his heart and listening to his heart and he said he was dead."

"While this was going on," Burden said, "where were your husband and your other son?"

"Osman was at work. My husband was upstairs in bed. He was ill with flu. He heard that man fall and he called out to me to know what the sound was. I went up and told him it was something out in the street. It was ten minutes to four, and Ahmed said we must hide the man's body while we thought what to do next. We had to put it somewhere Osman wouldn't see it. We carried it through into the place next door."

She was cool and calm. Burden thought this was probably the way she had been when Ahmed hit Targo and later found he had killed him. He had noticed her extraordinary dignity before, the way she could sit still for long periods without fidgeting, without even moving her eyes. "So what did you do next?"

"Took the car away," she said calmly. "We waited till the nighttime. Took it a long way to where my cousin Mr. Mansoor who is the postmaster lives. It is a place called Melstead. Mr. Mansoor knows nothing. He wasn't even there, he was at his home in Thaxted."

In the next room Wexford was saying, "If he wasn't dead when he fell on the floor, why didn't you call an ambulance? You say it was an accident, it wasn't your fault."

"I don't know if he was dead then, but he soon was. I knew that because the blood stopped flowing. That means a person is dead, doesn't it?" Ahmed didn't wait for an answer. "I thought no one would believe me if I said it was an accident."

Wexford said drily, "We sometimes believe what people tell us. It's more difficult to believe when those same people try to cover up an offence by concealing a body and going to considerable lengths to deceive as you did. I refer to the little games you played with Mr. Targo's car. What did you do? Drive it up to the place in Essex where some cousin of yours lives to make it look as if Mr. Targo had left the country through Stansted Airport?"

"I'll tell you what we did. As soon as we knew he was dead, we took the body next door into the shop. There's a door in our living room that leads into the room where we hid him. We had it put in when we had the conversion done. Then we waited till it got late and there was no one about. I drove Targo's Mercedes and my mother followed, driving our car. It was a piece of luck that my father was ill with an infectious illness, so my mother was sleeping in Tamima's room and my father didn't notice she wasn't there."

"Why not go to Gatwick?"

"It was too near," Ahmed said. "The car would have been found next day."

"Who worked on the cupboard in the shop next door? You, I suppose?"

"I wrapped the body up, made a sort of parcel of it, and put it in the back of the cupboard. Then I sort of boarded it up. I bought some sheets of hardboard, screwed it in place, and painted over the lot."

Wexford sat back in his chair, silent.

Hannah said, "Where is your sister, Ahmed?"

"I don't know. I only wish I knew. He didn't kill her, I know that. At least I prevented that."

Unless he did it before he spoke to you, Wexford thought. "It was you phoned Mrs. Targo with a message allegedly coming from her husband?" The strangely familiar voice, he thought. The voice of someone who had worked in the house as Ahmed had when he'd set up the computer.

"Oh, yes," Ahmed said wearily. "That was me."

Later that night Yasmin Rahman was released on police bail, but her son remained in one of the station's two cells for further questioning in the morning.

22

MANSLAUGHTER WOULD BE the charge or perhaps unlawful killing, consistent with Dr. Mavrikian's findings when he examined Targo's body. Death had resulted from that single deep wound to the skull, which corresponded to the sharp, two-inch-deep corner of the granite mantelpiece at 34 Glebe Road. There was also bruising to the left-hand side of Targo's jaw—incidentally in the centre of where the naevus had been—where right-handed Ahmed Rahman had struck him. Yasmin Rahman would be charged only with assisting an offender in concealing a death and would probably, Wexford thought, receive a suspended sentence. He hoped Ahmed would serve no more than two or three years in prison, and if it was less, Wexford wouldn't be sorry. The man had rid the world of a monster who, though old, had been strong and might have lived another twenty years of natural life. This, of course, was no way for a detective chief inspector to think.

He himself took to Mavis Targo, if not the news of her husband's death, the details of it and as much of an explanation as he thought good for her to hear. Sentimentality would have it that Ming the Tibetan died of grief, but it seemed to have got over missing its master and, when Wexford called, was helping Sweetheart eat the Chinese carpet. Mavis may have been equally indifferent to Targo's passing. At any rate, she showed no emotion but spoke only of her worries as to how to dispose of the menagerie. Although Targo had left most of his properties and his stock to his children, the house was hers, and as soon as she could, she intended to sell it and buy a flat in central London.

"You asked me if my marriage was happy," she said to Wexford, "and of course I wasn't going to say it wasn't, was I? The fact is, we were going to split up. What I say is, thank God we never got around to it. Once we'd done that, he'd have changed his will."

"What I can't understand," Burden said later, "is how he got all those women to marry him. Ugly little chap with that birthmark before he had it taken off, it's beyond comprehension."

"Anthony Powell," said Wexford, the reader, "says somewhere that while women are rather choosy about whom they sleep with, they will marry anyone. Women are said to like power in a man, and Targo exuded that."

They were on their way to pay a first visit to Rectangle Road, Stowerton, and the Hanif family. It was four thirty in the afternoon and Rashid was due home from Carisbrooke Sixth Form College and his formidable A Level programme of maths, biology, and physics. After they had listened for about fifteen minutes to Fata Hanif's highly laudatory curriculum vitae of her eldest son while she spooned pureed apple into the mouth of her youngest, Rashid hobbled in on a single crutch, his leg in plaster up to the knee.

Before either of them could say a word, Rashid had plunged into a defence of himself, his mother backing him up as soon as he drew breath.

"I haven't seen her for weeks, not for months. I don't know where she is, so it's no good asking me."

"Of course he hasn't. My son's a good boy. He's obedient, he respects his parents."

"All right," Wexford said. "Wait a minute. Tamima is missing. Her parents have no idea where she is. None of her relatives have any idea where she may be. Now, I must tell you that we have witnesses who have seen you about with her, at one time if not recently. They may not be reliable, I don't know. Certainly, Tamima has been seen about with a white man or boy, and you are white, Rashid."

Mrs. Hanif set down the apple-puree spoon, wiped the child's face, and said, almost spitting the words, "The police are institutionally racist, that's a well-known fact."

"And you," said Burden, "are a British citizen, a white woman from a family in the former Yugoslavia. Where's the racism?"

"My husband's Asian."

"Maybe. But Rashid is pale-skinned and blue-eyed," said Wexford. "If witnesses say they've seen Tamima with a white boy, the chances are it's Rashid, but he says no, and for the present we must take his word for it. You would like Tamima to be found, wouldn't you, Rashid?"

"He doesn't care!" Mrs. Hanif shouted.

Equally loudly, Rashid forgot respect and said, "Oh, do shut up, Mum!"

The baby began to cry, drumming his heels on the footrest of the high chair. "See what you've done." But Mrs. Hanif spoke in a low, petulant tone, subdued by Rashid's unaccustomed defiance.

"Tamima has to be found," Wexford said. "I think you'd like to help us, Rashid, I want you to come down to the station and make a statement."

Rashid's mouth fell open. "What about?"

"The last time you saw Tamima, what she said to you, any phone calls you've had from her, that sort of thing. You can come with us now. No need for you to walk anywhere."

WEXFORD CONSIDERED ASKING Mohammed and Yasmin Rahman to go on television and appeal to the public to find their lost daughter—considered and rejected it. Clever, gentle Mohammed might make a good impression, but his wife would not. Viewers would tend to be set against her by her stern features, steady eyes, and rigidity of expression. She reminded him of a bust he had once seen in Greece of Athene, and he thought that the helmet the goddess had been wearing would have become her. Besides, she was associated with her son in the unlawful killing of Targo. Better send out photographs of Tamima, which the Rahmans were happy to provide. She was good-looking, if rather too like her mother ever to be called pretty, yet with her dark skin and black eyes and the hijab she often if not invariably wore, a big percentage of the public would fail to distinguish her from any other Asian girl.

Rashid said in his statement that he and Tamima had once been good friends but "nothing more." The last time he saw her had been a month ago when he talked to her in her uncle's shop, the Raj Emporium. That had been just before she went to London to stay with her aunt Mrs. Qasi.

The newspaper photographs had no effect, or none of the kind Wexford wanted. A great many people claimed to have seen Tamima, but in every case it was a different Asian girl they had seen. He began to wonder if it was possible Targo had murdered Tamima *before* he made his offer to Ahmed, and he recalled what Osman had said: "You think he killed her just the same?" It was possible, and in a strange way it would have been just like Targo. Suppose he had found Tamima, had strangled her—what had he done with her body?—then gone to Ahmed to ask if he wanted his sister killed. If the answer had been yes, he would have said the deed was already done. Wexford could almost hear him saying, "It's all done. I don't want payment. Glad to be of service."

It made Wexford shiver because it seemed possible. Then he thought of the menagerie, the carnivorous animals, and began to feel sick. No, he was imagining too much. . . . When he was younger, he had never felt like this. He had been tougher. Banish ugly and dreadful images, he thought, put them in a box and send the box to the deep recesses of his psyche—but this faculty seemed to be deserting him now.

He went to London to see Jacqueline Clarke and Clare Cooper and learned more from them than Hannah had. It seemed that though Tamima had come to their flat intending to get a job and stay there for some weeks, even until Christmas, she had in fact left after a week, saying she was going home to Kingsmarkham.

"Did she ever mention a man called Eric Targo, an old man?"

"I don't think so," Clare said. "She didn't mention anyone much when she first came, and then after a day or two she was always on her mobile, answering calls more than making them, I think."

"Were any of those calls from Rashid Hanif?"

"I don't know who they were from. We didn't like to ask."

Jacqueline Clarke said, as if she had just remembered, "There was a man came here once to call for her. He wouldn't come in, I don't know why not. Tamima went down to answer the door and came back upstairs for something. She left him standing on the doorstep. I looked out of the window and saw him. It was dark, though."

"What was he like?" Wexford asked quickly.

"Young. Quite tall. I think his hair was brown, not very dark. I couldn't tell you the colour of his eyes."

Definitely not Targo, he thought. Rashid Hanif? Quite possibly. But wherever she was, if she was alive, she wasn't with Rashid now. But it was impossible. The timing was wrong. He could only have killed her if he could have been absolutely confident that Ahmed would leap at his offer and not go to the police.

WEXFORD HAD GOT into the habit of calling on the Rahmans every day. It was unorthodox behaviour if not absolutely against the rules. Released on police bail, Yasmin was at home, but he never saw her. She seemed to know it was wise to keep apart when he called and not to speak to him. She made tea or coffee and sent it in by one of her menfolk. Mohammed and Osman had both gone back to work, so Wexford called on his way home in the early evening. Nothing much was said—nothing at all, that is, about the killing of Targo and the concealment of the body. When they talked, it was about Tamima. Sometimes Hannah came too, and then they would ask questions as to all the people the missing girl had ever known right back into her early childhood, trying to find out whom she might now be with and where she might have gone, always supposing she was still alive.

Webb and Cobb was no longer a crime scene, and Mohammed's plan was to decorate the shop area and try to let it, to paint the exterior at the same time after replacing the windows in the top flat. This was necessarily delayed, and Sharon Scott moved out, leaving the tenancy to her husband, Ian Scott, whom she was divorcing.

Yasmin Rahman's strict morality made her disapprove of Scott's bringing to live there with him a woman he wasn't married to. In Yasmin's absence one evening, this was a topic of conversation between Wexford, Hannah, Mohammed, and Osman. The Rahman men were more easygoing. Osman took the robust view that Scott's morals were no concern of theirs so long as he paid the rent. Mohammed was against sitting in judgment. Besides, times had changed and we must change with them, but he didn't know how to talk his wife round. Not for the first time, Wexford marvelled at people's selective morality. Presumably, it was all right for Yasmin to help her son conceal the body of a man he had killed and attempt to deceive the police by taking part in a plan to hide that dead man's car, while all wrong to rent out her property to a cohabiting couple.

Wexford had no intention of visiting Mavis Targo again, but one day, a week or so before Christmas, he met her in Kingsmarkham High Street. With two full shopping bags on the pavement beside her, she was contemplating the Mercedes, recently returned to her, and the yellow-painted metal clamp fastened to its rear, nearside wheel. Ming and Sweetheart, bouncing about on the backseat, were both barking hysterically.

"Do something, can't you?" she said to Wexford.

"Nothing to do with me, Mrs. Targo." Resisting the temptation to tell her he was not a traffic cop, he took a little pity on her. "Just phone the number they give and pay the fine and they'll release you in no time."

"I knew it was a mistake to drive that bloody car. It's always brought me bad luck."

He said nothing about the menagerie or the house. The sight of her reminded him of his failure. Targo might be dead, but he had died in what was an accident, no more retributive or judicial than if he had met his death in a road crash. And now, even if they ultimately found Tamima's body concealed somewhere, buried or at the bottom of a lake or a river or butchered and therefore more easily hidden, Targo could not be responsible. Yet he felt he must find the girl, dead or alive, he must find her. It was terrible to him that the police forces of the whole country had searched for her, her picture had been all over the media, but she remained missing. He tried to comfort himself with the knowledge that it is much easier to hide a living person or for that living person to hide herself, than to conceal a corpse. The dead body cannot move, cannot pick itself up and find a new hiding place. Inert, it lies where it has been left or placed, but that place may be deep under the earth.

THE WINDOWS AT Webb and Cobb had been replaced and the exterior painted before Ian Scott moved in. Apparently, his private life no longer concerned Yasmin Rahman. She had other things to worry about. Her son Ahmed would come up for trial in February, and she had no reason to think that her daughter Tamima would be found before that—if found she ever was.

Christmas came and went. Mavis Targo sold Wymondham Lodge and moved. Dora Wexford got the flu and had to stay in bed while her daughter Sylvia came in to look after her. While he manfully limped to his sixth-form college, Rashid Hanif's broken ankle refused to mend and required an operation. A vast overhaul of the police station started with builders and decorators moving in and the working lives of a dozen officers disrupted. Then at the end of January when the weather had turned very cold, the trees were silvered with hoarfrost, and the pavements had disappeared under a light covering of snow, Wexford met Yasmin Rahman crossing the high street from Glebe Road.

He was on his way to join Burden for lunch at the Indus when he saw her. He had spotted her on the other side of the road, noticed the thick black scarf she wore wound round her head and the unflattering floor-length, belted, black coat, buttoned from neck to foot and just exposing clumping black brogues. In spite of all this, how beautiful she must have been when young, he thought, reflecting at the same time that this was a truly dreadful thing to say of a woman, as if beauty were necessarily and invariably confined to youth.

She crossed the street when the light turned red and advanced on him. Something in her face he couldn't at first define. Her first words gave an explanation.

"I've had a shock. I don't know what to do." She frowned, shifting blame onto him as was her way. "If you are on your way out, I suppose I shall have to go back home."

He had no idea what could have happened. They were outside a small café that specialised in "natural" foods but also served coffee and tea. "Let me buy you a cup of coffee, Mrs. Rahman. You've made enough for me in recent months."

If she had refused, it would have come as no surprise. She seemed to enjoy negativity. But she accepted with a reluctant nod. "I think perhaps I shouldn't be talking to you. I am a convict now, aren't I?"

If she meant she would soon have a criminal record, he was bound to agree with her, but all he said was "That's all right. Don't worry about it."

Inside, he pulled out a chair for her close to the window. Only two other people were in the café, but still she looked to either side of her and over her shoulder to make sure she wasn't overheard. Wexford ordered two coffees, which the waitress insisted on calling "Americanos." Yasmin Rahman preserved silence until she had gone, then said in a steady, determined voice, "I've seen my daughter. I've seen Tamima."

He said nothing, looked at her.

"I saw her yesterday, but I couldn't quite believe my eyes." She spoke slowly and deliberately. "I thought I was having a delusion, I've been so worried, you see."

"Of course you have."

"But I saw her again this morning. At the window. She was half behind the curtain, but I saw her, I knew her. Of course I know my own child."

As others had disbelieved him, so he gave this no credence. "Are you quite sure, Mrs. Rahman?"

"I'm sure. I know my child. It was Tamima."

"Which window was this? Where did you see her?"

The waitress arrived with their coffee. As soon as she appeared, Yasmin Rahman clamped her lips together, sat statue-still, staring at the roadwork outside the window. The waitress seemed to be purposely taking her time, setting out

milk and sugar, then recalling that the bowl of packet sweet-
eners was still on her tray. Yasmin continued to watch the
man with the mechanical digger and the man with the pneu-
matic drill.

"Which window was it?" Wexford repeated once the waitress had finally gone.

Yasmin expelled a heavy sigh as she turned her head back.
"One of the new ones. In the top flat, Mr. Scott's flat."

"Above Webb and Cobb, do you mean?"

"If you choose to put it like that." Yasmin's black sleeve fell
back a little, exposing several heavy gold bracelets on her narrow, fragile-looking wrist. He noticed how impossibly long
and thin her hands were. "I thought that man had killed her.
From the moment he made that offer to me and Ahmed, I
feared he had already killed her. And then I saw my daughter
at that window. She was looking out between the curtains."

"Did she see you?"

"I don't know. I haven't said anything to my husband. It
was only an hour ago and he was at work."

Wexford finished his coffee, said, "We'll go there now. I'll
take Sergeant Goldsmith with us."

He went to pay the bill, returned to hear her say, "Can it
be someone else?" She spoke in her usual austere, dignified
way, but her words were harsh. "I dislike that woman. I dislike being patronised."

How upset Hannah would be, he thought, that she of all
police officers might be found wanting in the very area of
race relations, where she so much desired to meet her own
standard of treating black, Asian, and white people all with
perfect equity. At the same time he admired this woman's
nerve in attempting to make the rules for the law. But he
gave in. A call to Burden fetched him to the café, and they

all went up Glebe Road together on foot. Glancing at the black-robed figure beside him, Wexford wondered if this was the first time Yasmin Rahman had ever walked in the public streets accompanied by two men other than close male relatives.

A sign attached to the ground-floor window of Webb and Cobb proclaimed it as shop premises to let, with, underneath, the name of a firm of agents to apply to. The flat immediately above looked empty. At the top, because the winter's day had turned dull, a light was on behind the drawn curtains in Ian Scott's.

"Someone's in," Burden said. "We ring the bell, do we?"

"It's the top one."

Yasmin rang it, but nothing happened and no one came. She pressed the bell again. The light upstairs went out and the curtain was twitched. There was no entry phone, but there was a letter box. Wexford pushed the flap inwards and called in his strong, resonant voice, "Police. Open the door, please."

Again there was no response.

"Please, may I try?" Yasmin's humble words were at variance with her imperious tone. She called through the letter box, "Tamima, this is your mother. You must open the door." She turned to Wexford. "Or you'll break it down, is that right?"

"I hope we shan't have to do that."

But as she called out "They will break it down!" a youngish man with blue eyes and brown hair opened the door. He wore a white vest and jeans, a bath towel draped over his shoulders. "I was having a shave. It's bloody freezing out here," he said. "What do you want?"

"You know what we want, Mr. Scott." Wexford didn't wait

for further discussion but headed for the stairs, followed by Yasmin and Burden. The stairs twisted round outside the lower flat before going on up. When Wexford had set foot on the second stair of the second flight, he looked up and saw, standing at the top, the girl he had last seen coming home from school with a satchel on her back.

23

A T THE TOP, in Scott's sparsely furnished flat, Tamima sat on one end of the bed, her mother on the other. They avoided looking at each other. Wexford sat on the only chair in the room, Burden and Scott on stools Scott brought in from the kitchen. Wexford broke the silence.

"How long have you been living here, Mr. Scott?"

"Since the middle of November." He spoke sullenly, then said with energy, "I've a right to be here. I'm the tenant."

"And you have been here with him all this time?" Wexford addressed Tamima.

She shrugged. "Since maybe the end of November, whatever." As in the case of her lover, speaking spurred her on to animation. "I've been so bored of everything. I'm bored out of my head. He said he was taking me to a luxury apartment. But he never did, he brought me to this shithole and in the night too, so nobody should see."

She met her mother's eyes. Veiled and gowned in austere black, Yasmin Rahman was taking in every detail of Tamima's clothes. Probably she had never seen her daughter dressed like this before, had never seen any good Moslem girl dressed like this, from the low-cut top and the ultrashort miniskirt to the fishnet tights and the cheap, high-heeled, scarlet shoes. Yasmin lifted her head gracefully and turned away.

"Didn't you see any newspapers? Didn't you watch television?" This was Burden. "There's been a nationwide search for you. Didn't you know?" He looked at Scott. "Didn't *you*?"

"She was scared of her family."

"I was going to tell them," Tamima said. "I *was*. Every day I meant to go next door and tell them. But I don't know, I don't know why I didn't. Well, yes, I do. I didn't want my mum and dad to hate me. It wasn't that I was scared of them taking me away from *him*. I'm sick of him."

"Charming," said Scott. "Thanks very much."

"I suppose you first saw Miss Rahman while you were living here with your wife," Wexford said.

"That's one way of putting it," Scott said.

"Is there another?"

"I don't know what I've done to be questioned like this. I've done nothing wrong." A frightening thought occurred to him. "She is over sixteen, isn't she?"

"Of course I bloody am. I don't know how many times I've told you." Tamima's bravado suddenly left her. Her face turned red and she stuck out her lower lip like a child half her age. "I want to go home," she wailed, and turning to her mother, threw herself upon her, clutching her shoulders.

Yasmin remained stiff and unresponsive for a moment. Then, her expression softening, she slowly put her arms round Tamima, holding the girl's cheek against her own. She stroked the long black hair and began whispering to her in what must have been Urdu. Wexford watched them for a moment. Then he turned his eyes on Ian Scott. The man had been correct to say he had done nothing wrong. His follies were minor compared to what Tamima's brother had done, what her mother had done.

Wexford got up. "There's nothing for us to do here," he said to Burden, and together they went down the stairs and out into Glebe Road.

"JENNY WILL BE pleased nothing's happened to her," Burden said when they were partaking of the lunch that had long been postponed. "She was worried about a forced marriage if not an honour killing."

Hoping for the drama of it, Wexford thought uncharitably.

"Not that I ever believed in either," said Burden.

"I am going to have kedgeree," said Wexford, "which I don't believe is Indian at all, let alone Kashmiri. I think we invented it in the days of our supremacy." They ordered. "We shall be able to tell Hannah we told her so."

"I suppose it was Scott she saw hanging around in the Raj Emporium."

"And Scott Targo saw with her, which made him think the Rahmans would want her killed."

"I'm afraid the kedgeree is off," said the waitress. "There has been quite a run on it."

"All right. I'll have the chicken tikka marsala, which I believe is another colonial invention."

"So will I," said Burden. "All this has made me wonder just how common these forced marriages are. Or these honour killings, come to that."

"Common enough in Asia, I fear, less so here. I daresay we shall hear no more of them."

Some undefined unease took away Wexford's appetite. He left half his main course and wanted nothing more. Burden ate heartily as usual, finishing with what he called that "well-known Kashmiri speciality," a large slice of apple pie with cream. It was half past two. While they had been in the restaurant, the winter's afternoon had turned colder, and an icy north wind blew out of every narrow side street and alley. Wexford had no belief in telepathy, premonitions, clairvoyance, or portents, yet as he walked along in the bitter cold, he was increasingly aware of some foreboding, some horror which lay ahead, and he quickened his pace, prompting Burden to ask what was the hurry.

The warmth which met them as they passed through the swing doors into the police-station foyer was so relieving as for a moment to banish all other sensation. Then Wexford saw Hannah bearing down upon them, phone in hand. Something in her face told him he wouldn't be passing on triumphant news about Tamima that day.

"I was just calling you, guv." As she spoke, his phone began to ring. "There's been an honour killing. It's really happened. A woman in Stowerton found dead in the room she was renting, her throat cut. She'd left her husband of a year, and the husband and her father swore they'd kill her. I'm going there now."

"We'll all go there now," said Wexford, and, silently to himself, at least I know it can't be Targo this time.

AFTERWARDS

THE YEARS PASSED, two or three of them. As Wexford had predicted, Yasmin Rahman received a suspended sentence for assisting an offender, the offender being her son Ahmed, convicted for the unlawful killing of Eric Targo. Ahmed spent the last year of his sentence in an open prison and was released on licence. By that time his family had moved away from Glebe Road, where some of their neighbours, notably Ian Scott—now with a new partner—and the occupants of Burden's old home, had made life uncomfortable for them. Having secured three fairly good A Levels at Carisbrooke Sixth Form College, Tamima had just begun on a four-year course in Islamic studies at a university in the Midlands.

The Rahmans now lived in Myringham, where Mohammed still worked but inside the office, the head of Social Services having decided it would be unwise for him to risk catcalls and other abuse from clients. Yasmin's criminal record made little difference to her life. As for Osman, he had given up nursing and was at University College London, studying for a medical degree.

On a Sunday in summer, Ahmed came to Wexford's house. Once more without a gardener, Wexford was at home mowing the lawn or, rather, after half-mowing the lawn, had given

up in disgust and was sitting in a deeply cushioned cane
chair outside the French windows, reading a novel by Ivy
Compton-Burnett. Ahmed hadn't come through the house.
He must have entered the front garden on his way to the
front door and seen Wexford from there. He walked softly
over to within a few feet of him and cleared his throat. Wexford looked up.

"I'm afraid I'm disturbing you," Ahmed said.

"That's all right. How are you?"

"Not bad. Better than I have been."

Wexford laid his book facedown on the table beside him.
"What brings you here?"

"I want to tell you something. A confession really. May I
sit down?"

For a moment the sun seemed to have darkened and
someone else, something invisible yet grimly present, to have
entered the garden and strutted up on to the paving. No one
was there, yet Wexford could see a shadow fall, the stocky,
muscular figure, the white hair and the thick blue-and-white
scarf wound round its neck.

Ahmed repeated his last words: "May I sit down?"

"No, Ahmed, I don't think you may, because I don't want
to hear what you have to say."

"I have to tell you. I think you'll be pleased. You hated him
too. When my mother was out of the room, I did—"

Wexford interrupted quietly but with firmness and got up.
"I'm not hearing this. I'm hearing none of it. I haven't even
seen you." He went into the house by way of the French windows, closing them behind him.

Ahmed stood outside for a moment, mouthing something, holding up his hands, but the image of Targo, which
had never really been visible, had gone. Was he going to say

what I think he was? Wexford asked himself. What else could he have been about to confess? But I won't think of it. I will never think of it again but put the monster back in its box and throw the box onto the rubbish heap. The best place, the only place, for him.

About the Author

Ruth Rendell has won numerous awards, including three Edgars, the highest accolade from Mystery Writers of America, as well as three Gold Daggers, a Silver Dagger, and a Diamond Dagger for outstanding contribution to the genre from England's prestigious Crime Writers' Association. A member of the House of Lords, she lives in London.

Turn the page for a special excerpt from
Ruth Rendell's latest novel

PORTOBELLO

Available from Scribner in September 2010

"Impossible to put down . . . *Portobello* is as brilliant as
anything she has ever written."

—*Evening Standard*

"The reader who is tired of Ruth Rendell's novels of
London is tired of life."

—*The Independent*

1

I T IS CALLED the Portobello Road because a long time ago a sea captain called Robert Jenkins stood in front of a committee of the House of Commons and held up his amputated ear. Spanish coast guards, he said, had boarded his ship in the Caribbean, cut off his ear, pillaged the vessel, then set it adrift. Public opinion had already been aroused by other Spanish outrages, and the Jenkins episode was the last straw to those elements in Parliament which opposed Walpole's government. They demanded British vengeance and so began the War of Jenkins's Ear.

In the following year, 1739, Admiral Vernon captured the city of Puerto Bello in the Caribbean. It was one of those successes that are popular with patriotic Englishmen, though many hardly knew what the point of it was. In the words of a poet writing about another battle and another war: "That I cannot tell, said he, but 'twas a famous victory." Vernon's triumph put Puerto Bello on the map and gave rise to a number of commemorative names. Notting Hill and Kensal were open country then where sheep and cattle grazed, and one landowner called his fields Portobello Farm. In time the lane that led to it became the Portobello Road. But for Jenkins's ear it would have been called something else.

Street markets abounded in the area, in Kenley Street, Sirdar Road, Norland Road, Crescent Street, and Golborne Road. The one to survive was the Portobello, and from 1927 onwards a daily market was held there from eight in the morning to eight in the evening and 8 a.m. till 9 p.m. on Saturdays. It still is, and in a much reduced state on Sundays too. The street is long, like a centipede snaking up from Pembridge Road in the south to Kensal Town in the north, its legs splaying out all the way and almost reaching the Great Western main line and the Grand Union Canal. Shops line it and spill into the legs, which are its side streets. Stalls fill most of the centre, for though traffic crosses it and some cars crawl patiently along it among the people, few use it as a thoroughfare. The Portobello has a rich personality, vibrant, brilliant in colour, noisy, with graffiti that approach art, bizarre and splendid. An indefinable edge to it adds a spice of danger. There is nothing safe about the Portobello, nothing suburban. It is as far from an average shopping street as can be imagined. Those who love and those who barely know it have called it the world's finest street market.

You can buy anything there. Everything on earth is on sale: furniture, antiques, clothes, bedding, hardware, music, food and food and more food. Vegetables and fruit, meat and fish, and cheese and chocolate. The stalls sell jewellery, hats, masks, prints, postcards old and new, shawls and scarves, shoes and boots, pots and pans, flowers real and artificial, furs and fake furs, lamps and musical instruments. You can buy a harp there or a birdcage, a stuffed bear or a wedding dress, or the latest bestseller. If you want to eat your lunch in the street, you can buy paella or pancakes, piping hot from a stall. But no live animals or birds are for sale.

Cheap books in excellent condition are on sale in the Oxfam shop. A little way up the road is the Spanish deli which sells, mysteriously, along with all its groceries, fine earthenware pots and bowls and dishes. There is a minimarket in most of the centipede's legs and at Portobello Green a covered market under a peaked tent like a poor man's Sydney Opera House. In Tavistock Road the house fronts are painted red and green and yellow and gray.

The moment you turn out of Pembridge Road or Westbourne Grove or Chepstow Villas and set foot in the market, you feel a touch of excitement, an indrawing of breath, a pinch in the heart. And once you have been, you have to go again. Thousands of visitors wander up and down it on Saturdays. It has caught them in the way a beauty spot can catch you and it pulls you back. Its thread attaches itself to you and a twitch on it summons you to return.

QUITE A LONG way up the Portobello Road, a glossy arcade now leads visitors into the hinterland. There is a children's clothes shop, for the children of the wealthy who go to select private schools, a shop that sells handmade soaps, pink and green and brown and highly scented, another where you can buy jerseys and T-shirts but exclusively cashmere, and a place that calls itself a studio, which offers for sale small watercolours and even smaller marble obelisks. It was here, long before the arcade came into being, that Arnold Wren had his gallery. He never called it that but preferred the humbler designation *shop*.

Stalls filled the pavement outside. Mostly fruit and vegetables up here. When Arnold's son, Eugene, was a little boy, the vegetables and fruit were of a kind that had been sold in English markets for generations. Eugene's grandmother could remember when the first tomato appeared, and he, now a man of fifty, saw the first avocado appear on old Mr. Gibson's stall. The boy's mother didn't like the taste, she said she might as well be eating green soap.

Arnold sold paintings and prints, and small pieces of sculpture. In rooms at the back of the shop stacks of paintings occupied most of the available space. He made enough money to keep himself, his wife, and his only son in comfort in their unprepossessing but quite comfortable house in Chesterton Road. Then, one day when the boy was in his teens, his father took his family on holiday to Vienna. There, in an exhibition, Arnold saw paintings by the Swiss symbolist Arnold Böcklin on loan from various European galleries. The Christian name struck him because it was the same as his own. Arnold Wren never forgot the paintings; they haunted his dreams and later on he could have described some of Böcklin's works in the greatest detail entirely from memory, *The Isle of the Dead*, the frightening self-portrait with the skeleton's hand on Böcklin's shoulder, the *Centaurs Fighting*.

He had forgotten where most of the paintings in the rooms behind the shop came from. Some had been inherited from his father. Others were sold to him for shillings rather than pounds by people clearing out their attics. There were thousands of attics in old Notting Hill. But looking through the paintings one day, wondering if this one or that one was worth keeping at all, he came upon a picture that reminded him of Vienna. It wasn't at all like *The Isle of the Dead* or *The*

Centaur at the Forge, but it had the scent of Böcklin about it, which made him catch his breath.

It was a painting of a mermaid swimming inside a glass vase with a narrow neck, trying perhaps—from the expression on her face of fear and desperation—to climb out of the water and the vase. All was glaucous green but for her rosy flesh and her long golden hair. Arnold Wren called the picture *Undine in a Goldfish Bowl* and showed it to an expert without telling him what he suspected. The expert said, "Well, Mr. Wren, I am ninety-nine percent certain this is by Arnold Böcklin."

Arnold was an honest man and he said to the potential purchaser of the painting, "I'm ninety-nine percent sure this is a Böcklin," but Morris Stemmer, rich and arrogant, fancied himself an expert and was a hundred percent sure. He paid Arnold the sort of sum usually said to be "beyond one's wildest dreams." This enabled Arnold to buy a house in Chepstow Villas, a Jaguar, and to go farther afield than Vienna on his holidays. His was a Portobello Road success story while old Mr. Gibson was a failure. Or so it appeared on the surface.

When his father died, Eugene Wren moved the business to premises in upmarket Kensington Church Street and referred to it as "the gallery." The name in gilded letters on a dark green background was EUGENE WREN, FINE ART and, partly through luck and partly due to Eugene's flair for spotting new young artists and what from times past was about to become fashionable, made him a great deal of money.

Without being a thief himself, Albert Gibson the stallholder married into a family of thieves. His only son, Gilbert, had been in and out of prison more times than his wife, Ivy, cared to count. That, she told her relatives, was why they had no children. Gib was never home for long enough. She was living in Blagrove Road when they built the Westway, which cut the street in two and turned 2 Blagrove Villas into a detached house. The Aclam Road minimarket separated it from the overhead road and the train line, and the Portobello Road was a stone's throw away if you were a marksman with a strong arm and a steady eye.

2

Joel Roseman never walked with a purpose, a destination. He wasn't going anywhere but mostly round in a sort of circle from his flat in a mansion block at the eastern end of Notting Hill Gate and back again. Once, when he first tried it, he had attempted going out in the late afternoon, but it was March and still broad daylight. Next time he went out after dark and that was better. Sometimes he walked clockwise into Bayswater, down to the Bayswater Road and home again, sometimes widdershins, in a loop up to Campden Hill and back to the high street. Mostly he wandered aimlessly.

For a long time now he had found life better in darkness. That was why he dreaded the summer, when it wouldn't start getting dark till ten. But now it was April and exceptionally warm, light too in the evenings but dusk coming at seven. He wore sunglasses, a special pair in which the lenses were darker than usual. At home he had several pairs of sunglasses but none with lenses as black and smoky as these.

The allowance Pa had paid into his account regularly on the tenth of the month had just come in on the previous day. Joel brooded on Pa as he walked along, wondering in despair what made him tick, why he was so cruel, and how it was possible that a man whose child had drowned could have that picture hanging up in his house. He stopped thinking about it when he found a cash dispenser in a bank wall at the bottom of Pembridge Road. The sunglasses had to come off briefly while he drew out 140 pounds. It came in twenty- and ten- and five-pound notes. Carefully looking over his shoulder (as the bank said you should) he put twenty-five pounds into the pocket of his jeans and the rest into an envelope. This went into an inside breast pocket of his rainproof jacket. There was no sign of rain, but Joel possessed few clothes and this jacket had happened to be hanging up, in the dark, just inside his front door.

He was taking these precautions with his money because he intended walking up the Portobello Road. It would be his first visit. He put his sunglasses on again and the world went dark and rather foggy. When she was young, his mother had lived in Notting Hill, and she had told him—she went on speaking to him when Pa did not—that if your house was burgled and your silver stolen, the police would advise you to go look for it on the stalls in the Portobello Road, where you were likely to find it up for sale. This had made Joel think that the market was a dangerous place, somewhere to be careful, but he had decided that the stallholders would be packing up by seven thirty. He was surprised to see that this was not so. The place was blazing with light and colour, packed with jostling people, voices and music, a flourishing trade still going on. When the natural light was dying, they had to make up for it artificially. They never thought what it was like for people of his sort. He blinked behind his glasses. According to his mother, Pa called him a mole and sometimes an earthworm.

No one took any notice of him. He walked up the western side, past knitwear shops and blanket shops and print and china shops. It surprised him to see any shops at all because he had expected only stalls. These were there in abundance, shops on the left, stalls on the right, and people, hundreds of people, walking, dawdling, strolling between them and up the roadway itself. All the people looked busy and happy. Joel could always spot happiness, he was an expert at noticing it, perhaps because in everyone he personally knew it was absent. On the other side of the road crowds were going home, heading southwards for the tube and the buses. They looked happy too and, the ones carrying bags and packages, satisfied or excited. He went on, not stopping, not considering buying anything. He never needed anything except food and not much of that. He shopped for nothing else. The special sunglasses were his last buy and he had had them for two years.

By the time he had been walking fairly steadily for twenty minutes, he came to the pub Ma had mentioned called the Earl of Lonsdale. He crossed the road and turned down Westbourne Grove. No one had looked menacingly at him while he was in the market, and he was beginning to think reports of the place had been exaggerated. But it was still a relief to find himself among the genteel boutiques and soon the gracious houses of this corner of Notting Hill. He had begun to feel a little tired. Well, they told him he had a heart problem. Young as he was, he had a bad heart.

It was quiet. The poor live among strident voices, clatter, crashes, deafening music, barking dogs, shrieking children, but places inhabited by the rich are always silent. Tall trees, burgeoning into spring leaf, line their streets and their gardens bloom with appropriate flowers all the year round. Joel was reminded by the silence, if by nothing else, of Hampstead Garden Suburb, where Pa and Ma had a big, low-roofed house squatting in landscaped grounds. Around here wasn't much like that, but the peace and quiet were the same, yet somehow uneasy, almost uncanny.

No one was about but for two men, not much more than boys, loitering on an opposite corner. They wore jackets or coats with hoods pulled down over their eyes, and Joel had learnt from newspapers he occasionally saw that hoods meant their wearers were up to no good. They looked at him and he looked at them, and he told himself that they would do nothing to him because they could see he was young and tall and they didn't know that his pockets were full of money. He looked poor in his old clothes, his ragged jeans and that jacket with one sleeve torn and the other stained.

He had once read somewhere about the assassination of the Empress Elisabeth of Austria, how she had been walking onto a boat, which was to take her across Lake Geneva, when she had felt someone jostle her and she received a mild enough blow in the chest. Only when she was in her stateroom, some minutes later, was it realised she had been stabbed and was about to die. This was how Joel thought afterwards of what happened to him on the corner of Pembridge Crescent and Chepstow Road. He had been struck not in the chest, but on the left shoulder and from the back. He felt the pain grip him with iron claws down his upper left arm.

Perhaps he cried out. He never knew. He fell or sank or plunged to the ground. But he must have leant backwards at some point for his head struck against the bell push in a plastered brick pillar, which was one of the gateposts of the house on the corner. Had someone assaulted him, as someone had assaulted the Empress Elisabeth? He forgot that he had a bad heart, he forgot everything as he lost consciousness.

THE TWO BOYS in the hoods crossed the street and stared fearfully at this shabby, long-haired man who lay spread-eagled on the pavement. They thought he was dead. The front door of the house behind those pillars opened. They ran.

If Joel had fallen forwards, his mother told him, no one and nothing would have pressed that bell. He would have died. What she didn't tell him, until a lot later and she was in a temper, was that his father had said it was a pity he hadn't. As it was, the occupants of the house had come out to see why their chimes were ringing and ringing. They found him slumped against the pillar and called an ambulance.